TRAVELER

TRAVELER

L. E. DELANO

Swoon READS

Swoon Reads | NEW YORK

A Swoon Reads Book
An Imprint of Feiwel and Friends and Macmillan Publishing Group, LLC

Traveler. Copyright © 2017 by L. E. DeLano. All rights reserved.
Printed in the United States of America by LSC Communications,
Harrisonburg, Virginia
For information, address Swoon Reads,
175 Fifth Avenue, New York, N.Y. 10010.

Our books may be purchased in bulk for promotional, educational,
or business use. Please contact your local bookseller or the Macmillan
Corporate and Premium Sales Department at (800) 221-7945 ext. 5442
or by e-mail at MacmillanSpecialMarkets@macmillan.com.

Library of Congress Cataloging-in-Publication Data is available.

ISBN 978-1-250-10040-5 (trade paperback) / ISBN 978-1-250-10041-2 (ebook)

Book design by Vikki Sheatsley

First Edition—2017

10 9 8 7 6 5 4 3 2 1

swoonreads.com

This one is for my fiercely resilient daughter and
my amazing, indomitable son. You've been so
patient while Mom went after her dream.
I promise, I'll return that favor until the breath
leaves my body. The world is yours. This world,
every world, and I'll love you in them all.

Prologue

HE RAN FOR THE TREES AS HARD AS HE COULD, HIS LEGS burning and his lungs trying frantically to suck in enough air to keep him going. He had to lead them away.

A shot ricocheted off a large rock nearby, splintering him with fragments as he ran on, not daring to take the time to look back. If he could get into the woods, he could probably lose them. Most of the trees were decayed or fallen, and it was hard to navigate if you didn't know your way around. There was a drop-off just a few hundred yards past the tree line, with a series of shallow caves just underneath it. He knew the safe way down; he just had to keep his lead.

Another shot rang out, and then another as a whoop went up from one of his pursuers. He'd finally made the tree line, so he risked a glance back, his green eyes wide and frightened. They'd broken off pursuit and were now running back, meeting the other members of their band as they dragged someone, kicking and screaming, down to the edge of the riverbank.

They'd found her.

"No!" he shouted. "Over here! Over here! Over here!"

He jumped up and down, waving his arms wildly. They gave him a cursory glance and then turned their backs on him, returning to their quarry.

The girl's blond hair was matted with sweat and blood from where she'd fought off her captors. He made a short, abortive movement as though he was going to attack, but there were too many of them. He'd only have one chance. They were circling her now, but her eyes weren't on them. They were on him, and she held his gaze as she mouthed the words.

Do it.

He took a deep, shuddering breath and set his jaw, again running as hard as he could toward them all, grabbing one by the shoulder and jerking him out of the way as he pulled back his arm and let the knife fly as hard as he could.

She made a strangled sound as it buried itself in her chest, and she bubbled the word "Thanks" through bloody lips as she sank to the ground.

He kept running, hearing their shouts, not caring if they shot him, and he leaped into the river below, feeling the rushing current pull him away from them all.

But not away from the memory of her face.

1

Remnant

THERE ARE FEW THINGS IN THE WORLD THAT I FIND more painful than being forced to sit on a cold metal folding chair in front of a home improvement store selling candy for the Spanish Club. Slightly higher on that list would be a root canal without anesthesia, and sitting at the candy-selling table when no one brought the candy.

"I don't know how I let you talk me into this," I grumble, folding my arms and sliding down on my chair.

"It's not my fault," Ben answers. He's on the phone with Mr. Fielding, sponsor of the Spanish Club, who seems as clueless as we are about the whole situation.

I roll my eyes and reach into my backpack to pull out my favorite Moleskine journal. I might as well get some writing done while we're waiting. I've had an idea burning in my head since I woke up this morning, and I know if I don't get it down on paper, I'm going to lose it.

I start flipping through it until I find what I want. On the page before me is the remnant of the dream.

Green eyes, dark hair.

Ski lift? Or some kind of gondola? I'm riding with him and it jerks to a stop, throwing me out. I dangle for a moment before I fall, with his scream echoing as the air rushes by me. . . .

I add *redbrick building* to the list, then review it all again, chewing the end of my pen as I stare at the paper. I've almost got it figured out—how I'm going to turn this bit of a dream into an idea and then into a story outline with plot points and a clear beginning, and I've even got an idea of how I want it to end. I'm just missing the middle.

The story of my life.

I know the beginning—who I am and where I came from. I know I want to be a writer, maybe even a journalist who turns novelist and wins a Pulitzer in both categories. And I'm going to travel—a lot. I'm going to see the world and write about it all and invent new stories about old places. That's the endgame.

I'm just lacking a middle, and there's nothing I can do to change that while I'm still in high school and will be for eight more months. After that, it's on to college, if all my financial aid comes through, and I can start really experiencing life.

That is, if I'm not cut down in the prime of life by an angry mob of sugar-starved, impatient people. I look up as a balding, middle-aged man with a rounded stomach moves up to the table.

"Any word yet?"

The guy is wearing a vivid red sweatshirt and a neon-green hat and has been bugging us at five-minute intervals for the last half hour. Clearly he's too concerned with candy to worry much about fashion. I smile apologetically.

"Any minute now," I promise, silently vowing to myself I will never volunteer for this stuff again, no matter how pathetically Ben begs me to.

"You said that last time I asked," the guy persists.

"You can buy candy next door at the dollar store, you know," Ben points out.

"They don't have Giant Pixy Stix," the guy gripes, then lumbers off.

Ben leans in and lowers his voice.

"If he asks me one more time . . ."

"Be nice," I say. "We've been promising him five minutes for half an hour now."

"How'd we get talked into this, anyway?" he complains.

I look over at him with raised brows. "You volunteered."

"Why in hell did I do that?"

"You volunteered both of us," I add. Then I drop my voice in pitch to mimic him. "Mr. Fielding? Jessa and I can take the first shift. We don't have anything better to do. Like homework. Or a social life, in general."

"I'm not enough social life for you?"

I give him a look and check my phone for the time once more.

"I'm only kidding you, St. Clair." He reaches out to playfully punch my arm. "If you had somewhere else to be, you could have told me. I'd've picked a different shift."

"What if somewhere else to be was 'anywhere but here'?" I grumble. "This chair is hard. And cold. It's messing with my concentration."

I look back down at my list and close my eyes tight, pulling my dream guy's face up once more in my memory. There's a weariness to him. Like he's seen too much that he shouldn't have seen, but at the same time he's not one to wallow. I like characters like that. The ones who just keep going.

He's got a rough edge, this guy. I can feel his desperation, see the pain on his face as my hand slips through his fingers.

I imagine his green eyes wide with horror as I fall away from him. I see him punch the bar on the ski lift. His hands fist in his hair and—

I'm about to put my pen back on the paper again and work through the scenario when Ben bumps my elbow as he's putting his phone away, sending the pen scratching across the paper, leaving a jagged line across one of my paragraphs.

"Hey!"

"Sorry," he says apologetically. I start to close my journal but find Ben's hand in the way.

"What is this, anyway?" he asks. "Talk to me. I'm bored."

I push his hand aside, closing the journal.

"It's nothing. Just a list."

"Dark hair? Green eyes?" He looks at me curiously. "Anybody I know?"

"No. It's stupid. Just something for creative writing class."

"You can always write about me. I'll even model for you." He flexes his bicep.

"Impressive. But I'm afraid I'd never do justice to that physique."

"So write about my outstanding knowledge and application of vocabulary," he suggests.

You'd never know Ben was such a nerd. He's over six feet, muscular but not bulky, with raven hair and deep-brown eyes. Basically he's the epitome of "tall, dark, and handsome." His mother is native Hawaiian, and Ben has that great allover tan that came with his islander heritage.

"I'll keep that in mind," I promise. "You can star in my next novel—the one that will be published after I die on a cold metal chair."

"Well, the candy is supposedly on its way, courtesy of the brother of a friend of Mr. Fielding's."

"That's not helping us," I fume. "We've got people staring at us with hunger in their eyes, and that's not because I'm looking hot today. They need their chocolate."

"Speaking of hunger . . . you wanna hit Mugsy's after this?"

"Can't today. I have to get right home. I promised Danny I'd help him make some of the decorations for the party at the library next week, and I have to get that translation project done for Spanish."

"Did he get Volunteer of the Year again?"

"Yes, but this is the library's birthday party. Fifty years. Which is only half as long as we've been sitting at this table."

He leans back on his chair, tilting dangerously on the uneven concrete. "I'm fixing to leave and grab McDonald's if they don't show up soon. I was planning on eating candy for dinner, but I guess that's a bust."

I can't help but smile. Ben always uses that phrase. He's *fixing to go* or *fixing to do* stuff all the time.

"Candy isn't dinner," I remind him. "How about Mugsy's tomorrow after school?"

"Can't. I've got chorus rehearsal."

"Ah yes," I sigh. "Bringing badly needed culture and excitement to our small-town lives."

"It's just chorus." He plays absently with the zipper on his hoodie, zipping it back and forth. "Now if I was a drummer . . ."

"Too ordinary."

"Girls like ordinary," he says.

"*Ordinary* girls like ordinary," I correct him. "You can aim higher."

I can tell he's pleased with my backhanded compliment.

"Okay," he says with a grin. "I'll test the next one by making her sit on a cold metal chair for hours. She has to be up to the challenge."

"You'll have a hard time replacing me," I say. "I think I'm frozen to the seat. You'll have to chip me out of here."

He reaches for my hand and clasps it, pulling it up to his chest. "I'll stay by your side through the bleak, cold winter. I'll even sing to you. *Ninety-nine candy bars on the wall, ninety-nine candy bars . . .*," he sings. I pull my hand away, laughing.

"Great. Now everybody's looking at us."

"Let 'em look," he says. "Maybe I should grow out my hair more." His fingers comb through it. "It's easier short, but if I'm going to join a boy band that I'll eventually up and leave for my solo career, I need a better look."

"Thought you were going to go pro in soccer."

"That was last week. Keep up."

"No, you were a cultural anthropologist last week."

"I'm investigating all my options," he says. "I'll keep you posted." He tilts back in his chair again, bracing his knees under the table as he rocks gently back and forth. The table is rocking with him, but it's not a big deal—we've got nothing on it anyway.

I shift again on the hard chair, and my hand moves unconsciously to rest on my journal.

Green eyes, so clear they're like looking at the bottom of a mountain lake, where the rocks are covered in moss. He jumps off the ski lift and pushes the hair out of his eyes and then . . . and then . . .

"You're zoning out on me again, St. Clair," Ben teases.

It's gone. The perfect half-formed story in my head and it's gone now. My fingers curl into a frustrated fist, but I make myself smile so Ben doesn't see that he irritated me. It's not his fault.

My mind replays the dream in my head once more, and I see him. I have vague memories of calling my dream guy by name, but that name vanished before I woke. It's frustrating in the extreme.

"When's the candy going to be here?" This from one of two girls in drill team uniforms, who are madly texting as they wait near the front of the table.

"It won't be long," Ben reassures them.

"Do they know what happened to the delivery?" asks the guy in the red shirt again.

"It was supposed to have gotten to the school earlier today, but the truck broke down," Ben says. "It's possible that's just a cover and they're driving it straight to Tijuana to sell it on the black market."

I pinch Ben's leg under the table and bite my lip to keep from laughing as Red Shirt Guy stomps off in a huff, and then I hastily scrawl out a sign for the remaining masses who still don't realize that this is, in fact, just a table and not a candy table. Maybe if we tell them to come back in half an hour, the candy will finally arrive. Then Ben could deal with them instead of me, since I only agreed to do the first half of the shift.

Once the sign is taped to the end of the table, I open up my journal and stare at my list again.

Dark hair, green eyes . . .

I pull out my phone and aimlessly Google "Top Boy Baby Names" to see if I might recognize something, or maybe find one I can use that seems to fit the person in my head. None of them feel right, so I guess I'll just keep calling him Green Eyes for now. He's the face I see in every story. The name has to be perfect.

This was someone I've seen before, but where? That's what dreams are, anyway, according to my creative writing teacher. She claims that your subconscious holds the memories of people you've met or even seen on the street or on TV, and then creates scenarios for you to live out in your dreams, featuring all of them. You never really dream of anyone unknown. So what was my subconscious trying to tell me?

Probably to get a life, I think.

Fingers tickle my neck and break me out of my thoughts. I shrug in reaction, and Ben lets out a low chuckle.

"Is it time to go already?" I ask hopefully.

"Nice try. I think this is the goods."

Sure enough, a van rolls up and the delivery guy hops out and starts unloading.

I turn around in my chair to look at the boxes of candy being set down behind me.

"Sorry I'm so late," Delivery Guy says. "Traffic."

"No problem. Everyone!" Ben exclaims, getting to his feet

behind the table. "Candy table's open! Just give us a few minutes to set up!"

He rips off the sign I just made, and then he picks up my journal and hands it to me. "Let's clear this off and you just start handing me stuff," he suggests.

I shove the journal into my bag and get out of my chair to start opening boxes. I turn just as the delivery guy is straightening back up, and the world suddenly tilts on its axis as I see who is leaning against the wall of the store, just behind the delivery guy.

Dark hair. Green eyes.

2

Encounter

"CAN YOU TAKE THIS?" DELIVERY GUY ASKS, HANDING me a box. I am mute. I can't stop staring over his shoulder.

"Miss?" he says impatiently.

"St. Clair! Come on, hand it over!" Ben calls out. I force my arms to move, reaching out for the box the deliveryman is passing to me. I'm trying very hard not to stare at the guy leaning on the wall.

Which is difficult to do, because he's staring at me.

I force myself to look away, and in minutes we have the boxes unpacked. A few more minutes after that, everything is displayed or stored under the table, and the first wave of candy buyers is crowding us. I know this is a seriously lousy thing to do, but I grab my backpack.

"Ben, I have to go," I say abruptly.

"What?" He looks at me over his shoulder. "You can't give me ten minutes?"

"I—"

I look over at the wall, where my mystery guy had been standing, and he's gone. I blink hard, and stare even harder, like I'm trying to will him to be there.

"You with me, St. Clair?"

"Huh?" I look back at him. "Yeah, I guess I can give you ten more minutes."

"You did just finally get the chair warm," he points out. He cranes his neck to look over his shoulder, following my gaze.

"What are you looking at? You look like you've seen a ghost."

"I just . . . it was nothing," I finish lamely. I reach for the little metal box we're keeping the money in, and hand Red Shirt Guy three Giant Pixy Stix. The next several minutes pass in a flurry of candy and money changing hands until the crowd thins out.

Did I imagine him? I look back over my shoulder once more. He's not there.

But he could have gone into the store. Maybe he's shopping.

"What time is it?" I ask Ben as I reach for my bag again.

He looks over at me as he rummages through a pile of licorice.

"It's almost five thirty."

"Crap!" I jump to my feet. My mom will be here any minute. "I have to go, Ben. I'm sorry—I know you're swamped but I can't stay. I'll make it up to you!"

Ben raises a hand that's clutching a half dozen Twizzlers. "You owe me big!" he calls out before he turns back to the table.

I don't have long to try to find him before my mom shows up to whisk me away. It's doubtful that he's still around. I could look in the store. It's worth a try.

I head through the doors into the store, glancing around but not seeing him. I finally decide to start at one end and just methodically—and hopefully not too obviously—glance down the aisles. I start down in lumber and am almost at the other end of the store with the lawn and garden stuff when a voice calls my name.

"Jessa." The voice comes again. "Over here."

I look in the direction of the voice, and there he is—dream guy—only this time he's leaning against the wall back by the entrance to the outdoor stuff, and he's motioning to me.

I stand frozen in the middle of the aisle, and my mind tries to make sense out of this, because this can't be happening. I had half convinced myself that I'd been seeing things, maybe just some wishful thinking, since I had the dream running around in my head. I had expected to *possibly* see some guy who might just *potentially* bear a passing resemblance to the man of my dreams. To have him fit the mold perfectly, two dozen feet away and calling me by name, is freaking me out in a serious way.

I wet my lips nervously and then I glance around. After all, some guy I saw in a dream—who somehow knows my name—is motioning me to walk over to a dim corner with him. This has classic-horror-movie scenario written all over it. The attractive stranger who turns out to be a serial killer or something. I don't even know him, really.

Except, I do. Or at least I feel like I do. I know the way he stands, the shift of his weight from one foot to the other as he waits for me to answer. I know that if he smiles, he'll have a dimple on one side. I know just how far my arms need to reach to circle his neck.

I take a deep breath, and then walk over to stand in front of him.

"Do I know you?" I ask. He's still staring at me, straight on, like he's trying to absorb every detail. It makes a shiver run down my spine.

"Sort of," he says finally.

"That's not an answer."

"Yes, it is. It's just not one you like." He shoves his hands in his pockets and rocks back and forth on his heels. Is he nervous?

"So . . ."

"So . . . ?" He says it like the ball is in my court, but he's the one who's playing the game. He's starting to irritate me now.

"You called *me* over, remember?"

"Yes, I did." He takes an audible breath. "My name's Finn."

Something in me shifts and clicks, like gears that were put into motion and then locked into place. Finn. His name is Finn and my only thought is, *Yes, that's right.*

"Seriously, how do I know you?" I ask him. "I know we've met before, but I don't think you go to my school."

"No, I don't," he says. But he doesn't expand on that, and I'm starting to get tired of being the only one having a conversation here.

"So how do you know my name?" I narrow my eyes when I ask, so he knows I don't think this is funny. It has zero effect, because apparently, he disagrees with me. The corner of his mouth lifts.

"We've met, but you probably don't remember where." He's looking at me in a way that seems really familiar, but he isn't giving me any more details.

"Why did you want to talk to me?"

I look over my shoulder at the sound of beeping behind me. There's a worker driving one of those tiny forklifts, getting something off a shelf nearby. I turn back to Finn, and I try to seem like I'm in control, when in reality, I am still trying to wrap my head around this. He's got me off balance, and I don't like it at all.

Finn must finally realize how he's coming across, because his voice softens.

"I was wondering if you wanted to . . . go get coffee or something. Then we can talk a little more. Get to know each other."

"I don't usually get coffee with secretive guys. And my mom will be here soon." He arches a brow at me but says nothing more, and I stand there awkwardly, trying to think of a graceful way out. He knows he's making me uncomfortable, too. I can see it on his face.

I am just about to say something rude when my phone chirps. It's my mom, and I'm torn between relief and frustration. I don't know how much longer I can stand here and be stared at by a guy with no social skills, but at the same time . . .

This is crazy.

"I have to go," I say, backing away. Only I'm not watching where I'm going, and I nearly walk into the forklift, and the guy operating it lets out a startled sound and hits reverse. Finn lunges forward and pulls me toward him just as a large pallet of paving stones slams into the ground where I had been standing.

"Oh my God!" the forklift driver says. "Are you okay?"

"I'm fine," I gasp, looking up at Finn. He's let me go and moved himself between the forklift and me. I have to look around him to see the driver.

"Really," I reassure the guy. "I'm okay. Sorry I walked into you."

He surveys the pallet of mostly broken stones with dismay. "I've got a customer waiting for these," he says, rubbing the back of his neck. "When my boss sees this, he's gonna have a cow."

"I'm sorry," I say again. "I'll tell him it's my fault if you want."

"You sure you're all right?" Finn asks.

"If you're hurt, I have to fill out a report," Forklift Guy says uneasily.

My phone chirps again.

"I'm fine," I repeat to both of them. "I really have to leave."

On shaky legs, I turn and walk toward the doors.

"Give me your phone number, at least," Finn says, falling into step behind me.

I shake my head, repeating, "I have to go."

My mom is waiting at the curb as we walk through the doors, but I feel like I owe him something.

"Finn," I say, trying the name on for size.

"Jessa." He raises his brows and looks at me.

"Thanks for pulling me out of the way." *Even though it's your fault I wasn't paying attention.*

He nods, and I open the car door.

"I have an incredible memory," I say pointedly. "Sooner or later, you'll come back to me."

"I'm counting on it," he says, and something in his eyes makes me hesitate before I finally slide in and close the door. The car pulls away from the curb, and Finn stands watching us with his hands jammed down in his pockets as we drive away.

3

Welcome to My Life

I OPEN THE DOOR TO MY HOUSE, EAGER TO FIND A QUIET place for my thoughts, and I find chaos instead.

My brother, Danny, is two years older than me, five inches taller, sixty pounds heavier, and at this moment he's kicking the wall over and over and shouting at the top of his lungs.

"Won't work! Won't work! It doesn't *work!*"

I toss my bag down on the floor.

"Danny. Danny!" I put my hands on his shoulders cautiously, and he turns tear-filled eyes to meet mine for a brief moment.

"The batteries won't work. They won't work. The batteries won't work," he repeats, clearly frustrated.

"Stop kicking," I say, leading him away from the wall. I rub his back in a soothing motion. "Now tell me slow. *Where* don't the batteries work?"

"In the remote. For the Xbox. I put them in and they don't work." He covers his eyes with his fingers, pressing hard.

"Did they fit?" Maybe he grabbed the wrong size or something.

"They don't work. I put them in and they don't work." His voice rises again with pure frustration.

I hold out my hand. "Let me see."

Danny rubs his eyes once more, then walks over to the end table next to the couch and picks up the remote control for the Xbox, handing it to me.

"Those batteries are bad. They don't work."

I pull the door off the battery compartment and see the problem immediately.

"They're in wrong, Danny. See? One goes this way, and the other one goes that way. Opposite." I turn one of the batteries around, and the remote's indicator buttons light up.

"See?" I say. "Danny? Danny, look at me."

He takes his eyes off the TV, finally making eye contact.

"Look at what I did with the batteries, so you know for next time, okay? One this way, one that way. And if it doesn't work, try going opposite again. Okay?"

"Okay. It didn't work."

"I know, but it works now."

"Did you fix it?"

"I fixed it."

"And it works now?"

"Yes," I sigh. "Do you want to work on the library decorations now? I promised you."

He sits down on the couch, reaching for the bag of Goldfish crackers he's always munching on.

"No. I want to do it later. I'm playing Super Mario Galaxy. Is the remote fixed?"

I reassure him again that it's working as he starts the game up and sees it for himself. Most days Danny is no problem, beyond the usual annoying sibling-type stuff. But when something upsets him, he gets stuck on it and won't let it go. He's probably going to talk about that remote for the rest of the night and mention the batteries again the next time he picks it up, too.

Sometimes, autism can be really tiring.

"Where's Mom?" he calls out as I scout the cupboard in the kitchen for a Pop-Tart.

"She told me she was going to rake the leaves," I call back.

"Is she using the rake with the green handle?"

Why this is important, only Danny knows.

"I think so," I answer.

I pour myself some iced tea to go with the Pop-Tart, scoop up my bag off the floor, and try to get Danny's attention by waving at him. "Danny! Tell Mom I'm in my room."

Danny doesn't hear me at all. He's too focused on the game now. I climb the stairs to my room and flop down on the bed, then close my eyes and replay the events of the last hour.

You think I'd be a little more freaked out over the fact that I almost died, but that's nothing compared to the feeling of seeing the man of your dreams in the flesh. And how does he know me?

Obviously, we've met somewhere before, and I wasn't kidding when I told him I have an incredible memory. I really do. I certainly wouldn't have forgotten him. I know that face, from the glossy darkness of his hair to his long, long lashes to the way he gets a dimple on one side when he smiles.

This must be what going mad feels like.

How does he know me?

And why is he being so cryptic about everything?

I think I'm through being freaked out. I'm just angry now. Who does he think he is? Is this some kind of joke for him? Like he met me in passing once (and my mind registered him, of course—how could it not?), and now he's being all secretive just to mess with me. What a jerk.

The jerk who saved my life.

I flip open my notebook with a sound of disgust and try to concentrate on my Spanish assignment, but it's not working.

So the jerk sees me working the candy table (I further muse), and when he realizes I forgot his name, he decides to have a little fun at my expense. Maybe he gets a thrill out of creeping girls out. And then he asked me to meet him for coffee! He's got some serious nerve.

As I'm running the scenario through my head, I realize it would make a great beginning to a horror story. Halloween is right around the corner, and my creative writing teacher is sure to ask for something in the genre.

I glance down and can't help but laugh at myself, because I recently tried my hand at sketching my dream guy, but I am lousy at that kind of stuff. He looks like a bad pumpkin carving with a wig. If I need a thoroughly creepy monster for inspiration, this drawing would do the trick. Words are a better way to paint. Well, they are for me, anyway. I am just reaching for my pencil when my mother appears in the doorway.

"Hey, you," she says. "What do you want for dinner?"

She pulls a sweaty tendril of hair out of her eyes. At forty-six, her blond hair is showing some gray, but only if you catch it in the right light.

The hair color is one of the few traits we share. Everyone tells me I look like my mom, because my dad's hair is dark brown. When my parents were still together, everyone called Danny and me the "mini-me's," since we each resembled one parent more than the other. If you went beyond the superficial, you could easily see the differences. Not a lot of people do that, though.

I look up from my notebook. "What do we have to eat?"

"The usuals. Soup. Pasta. Bagel Bite Pizzas." She ticks the options off on her fingers. "I think we have some leftover taco meat from the other night," she offers.

None of it sounds good. Probably because it's always the same stuff—easy stuff that a mom with two jobs and a yard to take care of can make quickly.

"I'll just heat up the taco meat later," I say. "I'm kind of in the middle of something."

"Suit yourself," she says. She wipes her damp neck with the hem of her T-shirt, which unfortunately has dirt clinging to it.

"Mom. You just put dirt all over your throat."

"What?" She swipes at it again. "Better?"

"Worse. You look like you're growing a beard."

"Sexy. And itchy. I need a shower." She steps into the room, checking herself in the mirror over my dresser. "Finish what you're doing and then come down. I don't want you eating at nine o'clock at night."

"Mom! Can I have popcorn?" Danny's voice calls from downstairs.

"Danny!" she calls back. "It's dinnertime, buddy."

"I need my dinner so I can have popcorn!" he shouts.

She rolls her head on her shoulders. "Okay! I'm coming!"

I watch as she turns to go down the stairs. For as long as I can remember, Danny has been pampered like that. My mother's shower will have to wait until she makes him dinner and then he gets his popcorn. Danny comes first. It's just the way it is. The way it always is.

I get up and close my bedroom door to drown out the sounds of the Xbox and pots clanging as my mother starts dinner.

I rub my forehead with my fingers and pull my Spanish homework closer. Maybe I'm reading too much into this whole encounter. Finn is a guy I've obviously met somewhere before, and he bears a resemblance to a guy I've been dreaming about, so my stupid brain locked the two together and now I can't remember dream guy any other way. Finn was probably just trying to be friendly, but he's got bad social skills. He's not being a creep. He's just a normal guy.

I turn to get another notebook out of my backpack, and I catch a glimpse of myself in the mirror over my dresser.

"Snap out of it," I say to my reflection. "It's all just a coincidence."

Only it doesn't feel like a coincidence. It feels like fate.

4

Stalker

I SPENT A MOSTLY SLEEPLESS NIGHT THANKS TO A green-eyed somebody, and now I barely have enough time to get out the door this morning. Thursdays are always hard because Mom works her second job. Some days, she and Danny work together at the retirement home, but Thursdays she works early at the drugstore, and that means I have to make sure that Danny has his breakfast. He can put his own Toaster Strudel in the toaster, but sometimes he can't get the frosting pack open and he'll hack it apart with scissors trying to open it himself. Today he manages fine, but he can't find his favorite cup.

I finally locate it with the dirty dishes in the half-full dishwasher, clean it out, and hand it to him, and then I realize I am going to have to run all the way to school if I don't get a move on.

I wave good-bye to Danny, reminding him that I'll be home at two forty-five, and then I run down the steps and out onto the sidewalk. It's getting colder in the mornings now, but we haven't had snow yet. The neighborhood is decked out for Halloween, with pumpkins and scarecrows all over the place.

I've lived in Ardenville my whole life, grown up in the same house and walked the same street to school. When my parents divorced, Dad stayed in town, and he lives only a few blocks away, so the walk doesn't vary much. It's a nice place to grow up—if you like sameness and quiet and a place with no surprises.

The sound of footsteps coming up alongside me breaks into my thoughts.

"Can I walk you to school?"

I am seriously so startled I let out a shriek. He knows where I live? Now I am *really* starting to get alarmed. He's in my dreams, he's in my reality . . . and that can't be coincidence. Maybe my subconscious is trying to warn me. I try to keep my voice calm.

"I'm fine, thanks. The school is right down the next street." *So don't go thinking you can pull me into your murder van or anything.*

"The walk will go faster if you have company," he offers.

"I don't need company." I pick up my pace, nearly jogging because I'm walking so fast.

"Jessa . . . ," he says, holding his hands out. "I just want to talk."

"I have to go!" I start running and don't stop until I get to the doors of my school. When I look back, he's gone.

I end up spending most of my class time for the rest of the day worrying about whether I'm going to run into Finn again—and alternately kind of wishing I would. Which makes no sense. He could be a serial killer, for all I know of him.

Except he doesn't *seem* dangerous. Isn't that what people

always say about serial killers, though? *He was the nicest guy . . . really polite . . .* I have to stop letting him take over my brain.

When lunchtime comes, I pick at my food, glancing around because I half expect Finn to step out from behind the serving line, tearing off his hairnet and a lunchroom-lady mask to reveal that he's still watching me.

"You okay, St. Clair?" Ben asks.

"Yeah. I didn't sleep well."

"Hey, at least tomorrow's Friday and you can rest up. It's not like either of us ever have anything to do on a Friday night."

"You're not hanging with your soccer buddies?" I look nervously over my shoulder.

"Jessa." He gives me a look. "My father is a professor and my mother is a software developer. Who do you think I hang out with when I'm not working? Nerds like you."

"Thanks." I push my food away.

"Don't be like that. I just mean that between the two of us, maybe we can find something to do this weekend. What do you think?"

My only thought at the moment is that I probably haven't seen the last of Finn. And I really want to know how he knows where I live. It really should creep me out more, but it doesn't. Finn feels sort of . . . comfortable. Like a friend. Like Ben. Okay, maybe not like Ben. I'm not obsessing over Ben's eyes on a minute-by-minute basis. I'm sort of freaked out by how not-entirely-creepy this is, which really makes it kind of creepy. If that makes sense.

"I guess so," I finally answer Ben. "We'll figure it out tomorrow."

I make it home without any sign of Finn, but that doesn't keep my head from swiveling left and right as I walk. I reach the front door and laugh at myself for getting so worked up. Obviously, he got the hint.

I barely make it through the door when Danny asks if I'll play soccer with him out back. Ever since Ben started coming over, Danny's had a bro-crush on him. He's trying to learn how to play, and I need something to do besides sitting around worrying about crazy guys stepping out of my dreams, so I agree.

And of course, right on cue, Finn shows up. Our back lawn is unfenced, and he must've seen us from the sidewalk. He's standing there watching, and this time I'm not scared—I'm starting to get really annoyed instead.

I tuck the soccer ball under my arm and walk over to him.

"What are you doing here?" I ask. "This is private property."

He seems annoyed, too. "Don't act like you don't know me, Jessa."

"I *don't* know you. I just met you!"

"I'm not trying to make you uneasy," he says calmly. "I'm here for a very good reason, and if you'll just hear me out—"

"I can't talk right now," I say, gesturing back at Danny. "I'm playing soccer with my brother."

"Hi!" Finn says, raising his hand to wave at Danny.

"Hi!" Danny waves back.

"Stay away from him," I warn.

"I'm only saying hello. I thought he might be worried, since you seem like you're arguing with me."

"I *am* arguing with you. I want you to leave, and you won't go."

"Jessa . . ." He lowers his voice, and there's a sense of urgency in it. "I was sent here to warn you."

I look at him like he's nuts. Because he is. "Warn me?"

"You're in danger," he says. "And I want you to—"

I'm shaking my head as he's talking because I don't want to hear this. And I definitely don't want Danny to hear this.

"You need to leave." My voice is firm, but he keeps going.

"Please—Jessa. I'm not joking. You have to believe me."

"The only one who's causing me any problems here is *you*," I say. "Now leave."

"Jessa?"

Danny is walking over now. Great.

"Leave," I repeat.

Finn shakes his head. "You have to listen to me."

"Just go!" I've had it. I hit him with the soccer ball right in the chest, and hard. It ricochets off and rolls behind me.

"Bad manners, Jessa," Danny says, scooping up the ball. He tosses it to me, and I'm so flustered, it drops. Finn and I go for it at the same time, and we straighten up together. He's looking down at me and both our hands are on the ball, and for a moment, I feel such déjà vu my head swims with it.

"How do I know you, Finn? Really?"

"I can explain everything," he says softly. "Just give me a chance."

Danny trots up next to me. "You need to say sorry," he chides.

I roll my eyes, mostly because Finn is looking at me in a very smug way that makes me itch to hit him with the soccer ball again.

"Yes, Danny. I shouldn't have done that."

"You hit him with the ball," Danny reminds me.

"Yes, I did."

"Yes, you did," says Finn, clearly enjoying my brother pointing out my transgressions.

"You're in trouble, Jessa," Danny adds. "You're in trouble, Jessa Emeline St. Clair."

I groan audibly.

"*Emeline?*" Finn is smirking now.

"That's her trouble name," Danny supplies. "Jessa Emeline St. Clair."

Finn raises his eyebrows, so I explain. "Whenever my mom used to get really mad at us when we were kids, she'd use all three of our names. The dreaded 'triple name.' You had to really be in trouble if she used it."

"Emeline." He's nodding to himself, as if he thinks it suits me somehow, which irks me to no end.

"So what's your middle name?" I ask him. "Irving? Hubert? Darth?"

He shakes his head. "I'm just Finn. Nothing else."

"No middle name?"

"No middle name."

"Finn is his trouble name?" Danny asks.

I clutch the soccer ball, scowling in a threatening manner at Finn's smug face.

"Yes, Danny. Finn means trouble."

I grab Danny's arm and promise him popcorn to get him into the house. I don't look back at Finn. I spend the next hour trying to forget his words and the way he looked down at me, and how incredibly long his lashes were.

Danny is right. Finn means trouble.

5

Autumn Memory

"YOU SLEEPING OVER, ST. CLAIR?"

"What?" I look up from my journal to see Ben standing over me.

"Are you staying here all night? Class is over."

We'd been doing project presentations about colonial living in AP US History class, and once mine was done, I'd pulled out my journal and tried to muddle through the mess in my brain that belonged to Finn. It isn't working. I slam the journal shut.

"So what did you think?" I ask Ben as we walk to the door.

"What—your presentation?"

I make a face. "Was it boring?"

"Better than NyQuil," he teases. "I could barely keep my eyes open."

"Why did I pick agriculture?" I gripe. "What an absolute turd of an idea."

I'm almost through the door when Mr. Draper stops me.

"Don't forget your project, Jessa," he reminds me.

"Can I leave it here till the end of the day? My locker is pretty full."

Mr. Draper shakes his head apologetically. "I need the room on the table for the next class. Sorry."

I give him a tight smile. "It's fine. I'll take it."

My project consists of seeds, sprigs, and charts all mounted to a poster board. It won't fit in my messenger bag. And I can't roll it up—it's attached to cardboard so it could hold the weight of the seeds and plant cuttings. I really, really don't have room in my locker for this thing, so guess what? I get to carry a poster around to all the rest of my classes.

Perfect.

Ben walks with me toward creative writing, because his next class is in the same hall. He lets out a little snicker as I try to juggle the poster and readjust the strap on my messenger bag, since it's slipping off my shoulder. I shoot him a glare.

"You could give me a little help here," I point out.

"I'm not going to be seen carrying that thing," he says. "You could just throw it away, you know. It's made out of cardboard, paper, and dead plants. It's not like you broke the bank building it."

"I spent almost three hours on it, getting it right," I complain.

He rolls his eyes. "Where are you going to use this again? You just can't stand to throw it away. You're a pack rat."

"Am not."

"Yes, you are. You couldn't even put it in your locker if it fit, because your last six school projects are in there."

I don't answer him because it makes me mad that he's right. I just hate getting rid of stuff I worked so hard on. It doesn't seem fair somehow, even though it's all getting crushed and probably broken in my locker and I'm going to throw out the smashed mess at the end of the year anyway.

"Give it to me," Ben says, holding out his hands.

"Ben . . ."

"Come on. We're fixing to walk right past those big garbage cans outside the cafeteria. I can toss it on the way and you won't have to carry it around all day long."

"I don't know . . ."

"All. Day. Long." He raises his brows and stands there waiting. I finally put it in his hands with a disgusted look.

"Go ahead." I roll my eyes. "Just do it now before I change my mind."

He takes it, and I wince as he folds and crushes it into a ball. Then he jogs ahead a few paces, lobs the crumpled mass like a basketball, and sinks it perfectly on the top of the cafeteria trash, right by the door. Early lunch has already been dismissed, so it sits perched on top of the pile, resting against some tater tots. I keep walking, though I can't help but glance over at it guiltily as I pass.

"There," he says. "Taken care of. And I'll be checking the Dumpsters after school, so don't get any ideas about digging it out."

"Whatever."

He reaches out and holds me gently by the upper arms. "You'll get through this, Jessa," he says dramatically. "You're the strongest person I know."

"Have you ever taken a messenger bag to the face?"

He chucks me under the chin and trots off toward his class, calling out, "You're an inspiration!"

I'm still shaking my head at him as I walk into creative

writing class, where I find my seat, pull out my journal, and thumb through it until I find a blank page. Ms. Eversor is busy at the whiteboard putting up the day's theme assignment as I take my seat.

"All right, everyone," she calls out in her lilting French accent. "Quiet, please. We've got one more class until the publishing cutoff for this month's issue of *The Articulator*. As you know, we try to put a little bit of everything into each issue of the news-paper, and the flash fiction theme for November is usually some-thing like 'Thankful' or 'Thanksgiving,' but I think we need a change, yes?"

The class mumbles its agreement, and some of the students start calling out alternative topics—everything from "Feast" to "Death on the Dinner Table." Ms. Eversor shakes her head, laughing.

"No, no, no. In my mother's country, we have *Tabaski*. It is like Thanksgiving and Christmas all together in Côte d'Ivoire. But it is too easy to write about a holiday," she says. "Let's go entirely away from the Thanksgiving theme and choose something a bit more mysterious. How about autumn? You can explore the aging process, the colors, the coming winter. . . . There are a lot of ele-ments there, you see? It can be lovely, and it can be a warning of bleak things to come. So . . . autumn!"

Ms. Eversor waits a moment as we pull out our notebooks, laptops, and iPads. A few of the students move to the PCs at the back of the room. I remain seated, preferring the old-fashioned feel of paper and pen.

"Very well, everyone," Ms. Eversor calls out. "Five hundred words. Begin."

I look at the paper, letting my mind wander through the remnants of a dream I once had with leafy memories and the smell of pinecones and fireplaces. I set the pen to the paper and begin.

His hand was warm in hers as they walked through the park with feet that felt lighter due to the mere touching of their palms. The trees screamed their colors, competing with the distraction of the geese as they flew overhead. She looked up, realizing that the flock pointed in a perfect V.

"Can you believe it?" she asked. "It's almost as if they want us to find the place."

"We probably need to hurry," he urged. "But I don't want to rush you."

"It's okay." She let him pull her along, clenching his hand tighter.

Her step faltered over the root of a tree that grew into the path. His arm came around her automatically, and she found herself looking up into eyes that belonged to a green time, promising renewal and the exuberance of life.

She leaned into him, grateful to have his solid warmth. It was getting harder to walk.

"I'm cold," she gritted out, shivering.

"They said that would happen."

"I know."

Little by little, so much had been taken from her. Her glorious golden hair. Her body's ability to regulate temperature. The feeling on the soles of her feet.

Her love for him.

It still remained, but not as it had been—how could it?

Her love carried a terrible burden now. Every moment she loved him was another moment she encouraged him to love her in return. Every moment he loved her was one less, then one less, then one less that he could.

When she reached the end, she'd simply stop.

When he reached her end, he had to keep going.

He rubbed her arm, as if trying to put his own warmth into her skin.

"Not much farther," he said.

"No, not much farther." She shuffled now, her feet barely moving. She couldn't feel from the knees down but remembered how to move her legs back and forth, back and forth. The motion of her thighs said that she was moving, but slowly.

"I think I can see it!" He shouted it a bit too loudly, and the birds in the trees took flight, raining down a riot of red, purple, gold, and orange leaves that clung to her hair and crunched under her feet.

"You're going to get there. You're going to get there. You're going to get there."

He kept chanting it over and over like a mantra as he tugged her along, pulling so hard that her legs finally gave out. She rolled on her back, staring up at the trees and the light streaming through the mostly bare branches. The leaves were soft like snow, brushing her cheeks and pillowing her body. The sun was pale, but she felt its warmth.

"NO!" she heard him shout. "No! I can carry you! I'll carry you!"

She closed her eyes, sinking deep into the color and the

smell of autumn, wrapping herself tight within it as winter
began to creep in from her fingertips, where she felt his hand
no more.

I look up, blinking. Then I go back and make a few minor edits after counting my words and catching a repetitive phrase. The feeling of the moment still echoes inside me: the agony in his voice, and the look in his eyes.

His green eyes.

I slam the notebook shut and walk over to an empty PC terminal at the back of the class, where I sit and surf random Wikipedia articles, pretending to be doing research until class is over.

The rest of the day passes in a blur of classes and teachers and annoying classmates that all take too much time and focus away from my thoughts. Normally, I like school okay, but today, I just can't stand to be here.

I can't wait to be alone somewhere, just me and my journal, figuring things out. Luckily for me, my mom is off work early today, so she can hang with Danny and I can take my time getting home. So after school, I head over to Mugsy's, where I order my usual caramel mocha with cinnamon and then slump into a booth.

I try to distract myself by working on my flash fiction, but I'm just not feeling the flow. Finally, I push myself up and out of the booth, leaving my notebook, bag, and coat in place as I walk up to the counter to check out the selection of baked goods. I'm pretty much the only one here this time of day unless Ben comes along. Ever since we started hanging out, we've been semi-regulars at Mugsy's, as long as he doesn't have practice.

I take my time choosing between the cranberry-and-white-chocolate scones and the fresh, hot blueberry muffins that just came out of the oven.

Why do I have to keep seeing his eyes? And I'm not just seeing them, it's like I'm obsessing over him or something.

This has to stop. I have other homework to do. English lit and calculus have assignments due by tomorrow—maybe I should work on those instead of that stupid story. I make my purchase and return to my seat, only to find a disturbingly familiar somebody sitting across from my side of the booth, reading the story in my journal intently.

"Hey!" I snap, trying to tug it out of Finn's hands. "That's private."

"Then you shouldn't leave it open on the table where anyone could walk by and see it. Like me." His finger follows along, and he freezes for a moment. I hear him suck in an audible breath, and then he slowly pulls his hand back from the paper. His eyes are still down, but his hand is now clenched in a fist.

"You wrote this today?" he asks, still not looking up.

"It's an assignment. For creative writing class."

He looks up at me and starts to say something, but his jaw tightens and he clears his throat, like he's having a hard time getting the words out.

"It's really good," he says. "The imagery is fantastic."

I slide into the booth across from him, biting my lip so he won't see just how pleased I am with his comment.

His eyes meet mine, and the sadness in his gaze pulls at me. For a moment, I'm back in my story, looking up at those green, green eyes.

"But this is more than a story. You remember this, don't you?" he asks, pointing to the page.

My eyes flare, but I get a grip on myself. "It was based on a dream I had once."

He closes the journal and stares down at it until the silence becomes uncomfortable. I'm not sure what else to say.

"I remember it, too," he says softly. "I was there."

"You think that really happened?" I play with the paper wrapper on the muffin, unsure if I really want to know.

"I'd read about a new treatment being offered at a university across town," he says in a soft voice. "We didn't have change for the bus. You said you were strong enough to walk. I didn't realize how sick you really were." He stops a moment, swallows hard, and goes on. "Your heart gave out before we got there." His grief pulls at me, and I have to remind myself that this is not a well-balanced person I'm dealing with.

I can't help myself. I reach across the table and cover his hand with mine, and he looks up, startled. Then he smiles a slow, genuine smile, and I pull my hand back. God, what was I thinking, leading him on?

"Finn," I say, gently but firmly, "you have to realize that most people don't believe that dreams are real. And I think you need to talk to someone about that."

He stares at me. "You think I'm crazy." It's a statement, not a question, and an exasperated statement, at that.

"You have to admit, it's not . . . normal."

"You and I have an entirely different definition of 'normal.' And I can explain all of it to you if you'll just let me." He leans across the table. "Jessa, you are in danger." He punctuates the last word with his finger thumping the table.

I shake my head. "You said that before, but—"

He sits back, hands splayed on the table, and lets out a huff of air. "This isn't working," he says to himself. "We're running out of time. I'm going to have to do it."

I look at him warily. "Do what?"

He gets to his feet. "I'll see you tonight, Jessa."

"I—I have plans," I blurt out as he's walking away.

Finn just shakes his head, as if he doesn't care, and he keeps on walking.

He's crazy. He's honest-to-God crazy. *He thinks my dream was real.* There's just one problem with that.

The additional backstory he supplied about my writing project is exactly the backstory I had in my head, as well.

When you wonder if you're going crazy, doesn't that make you *not* crazy?

I cling to that hope.

6

Mario

I'M SITTING IN A CLASSROOM, AND IT'S EMPTY OF students, except for me. The walls are an unrelieved white, without a poster or even a clock to break them up. In one corner is a bright red door, sticking out like a sore thumb. The teacher is a middle-aged man with dark, curly hair and a wide smile. He's wearing a yellow polo shirt and khaki pants, and he's perched on the corner of the desk with one leg swinging carelessly.

"Are you ready to begin, Jessa?" His voice is friendly, polite.

I glance up at a whiteboard on the wall behind him, but there's no assignment to be seen. I look around for my backpack, and it's nowhere to be found.

"I'm not sure what I'm supposed to be doing," I finally say.

"Feeling lost without a notebook?" he asks sympathetically.

"Yeah."

"There you go," he says. "Feel free to take notes if you're more comfortable that way."

I glance down at the desk in front of me and flip open the Moleskine journal, sliding my pen from between the pages.

"Thanks, Mr.—" I look at him questioningly.

"Mario." He smiles at me warmly. "Just call me Mario."

"Thanks, Mario."

"Don't mention it." He shifts back, pulling both legs off the floor, and sits squarely in the middle of his desk. He folds his arms over his chest and stares at me for a moment.

"So . . . Finn tells me you're giving him a hard time."

My head snaps up, and I stare back at him warily. "You know Finn?"

"He and I just met," he tells me. "But you can't really say the same, can you?"

"I—I don't really know him," I stammer.

"But you've been dreaming about him for quite a while," he tells me. "Years." He pushes himself off the desk. "Though you've only just made the connection in the last few months."

I'm having a hard time getting words out of my suddenly dry throat. "How do you know that?"

"Because I know what you dream about. You're dreaming right now."

I look around me slowly. "I'm dreaming?"

He nods. "You're dreaming."

"Oh . . ." I close my notebook slowly. "This is . . . weird."

"I'm going to explain everything, I promise." He smiles at me again. "You might want to open the notebook back up," he suggests. "This is going to take a while to explain."

"Uh . . . sure," I say, flipping the cover back and grabbing my pen. It doesn't bother me that I'm dreaming. Part of my mind registers that this is going to make a really cool story. Might as well go with the flow.

"I'm here to speak with you because it's time for you to learn what you are," he tells me.

"And what is that?"

"You're a Traveler," he says, then gestures to himself. "And I am your Dreamer."

"What's a Dreamer?"

Mario goes to the front of the classroom, and the whiteboard behind him suddenly shimmers to life with a picture of a giant urn, the kind you'd see in a museum, with Greek figures drawn on it.

"Dreamers are—for lack of a more current term—*Fates*," Mario says.

"Fates? As in Greek mythology Fates?"

"I'm referencing that because you know it and it's close enough," Mario says. "We don't really decide anybody's fate outright. We're just in charge of keeping track of all the possibilities. Finn realized he was getting nowhere with you today, so he brought me in to talk to you."

"Wait," I say, touching my pen to my lips. "Is this going to be some kind of *Christmas Carol*–type thing? Like, Finn is the Ghost of Christmas Past or something? Is he visiting me to tell me how to fix my life?"

Mario laughs out loud, rich and full and genuine. "Oh, Jessa," he says. "You've always had the best imagination. But in a way, you're not far off. Finn is here to teach you, but also to keep an eye on you."

"Teach me what, exactly?" I close my notebook again.

He moves over to the desk in front of me, turning around in the seat and leaning a forearm on my desk.

"He's going to help me teach you how to travel between realities."

Before I can form a question, he lifts a hand to shush me. "I know that sounds far-fetched," he continues, "but bear with me. You're dreaming anyway, right? You might as well hear me out."

He's got a point. Might as well hear him out.

"Dreams are just another reality, and there are many, many realities," he explains. "Everyone can visit them in a dream state, though most people don't have the power to change anything. You and Finn can travel while you're awake, too. That's what makes you Travelers."

"*Everyone* goes to other realities in their dreams?"

"Sure they do." Mario shrugs. "The dreams show the other realities. Some realities are wildly different. Some are very close to what you know but just a little off." He leans in, warming to his subject. "Have you ever tried to describe a dream to someone? You say things like, 'I was in a house and it was my house except it looked like it was as big as a football field. And then we went down to the diner in town and that waitress who has the weird hair told me that my cousin murdered Matt Damon.'"

My eyes widen. "In another reality I'm related to someone who murders Matt Damon?"

He lifts a shoulder. "You never know."

I sit slowly back while I try to wrap my head around all this.

"So Finn and I travel through dreams?" I'm getting confused.

"No, you *observe* through your dreams. That's where I come in. There aren't a lot of Travelers, and each Traveler has a Dreamer.

We keep an eye on all the realities and their possibilities, and we ask a Traveler to step in when something needs a correction."

"A correction?"

He moves back to the front of the class again, and the whiteboard behind him shimmers once more. This time, it's a horizontal line that spans the width of the board.

"There's a ripple effect when a decision is made that changes reality," he explains. "Sometimes the ripples are no big deal, and the reality stream remains on course. Sometimes one decision"—he touches his finger to the line and it splits into two lines, now at right angles to each other—"can alter things dramatically, and a new reality shears off and is formed. Dreamers can see that and figure out the potential repercussions." He touches one of the lines again, and it branches into five more. "We brief you through your dreams and then dispatch you to make the necessary adjustments."

"And how do we do that? Is there a wormhole or something?"

"It's a lot simpler than that," Mario says. "I'll leave the hands-on training to Finn."

I set my pen carefully on the desk. "Look . . . Mario . . ."

"You're not sure if you believe me. And you want to wake up, write it all down in your journal, and make sense of it. I know," he says. "But that won't work. It won't make sense. Not until you're ready to believe."

"You have to admit, it's a lot to take in."

"It is. And you haven't even heard the rest of it."

"The rest of it?" How much more could there be? "I think I want to wake up now."

"We're not done here," Mario says. "I've invited some guests to join us." He gestures toward the bright red door in the corner.

"Right this way," he says.

I get up from the desk and move hesitantly toward him. "Where are we going?"

"Into the dreamscape."

"We're going into my dreams? I thought we were already there."

"The dreamscape is a place where Dreamers can observe all realities, and all the people who shape them. Including you."

I must be making a face, because he smiles at me to reassure me. "Nothing's going to hurt you here, Jessa. This is just an observational platform."

"Right," I say, trying to sound like this is all perfectly fine. "I'm right behind you."

He opens the door, and I take a deep breath.

I step through, and I'm in a baseball stadium. Thousands of fans are cheering around us, and Mario is somehow now eighty years old and wearing one of those cabbie caps that old guys like to wear to cover their bald spots. I have no idea how I know it's still him, but I do.

He takes the cap off and folds it in his hand. "Yankee Stadium," he says, gesturing with the flopping hat.

"I saw a game here once with my dad," I say. "It was a long time ago, though."

"Huh?" He leans in, cupping a hand to his ear.

"I said, I've been here before," I say loudly.

He nods. "It's too loud here, don't you think? Come on."

He walks back toward the red door again—which is visible in the wall behind the last row of seats—and we walk back through.

Instead of the classroom, we're standing next to a river, on the outskirts of a rain forest. Mario is now a woman, short and brown-skinned, with thick black hair.

"It's a lot more peaceful here," she says.

"You can go back and forth like this?" I ask, awestruck. "What are you—a shape-shifter or something?"

"It's the dreamscape." She shrugs. "I can look like anyone here. I can take you anywhere you want to go. Or show you anyone in any reality."

"Won't people notice us?"

"It's not real. Think of it like . . . an interactive movie. It feels real while you're here, but it's just a projection."

I glance around. "I don't think I've ever been here before."

"You haven't. Not this you, anyway." She motions me toward a nearby shack. There are fish hanging on a line, drying in the sun, and the red door stands out from its frame. She opens it and once again motions me through.

"How many realities are we going to visit?" I ask.

"Last one tonight," she says. "I promise."

We step through and we're in the middle of the desert. Scrub brush dots the landscape, and it's evening.

A fire has been built within a circle of red boulders, and Mario gestures for me to take a seat on one of the boulders. I do a double-take because he now looks like a young Native American boy, and he's beautiful. His hair is long and silky, and his high cheekbones and flawless skin make him look almost too perfect in the firelight. He catches me staring and smiles as he finds a boulder of his own.

Sitting next to him is a man in his early forties, blond-haired and steely-eyed with an impeccable haircut and dressed in a business suit—which really looks odd, considering we're sitting on rocks. And next to him . . .

"Hi," Finn says. "Glad you made it."

"Another face change?" the other man remarks to Mario in an amused tone.

"Variety," Mario says with a shrug.

"I like this place," Finn says, looking up at the sky. "I forget how beautiful the stars are out in the desert."

"Where are we, anyway?" I take a seat, doing my best to get comfortable on the boulder next to Finn.

"Arizona," Mario replies. "In this reality, your father got a job out here six years ago." He points off away from the foothills. "If you walk that way for about two miles, you'll be in your backyard."

"Ahem." Mario's companion clears his throat slightly, and Mario gestures to him.

"Jessa, this is Rudy. He's another Dreamer."

"Rudy?" I raise my brows. "Why don't you have old Greek names?"

"We're not Greek," Mario says. "I told you, that's only one of the mythologies we appear in. We predate your civilizations by quite a bit. These names will do fine."

"It's nice to meet you," I say, giving Rudy a nod.

"Rudy is my Dreamer," Finn says. "Mario invited us over so we could all have a discussion."

"Is that normal?"

"It's highly unusual," Rudy says. "But in this case, we feel a need to break protocol."

Mario threads his hands together, balancing his elbows on his knees, and looks over at me.

"Jessa, it's time to level with you," he says. "I haven't told you everything."

"I would imagine there's an awful lot more to know."

He shakes his head. "No, not the Traveler stuff. That'll come," he agrees. "You need to know why Finn is really here."

I look over at Finn, and I'm suddenly feeling uneasy. "What haven't you told me, Finn?"

He takes a deep breath. "I was sent by Rudy to find you. This you. Specifically."

"Me?" I clarify. "Why?"

"Because you're at risk," Rudy interjects.

Finn leans forward, running his hands through his hair. "Jessa, now you know that you exist in multiple realities. But the truth is, there are fewer and fewer of you every day.'"

"What's that supposed to mean?"

"It means," Mario finishes, "you're being killed off. One by one. Everywhere. In every reality."

I go cold inside. "Who?" I ask. "Who's killing me?"

Mario's face is full of sympathy, but Finn's voice chills me to the bone.

"I am."

7

The Target

I JUMP OFF THE BOULDER, MY MIND WHIRLING WITH panic. Oh my God, I knew it! I saw this coming! Another horrified thought invades my brain: *What if I'm not dreaming?* What if Finn drugged me or something and . . . that sounds improbable to the point of crazy, but then again, I think I'm talking to people in a dreamworld. And now they've brought me out into the middle of nowhere, where no one will hear me scream and no one will find my body.

"Jessa," Finn says, coming to his feet slowly. "Sit down. Just listen."

"Don't touch me!" I shriek. I scramble to put the boulder between me and the three of them. "I mean it! Don't come any closer!"

"Calm down," Rudy orders. "No one's going to hurt you."

"You're here to kill me!"

"Do we look like we're here to kill you?" Finn asks, spreading his hands wide.

"We're here to save you, not hurt you," Mario promises.

I stare at them all, wide-eyed.

"What is going on?" I demand. "I need you to tell me the truth—all of it. How can I protect myself if I don't know what I'm up against?"

"Jessa . . . ," Finn starts in again.

"I mean it," I snarl. "Somebody had better start talking!"

"Fine," Finn agrees. "But you really need to come out from behind that rock before you step on the damn snake."

I leap away so fast, Mario breaks into laughter. I stumble a little, then glance back to see that Finn was right. A snake lies coiled just behind my former refuge.

"It can't hurt you," Mario reminds me, "but I can imagine it would be hard for you to concentrate with a snake nearby. Let's move back to the classroom. Rudy looks like he's tired of sitting on a rock anyway."

"Indeed." Rudy stands, brushing off his pants. Mario stands as well, gesturing to the large boulder just behind me, and the red door set within it.

Finn opens the door, and I step through warily, still not over my encounter with the snake. The stark white of the classroom makes me squint my eyes after the darkness of the desert. I take my seat, and Finn slides into a desk beside me as Mario—who's back to his original self—and Rudy each lean on a corner of the teacher's desk.

"So . . ." I look over at Finn. "Why do you want to kill me?"

"I'm not the one trying to kill you," Finn clarifies. "But I am the one responsible."

I raise my eyebrows, failing to see the distinction. He rubs a hand over his face before going on.

"In almost every reality that you've died in," he says, "the cause lies indirectly with me. Either an accident or some other circumstance brings it about, but the bottom line of every situation is that if I weren't there, it wouldn't have happened."

"So you're involved in my death? Deaths?"

"I'm not doing it on purpose. In fact, most of the time, I'm trying to save you and failing." His eyes are haunted, gleaming in the firelight. "I can never see it coming, either."

"So you've watched me die . . . ?"

"Over and over again. Either directly or in the memories of the other Finns." His eyes are full of pain, so much that I have to look away.

"Why me?" I ask Mario. "What does the universe have against me?"

"We're not sure," Mario answers. "But it's happened too many times to be a coincidence. And since Finn is indirectly involved, I thought I'd reach out to Rudy and we could all work together on this."

Rudy nods. "When Mario approached me, we agreed to work together to figure out who was causing this kind of widespread targeting of one individual. It happens every so often," he explains. "A Traveler goes rogue, gets some idea in his or her head about challenging the order of things, seeking vengeance on somebody across realities. It's not unheard of to involve another Dreamer if you need to cast a larger web to track them down."

"We've never seen it quite to this level before, though," Mario says, and the concern is clear on his face. "Someone wants you gone, Jessa. All of you."

"I'm a nice person," I say. "I haven't done anything to piss anyone off—that I know of."

"Whoever is doing this is acting of their own accord," Rudy says.

"Can't you . . . ask around or something?" I ask. "If it's a Traveler, they have a Dreamer. I mean, the Dreamer had to have sent them, right?"

"That's not how it works," Finn says. "The Dreamers give us direction about where to travel and what to do when we get there, but we're not dependent on them for the ability to cross into other realities. We can do it anytime we want to."

"Really?" I look at Mario. "I could have been jumping into other realities on my own?"

"If you knew how," he says. "You're born with the ability, but we don't let you in on the secret until we feel that you're ready to accept the responsibility that comes with it."

"And sadly, it appears our faith has been misplaced," Rudy says. "This Traveler has their own agenda."

"You may not have done anything," says Finn. "Not in your own reality."

"Great." I fold my arms over myself. "So you're telling me that 'alternate me' royally hacked somebody off and now I'm marked for death?"

"That's how it looks," Finn says. "So I'm going to watch your back, and Mario and Rudy are going to watch everything else. Whoever it is, they'll have to tip their hand sooner or later."

"Well then," I say, standing up and dusting off my hands and behind. "Guess I'd better get back. How do I wake up?"

Finn looks at me funny. "You're taking this awfully well."

Mario gives me an all-too-knowing smile. "She thinks she's dreaming. She doesn't believe a word of what we've said."

"You *told* me I was dreaming," I point out.

"And so you are," Rudy says. "That doesn't mean we're not telling the truth."

"It's easy enough to prove," Mario says. "You've met Finn already in person."

"I met a cute guy and now I'm dreaming about him." I shrug. "What's so weird about that?

"You think I'm cute?" Finn looks surprised and pleased. Mario just rolls his eyes.

"I think you're all figments of my overactive imagination," I conclude. "But that's okay. I'll wake up and write it all in my dream journal and maybe I can use it in a story sometime."

"You do that," Finn suggests. "But before you go, why don't you give me your phone number?"

My eyes narrow. "You've already tried to get it, remember? I don't pass my number out to strangers."

"I'm not a stranger," Finn says. "And besides, it's only a dream."

"That's what she said," Mario agrees. "Nothing but a dream. Right, Jessa?"

I look at the two of them warily. "That's right."

Finn reaches over and picks up my pen, opens my notebook, and looks at me expectantly. I dictate the numbers, and he copies them down before closing the notebook and tucking it under his arm.

I get out of my seat and Mario gestures to the red door.

"Just open it and step through," he tells me. "You'll be back in your reality."

"All right," I sigh as I walk over. I grasp the knob and twist, pulling the door open. "It's time to wake—"

The next word is on my lips as I roll over in bed. My room is dark and the clock at my bedside reads 2:48 a.m. It takes me a moment to get my bearings.

And then my phone rings.

8

The Decision

I STARE AT THE PHONE, AND MY HAND FUMBLES WITH it as I switch off the ringer. The screen is still lit, and the glare of it seems ridiculously bright.

I reach for it again and pull my hand back, sure that it's going to stop ringing any second. I even glance around a bit, on the off chance that I'm actually still asleep. I can feel the vibration of it on the mattress, and I manage to pull in a breath despite the tightness in my chest. My hand reaches for the phone again, and I press answer.

"Hello?"

"You answered," Finn says.

"You didn't think I would?" My voice sounds entirely too high and thin. My heart is pounding.

"I had my doubts. Are you okay?"

"I'm not sure."

"Completely understandable. Are you ready to know more?"

"I—Finn, I need some time, okay? And I can't talk right now. I have to go to work early."

"What time are you done?" he asks.

I know I probably shouldn't tell him, but I do. "I'm off at twelve."

"Meet me at Mugsy's for lunch."

"I don't . . . I'm not sure."

"I'll be there," he promises. "Good-bye, Jessa."

"Bye."

I end the call, and I can't help but wonder if I'm suffering from some kind of delusion brought on by an undiagnosed brain tumor or something.

I groan and throw an arm across my eyes. *This is nuts. This is nuts. This is nuts.* I repeat it over and over in my mind, but even so, some part of me knows it's true.

I lie there awake for a few hours until I finally drag myself out of bed and into the shower, and then I spend entirely too long choosing exactly the right sweater to pair with my jeans. I am brushing my hair when a text lights up my phone.

Crap. I'd forgotten all about Ben.

> **where r u?**

he texts.

> **5 texts last night**
> **no answer**
> **U OK?**

I grab my phone, typing back:

> **Sorry**
> **Slept like the dead**
> **Everything's fine**

It only takes a minute for the reply:

> **Deathville Regatta @ 7:30**
> **U in?**

I pause a moment, considering. I'm really not in the mood for a horror movie. But then again, after lunch with Finn—or worse, without Finn, because this will have all been a delusion—I will probably need a little "normal."

> **OK**
> **Meet you there**
> **You get the tix**
> **I'll get the popcorn**

I put the phone away and brush my teeth. I add a touch of lip gloss and a swipe of mascara, and then I'm heading downstairs to the kitchen, where my mother is pouring a cup of coffee.

"Looks like I timed it just right," she says. "I thought I heard the water stop in the shower." She pushes the mug toward me. "I made pancakes, if you want some."

"Just one," I say distractedly.

She stares at me, a frown creasing the space between her eyes. "Everything okay?"

I look up guiltily. Am I that transparent? "I'm just tired. I didn't sleep well."

She puts a hand to my forehead. "You don't have a fever. But you don't work till later, right?"

"I work at nine today. Tomorrow's an afternoon shift." I take a sip of coffee. "Oh, by the way, I'm going to the movies with Ben tonight."

"We're going to the movies?" Danny calls out from across the room.

"It's a scary movie, Danny. You wouldn't like it."

Danny makes a face. "I want to see *Penguin Palooza*."

Mom smiles, shaking her head. "Danny, we're going to see it tomorrow, okay?"

"Okay." He goes back to his television show.

Mom turns to me. "We'll be at work till five, and then I promised Danny we'd get pizza. I'll see you when we get home. Why don't you go lie down for a little while—you've got time."

I give her a nod, but I know I won't get any more sleep.

I head back upstairs, whittling away the time by working on my homework. I'm hit with sudden inspiration and open up my dream journal, reading over the entries there. It's not surprising but definitely unsettling when I realize that I've been dreaming about Finn—who is now real and here with me—for months. I may not have known his name, but reading my notes brings the memories of the dreams back, and I connect the fragments easily into a picture of him. Or, more accurately, of us.

I've detailed walks in the park, trips to the beach, quiet

meetings in coffee shops, and bizarre memories of swimming with dolphins, eating fruit the size of my head, even dancing some-place with palm trees in the background.

And if he's telling the truth, I've lived every bit of it.

For as long as I can remember, I've been told I have a wild imagination. I've had vivid dreams and lost myself in daydreams, and I always felt that was a sign that I was meant to be a writer.

When I was four, my family visited the aquarium. My parents were, as usual, chasing after my six-year-old brother, who had no interest in fish but did have a strong obsession with running up and down the handicap ramps by each set of stairs.

He took off at one point, knocking into a stroller and nearly tipping it over. My mother ran over to make sure the baby inside was all right and apologize to the parents, and my father took off after Danny.

I wandered over to the dolphin display, watching the light behind the giant wall of glass filter through the water, daydream-ing about swimming with my dolphin friends in an underwater dolphin kingdom, when something odd happened.

I stood there, spellbound, staring with wide eyes at the girl staring back at me, and I was mesmerized by my own reflection.

They found me there nearly ten minutes later, and my mother scolded me even though Danny was the one who ran away first. She only remembers today that I was lost and scared her half to death.

But I remember these two things:

First, that Danny, as always, had all their attention.

Second, I remember the way my hair rippled and swirled in my reflection on the other side of the glass.

The years passed and things changed and yet they didn't. They say when you're left alone a lot as a child, you either act out to get attention or you turn inward, relying on your own creativity to keep yourself company.

This is why I write. If it's true, all of this has always been a part of me, and to find out there's a reason is a relief just as much as it makes me feel like a fraud. If it's true, I don't have a great imagination. I'm not creative or gifted or any of that. I've only been transcribing events that occurred to me someplace else.

Which makes me not as much of a writer, I think.

I slam the journal shut and do my best to ignore the rock in my stomach. It's not working. This is some serious freak-out-level crazy. And I have to decide whether I believe it or not.

I hear the door slam downstairs as my mother and Danny leave for work. I glance over at the clock, and I realize I have to leave for work soon myself. Then I have to meet Finn for lunch at Mugsy's.

If, of course, I actually believe a stranger is talking to me through my dreams and I should meet this stranger for lunch. Because that's a totally smart and sane thing to do.

I manage to make it through my shift at Wickley's market handing out samples of organic granola and gluten-free brownie bites that are surprisingly good. At the end of my shift, I have a couple of brownie samples left over that I shove into the pocket of my hoodie for Ben. That's against the rules, technically, since I'm supposed to throw them away, but that just seems wasteful to me. Ben will be happy to devour them.

I look down at my phone. It's five after twelve.

My eyes shift down Main Street toward Mugsy's, which is only a seven-block walk from here. But I'm not going there.

No, I'm not.

It's a pretty nice day, though. Founder's Park is only four blocks away in that same direction, and I could sit on a bench in the crisp air and look at all the trees turning colors while I write. It'll give me real-world inspiration.

With that half-formed thought in my head, I start walking. I find a good spot on a bench and yank my journal out of my bag, opening it to where I left off on my latest story, but of course, I have to thumb through a few pages to get there and doesn't my stupid thumb land right on the page I shouldn't be looking at.

Dark hair, green eyes.

I click the ballpoint on my pen a couple of times as I push past that page and find where I left off, and I put my pen to the paper almost hard enough to poke a hole in it. And I write.

I keep writing, glancing nervously at my phone—which is sitting on the bench next to me—at two-minute intervals. Finally, I slam the journal shut with a disgusted sound.

You are an idiot, Jessa. Just get it over with. Go to Mugsy's. Just be done with it.

I shove everything back in my bag.

This is crazy, and I know it's crazy.

I'm going anyway.

9

Through

I SLIDE INTO THE SEAT AT MUGSY'S ACROSS FROM FINN at seventeen minutes after twelve, setting my bag down next to me, and then I stare at him, uncertain of what to say.

"Still freaked out?" he asks.

"What do you think?" I ask in a fierce whisper. "People don't normally communicate between dreams and real life."

"I told you . . . we have a different definition of 'normal.'"

I gesture to the tall cup of coffee in front of me. "Is that supposed to be for me?"

Finn nods. "Caramel mocha with a dash of cinnamon."

"How do you know that?"

"Because I know you, and most of the time, you order that—or something like it."

"Most of the time?"

He takes a long drink. "I'll get to that later. But first, you have to let me prove this to you."

My eyes go wide, and I can feel my tightly clenched hands start to sweat.

"You mean . . . we're going to do it? Travel?"

"It's not painful," he reassures me. "Or even very hard. And we'll only stay as long as you want to."

He stands up and holds his hand out to me.

I have no idea why I take it.

I let him pull me along to the back of the shop, where the lone restroom stands unoccupied. Thank God. He opens the door, and with a quick glance around, we both step inside and he pulls the door shut behind him.

"We do this in the *bathroom*?"

He rolls his eyes. "We need a mirror. I'm going to show you the basics," he says, pulling me in front of him to face the mirror. "You're going to start by looking for the differences."

"What differences? It's a mirror." I look over my shoulder at him.

"It's a conduit that just *happens* to be a mirror. That's how you need to see it and every reflective surface from now on."

"You mean I could do this with anything I can see myself in?"

"That's right." He nods. "For now, we'll stick with mirrors because they're the clearest. Eventually we'll work up to other things. Lids on pots and pans. Teaspoons. Water. Even highly polished wood, if you're strong enough."

I look back at him in disbelief. "Polished wood? Really?"

"As long as you can see enough of yourself and you know where you want to go. You'll get the hang of it."

He gently takes my chin and guides my face forward again.

"Our counterparts have been prepped to travel by Mario and Rudy, so they'll be expecting us. We start by giving the signal."

He puts his hand to the mirror, touching it gently with his fingertips. Then he motions me to do the same.

"Now . . . look for the differences," he says.

I look carefully at the reflection in the mirror. My eyes sweep across the room, side to side, but nothing seems out of place. I touch the glass. There is no give to it. It remains solid and the room remains unchanged.

"This is useless," I huff. "I'm not this . . . *thing* you say I am. I'm not."

"You're a Traveler," Finn says firmly. "Just look. Concentrate. Look at only yourself and don't stop until you see the differences."

I turn back to the mirror, staring at my own eyes as they reflect back to me, first with irritation, then with boredom. She has the same dark-blond hair. The same blue-green eyes, which are mostly blue at the moment. The same deadpan expression. The same gray Hollister shirt. My eyebrows need to be plucked. Crap. I'd better remember to do that tonight before bed, if I have time after studying for the quiz in Spanish. My mind begins to drift, but I keep looking firmly at my own face, staring myself down until I feel sure that I've lost the ability to focus my eyes. I struggle back to reality, forcing myself not to zone out.

And then she blinks.

She blinks.

The other Jessa.

I draw in a startled breath and I'm about to turn away when Finn's hands come up to hold my head, keeping my face to the mirror.

"Steady," he murmurs quietly. "Keep looking. What else is different?"

I stare long and hard now, taking in every little nuance of the face in front of me, seeing the reflection as it really is: *not* me. What is that high on her left cheek? As I look harder, it seems to bloom before my eyes. It is a scar, semicircular and faded but visible.

The white paper-towel holder on the wall begins to shimmer, transforming before my eyes into a highly polished chrome. The one boring picture of a coffee mug in a brown wooden frame begins to fade, then grow, becoming larger and brighter until it changes into a brightly colored tapestry filled with bronze and copper colors, hanging from an enormous glittering golden bar attached to the wall.

"How . . . ?" I don't know what to say, much less what to do from here.

"Don't question, Jessa. Just push through. Go ahead."

I hesitate a moment. "You'll come, too?"

"I'll be right there with you. Promise."

I start to press my fingers in, and the glass now feels like stiff rubber. I take a deep, shaky breath and push harder. My hand slips through more easily this time, like pushing into a tightly pulled rubber band, but without the rebound effect. My arm follows my hand, and before I know it, the rest of me seems to just step through until I am there.

Wherever *there* is.

10

All That Glitters

I'M IN A GOLDEN RESTROOM. INSTEAD OF THE LONE porcelain toilet, there's a gilded, monstrous throne with an ornate braided pull rope hanging above it. A crystal chandelier hangs overhead and the walls are chrome, polished to a high shine. Light bounces off every surface, even the golden sink, blinding me and making me blink my eyes.

"What the—?" I let go of his hand, pressing my palms into my eyes. "Sheesh. This is a bit much."

"They're big on flair over here," Finn says. "It doesn't change the coffee much, but wait until you see the baked goods."

"So what happens to her?" I ask. "The other Jessa?"

"Simple," Finn says. "She's you. She's just in your reality now."

"Won't everyone notice she's different?"

"No."

"I don't understand. She's not *really* me."

"Yes, she is," he explains. "You're still you, no matter where you go. You're just you reacting to different circumstances. And because

66

you're a Traveler, you're more aware of yourself than most. The things that make you essentially you will always be preserved because of that. You also gain all her knowledge and she gains all yours the minute you transfer. You'll bring up the memories as you need them."

"This is seriously confusing. You know that, right? Some of this . . . it's just beyond comprehension."

He gives me a slight smile. "You get used to it. I'm trying not to overload you with too much at once. Come on. Let's see what's cooking on this side of the mirror."

"Wait," I say. "I'm not going to encounter an evil version of everyone, am I? My parents and Danny aren't going to have goatees or anything, right?"

Finn shrugs. "How do I know? Let's go see."

He reaches for the door handle, and as he opens it, a woman in a shiny silver coat guiding a young child steps back from where she'd been waiting to get into the restroom. She sees me coming out from behind Finn and gives us both a look that should incinerate us.

Finn gives her a nod that can only be described as regal, and I clap my hand over my mouth to keep from laughing as he pulls me past her and over to the counter.

"Oh my God," I say, in a hushed whisper. "She thinks we were . . ."

"Yes, she does."

He threads his fingers through mine and gives my hand a squeeze. We make our way to the front counter, and I can't stop looking at the glittering lights and polished chrome walls. Finn reaches up with his other hand and turns my head so that I'm looking full-on at the array of baked goods on display in a shining golden case with ornate prism crystal shelves.

Once again, I am dazzled. Everything looks like it was the prizewinning dessert on a Food Network showdown. There are brownies with gold leaf glittering on the top, cupcakes that sparkle and stand six inches high with shimmering, fluffy frosting over gilded golden wrappers. The cookies are glowing under the lights with silver and gold chips, and they're easily the size of my outstretched hand.

Finn nods to the girl behind the counter. "Two chocolate spice specials and two bowls of glitter mousse, please."

"No mocha with cinnamon?" I ask, still drooling over the cupcakes.

"That's not what they call it here. Think about it a moment—the memory will come to you."

He's right, and it does. Cinnamon is just referred to as "spice" here.

He pays the girl and takes our tray of treats, motioning me toward a booth in the corner with a tilt of his head. I slide in, staring at the small, circular pot of sparkling stuff in front of me. It looks like whipped cream, but in an eye-popping shade of silvery blue.

"Glitter mousse?" I ask. "What flavor is this?"

He shoves a spoonful in his mouth.

"Glitter," he says, raising his eyebrows.

I take a dab on the tip of my spoon and slide it into my mouth. The flavor explodes on my tongue, sweet and tart and screamingly delicious. My eyes are literally rolling back in my head.

"Mmmmmmmm!"

"Told you so," he says. "Now for the best part." He opens his mouth, smiling widely.

I suck my breath in, choking on a laugh. "You're *glowing!*" His teeth and tongue are shining like neon.

"Should have brought you here at night," he remarks. "The effects last for hours."

I bring my hand up to my mouth self-consciously. "How am I going to explain this? When we get back?"

Finn answers around another spoonful. "You won't have to. You'll be back as your other self. She didn't eat this stuff."

"In that case, maybe I'll have two."

He raises his brows. "I don't think the other you would appreciate it."

I look down at myself. My clothes detract a lot from the rest of me because they're pretty loud and flamboyant, but it's clear I weigh more here. I'm not obese or anything, but I am definitely overweight.

"Are you making a remark about my—our—weight?"

"Not like you think. I just know that this Jessa used to weigh more. A lot more. She's been working really hard to get in shape."

He's right. The memories of all the early morning workouts and the ways I've cut back come to me. Now I feel bad. I really shouldn't sabotage everything I've been working toward over here.

"Guess I'll stick with one."

I take another spoonful, sighing in contentment as it melts on my tongue.

"So . . . ," I muse.

"So . . . ?" He licks his spoon.

"You know me here." The memories are trickling in as I access them. "But we're not together."

"I know you everywhere." he replies, "and we're not officially together yet because I only just got to know you."

The memories are getting clearer now. Finn used to work here, and in a complete change of events, I told *him* that he was a Traveler.

"So just because I know I'm a Traveler in one reality doesn't mean I know it in another?" I ask. "I mean, I knew before you over here. We don't all become aware at the same moment?"

"No. What are you, Skynet?" he smirks.

"That," I say, pointing my spoon at him, "was a solid nerd joke. Ten points to Gryffindor."

He looks at me blankly.

"No Harry Potter, huh?"

He shrugs, still clueless. "No *Terminator*, either. I just happened to catch it on TV once, when I was traveling."

"So you're not from here?"

"Here?" He glances around at the shining chrome and sparkling chandeliers of glittery Mugsy's.

"There," I qualify. "Back where I'm from. You're not from my reality."

"No." He looks uncomfortable.

"Do you know me, where you're from?"

"I did."

I let that hang in the air for a minute before I bite my lip and ask.

"Did I move away?"

He holds my eyes.

"No."

"When—" I clear my throat. "When did it happen?" I can't bring myself to ask how it happened. I get the feeling he was there.

"Three years ago."

"I'm sorry," I say, and I really am. I can see the hurt in his eyes. Whoever we were to each other, we were obviously close.

"It's okay," he says. "Not like I really lost you, after all. We're Travelers. We're always around somewhere."

He gives me a stiff shrug, but it doesn't quite cover the pain in his voice. I can't help myself. I reach across the table for his hand. He rubs his thumb across the back of my knuckles, and the feel of his hand on mine is incredibly familiar.

"That's got to be weird, though. Seeing a different me every time."

"You get used to it."

He says it, but something in his voice tells me you don't, really.

"What if 'other me' kills somebody or OD's on drugs or something?" I ask.

"It's possible," he concurs, "but not likely. You're still you, after all."

"Not over here, I'm not."

"Yes, you are." He leans in, lowering his voice. "That's why you're a Traveler. You're still you, no matter where you are. You're just you, reacting to different circumstances." His fingers tighten on mine. "The things that make you fundamentally you won't change, Jessa."

"What if I had a hard life? Grew up on the streets? Hung out with murderers?"

"You'd still be you."

That makes me feel better. "So, that's why I can do this? Because none of it will change me?"

"I didn't say that," Finn replies. "You can't help but be shaped by the events around you, to some degree. But as a Traveler, you can recognize that they're all just random particles that swirl around you and might become part of a bigger plan. It's all transient. Maybe we're a little smarter, or braver . . . maybe just more resilient. I don't know. But we're this way for a reason."

"This is still wildly beyond comprehension," I sigh. "It really is."

"Don't sweat it," he tells me, scraping out the bottom of his bowl with his spoon. "Mario's got it all under control. He'll guide you along until you get the hang of it. I would imagine he'll give you your first official job soon."

I hold up a hand. "Whoa. Oh, no. Not yet. I'm not ready for a job yet. I haven't even agreed to sign up for this," I remind him.

"You're already signed up for this, Jessa," he points out. "And you've been seeing other realities for a while—you just didn't realize it. Now you can consciously travel. That's the only difference. I can help a little with some of it, teach you how to shift in dim light, or into water, or when your image is clouded or rippling. It just takes practice. Lots of practice."

"I haven't given an official answer about any of this," I protest.

"Jessa . . ."

I've had enough. I'm not ready to commit to this. "I want to go home," I say firmly. "Now."

"Come on . . ."

"*Now*, Finn."

He sits back in the booth. "So go ahead." He shrugs. "Go back."

"You're not coming?"

He crosses his arms. "No. Figure it out yourself. You know how."

I glance over at the restroom door, but it's closed and occupied.

"Great," I huff.

"You don't *have* to have a mirror, you know," he says, raising a brow. "Any reflective surface will work, so long as you can see yourself."

I glance around, and the polished chrome wall next to me in the booth catches my eye. I can see myself, and everything else behind me. I can see Finn, and his eyebrow's still raised in a way that really irks me.

I set my hand against the chrome and try to concentrate on my reflection.

"Don't let yourself get distracted," he warns. "You could end up somewhere you don't want to be."

"Quiet."

I take a second and look around me, so I have something to compare to when things start to change in the reflection. I look back at myself, and I try to see me sitting in a booth at my Mugsy's. I stare so long and hard, my eyes start to water.

"You're trying too hard," he says in a singsong voice, and it makes me even madder.

"Will you shut up? I'm new at this, remember?"

I straighten my shoulders and try again, and this time, everything behind me starts to get duller, more muted. I see the glittery, gold-speckled booths and gleaming, ornate decorations bend and morph into mundane photographs of coffee mugs and deep-red corduroy booth upholstery. Finn is saying something, but I tune him out, pushing my fingers into the chrome.

And I'm back.

I take a second to look around me. Mugsy's is half-full, but no one seems to have noticed me just appear. Then I realize that I was here anyway, or at least, other me was. What did I use, though? I turn the teaspoon over in my hand and see myself in the bowl. Wow, she must be good at this if she could travel through a teaspoon.

I stare at the other me for a moment.

"Hi," I whisper. "Bring me a cupcake next time."

I stare down at the humdrum chocolate chip cookie in front of me, and I wonder if I'll be able to resist the temptation to travel again.

11

Fate and the Social Norms

"YOU'RE HOLDING OUT ON ME, ST. CLAIR," BEN SAYS, tossing an entire fistful of Milk Duds in his mouth.

"Huh? What?" I realize I've been sitting here zoning out and haven't heard much of what he's said. The movie hasn't started yet, so I'm going to have to answer him.

"Are you even listening to me?" he complains.

"Sorry. Got a lot on my mind. What were you saying?"

"I was saying that the partner project in Draper's class is due on Wednesday, and I need your essay so that I can build the diorama and feature your key points."

"Crap! That's due Wednesday? We just finished the invention project!"

"Where have you been?" he laughs. "Draper announced it, like, a week ago."

"Sorry. I haven't even started. Can I e-mail it to you tomorrow night? Or maybe Monday morning? How much time do you need?"

"Relax." He throws an arm around me to pat my back, and he leaves his arm on my chair. "I can put it together in a night."

"Thanks."

I'm very much aware that he hasn't taken his arm off the back of my chair, so I lean forward and turn to him.

"Do you believe in fate, Ben?"

"Fate?"

"Like we're all part of some preordained plan or something. Destined to do things or meet certain people. Fate."

He eyes me speculatively. "Like, it's fate that we met? Is that what you mean?"

I roll my eyes. "Not that specific, but yeah, maybe you were meant to move all the way here from Texas—"

"New Mexico," he interrupts.

"Whatever. You sound like you're from Texas."

"That's because it's right next door to New Mexico," he reminds me. "And for the record, we were fated to be friends as soon as I realized that you knew my home state was actually a *state*. You'd be surprised how many of y'all ask me what my country's like."

"No, I wouldn't. But I'm talking fate in a general sense. Like there are some people that we're just supposed to meet, for whatever reason."

He takes a drink of his soda, considering for a minute. "Yeah. Yeah, I guess I do. I think we all have people that we were meant to meet. Not so sure about things we were meant to do, though."

"But how do you accept one and not the other?"

He shrugs. "I guess I'd like to think that I have a hand in

shaping my future for myself. Otherwise, why bother doing anything, right? Might as well just strap in and wait for the ride."

I start to lean back, but I remember his arm is there and shift forward again. "Yeah, I guess."

I hear his sigh as he moves his arm, but I'm not really looking at him. I'm a thousand miles away, thinking about what Finn said.

My logical brain tells me I shouldn't be getting mixed up in all this. But my gut is telling me that I trust him. I trust Finn because I know Finn.

And that's crazy. I realize that's crazy.

Ben drives me home after the movie, and we sit for a moment in the driveway, with the truck idling.

"You're awfully quiet tonight, St. Clair," he remarks. "Why so philosophical?"

I shake my head. "It's hard to explain."

"Try me."

"I need to stop having an existential crisis and go inside and write an essay," I remind him. "Or my project partner will hang me in effigy inside his diorama."

"Now there's a thought," he says, grinning widely.

I reach for the door handle. "I'll see you Monday."

"Yeah. See ya Monday." He stares at me expectantly for a moment, and then realizes he hasn't unlocked the door. He pushes the switch with a loud thunk, and I escape to my house and my room, where I hope to get a grip on myself.

That turns out to not be an easy thing. I am afraid to go to sleep.

I stay up as late as I can, finishing the essay and e-mailing it over to Ben before I tackle a new assignment for Ms. Eversor about a controversial subject. I choose "Internet Etiquette" and I realize halfway through writing it that I don't find it very controversial and I am probably the most boring person on earth.

I'd be a better writer if I'd ever done something, or been anywhere, or even met anyone interesting.

Like a hot guy who can travel through dreams and reality.

I catch my reflection in the mirror across from my bed and stick my tongue out at it. I am certifiably crazy.

I scroll through the received calls on my phone and look at his phone number. I want to dial it just so I can scream into the phone, *Why are you messing with my brain?*

But I guess that would definitely be crazy. Worse, he'll probably have an answer for that.

Come on, St. Clair. No guts, no glory.

Great. I sound like Ben now.

I finally text Finn.

> **Are you there?**

I press send. It's late. He's probably busy. Or asleep.

The phone rings less than thirty seconds later. I glance down at it in dismay. I let it ring twice more before I tap the answer button with entirely too much force.

"Why are you calling me? I *texted* you," I say angrily.

"I'm aware of that," he replies, completely unconcerned. "So what do you want? You reached out to me, remember?"

"And you were supposed to *text* me back," I say, still perturbed that he's broken a serious social rule here.

"Sorry. I prefer conversation." He lets out an audible sigh.

"What if—what if I don't want to do this?" I ask tentatively. "If I decide to be a normal person, maybe whoever it is that's hunting me will leave me alone."

"But you're not a normal person," he says. "It's a moot point. And that wouldn't stop them. They've killed you before, and they'll kill you again. They've already tried once."

"We don't know that for sure. That one was my fault. I walked into the forklift."

"You keep coming up with excuses," he says. "But this is your life now. You are a Traveler, and we need your help to figure out how to save you. Do you really want to ignore what you are and just be a sitting duck?"

I am suddenly incredibly tired.

"I don't want to hear any more about it, Finn."

"You *need* to hear it."

"No, I don't."

"Yes, you do. Or you wouldn't have called."

"*Texted.*"

"Whatever."

I punch the end button and throw the phone down on the bedcovers.

12

The Other Side

I WAKE THE NEXT MORNING TO DANNY, SITTING ON MY bed and shaking my shoulder so hard my teeth rattle.

"Ugh . . . ," I say. "Danny, get off." I yank at the covers he's sitting on, trying to roll over, but I give up. He won't be budged.

"You have to get up," he says. "You have to work soon."

I glance at the clock. "Not till one," I tell him. "It's only eleven."

"You have to get up," he insists. "Mom said to make sure."

"I'm up, I'm up." I sit up in bed so he'll leave, mentally cursing my mother as he shuts the door behind him.

I roll out of bed, spread the covers back up, and slide into some plain gray sweatpants and a black T-shirt before I brush my teeth. I took a shower before bed last night, and my hair is skewed from sleeping on it wet. I shove it back into a ponytail, and I'm staring at myself in the mirror.

My eyes shift away from the face in front of me, noting the hoodie hanging over the back of the chair behind me, the book on the edge of the bed, the messy coverlet. . . .

But I made my bed. I resist the urge to turn around and check. I know it, though. I had set the book on the end of my neatly made bed. I would bet money on it. As I look longer, the hoodie on the back of the chair seems to deepen from navy into black. My carpet gives way to hardwood, with a rug over it. My room seems to grow longer and wider, and a computer desk appears next to my bed.

I put my hand to the glass, and she does the same. A moment later, I am through.

My room is very different. She's really into black-light posters, for some reason. And it's messy—not only is the bed not made, but clothes are strewn everywhere and the dresser is cluttered. Books are lying on the floor, and I don't recognize the titles.

I move out of my room, down the stairs, and into the rest of the house, which appears to be quiet, for the most part. The place is wild to look at—the walls are all different colors than they are in my house, shades of blue and green instead of sand and tan. There are strange bohemian pictures and pieces of artwork everywhere, and the curtains have been replaced with pouffy, patterned scarves, draped artlessly over elaborate curtain rods.

"Interesting," I say. "It looks like Walt Disney threw up in here."

There's got to be somebody around somewhere. I realize that I know my way through the house, even though it's not really anything like mine.

I continue on through the house until I reach the French doors, which open up onto what I know before I see it is a spacious deck, overlooking a very large, very green backyard. The kitchen is off to the left, and I'm surprised for a moment to see my brother, rummaging through the cupboards. His hair is shorter, and he's not quite as chubby, though still solidly built.

"Danny? Hey, are you looking for something?" I ask.

He turns and looks me right in the eye. "Do you know where Mom put the Oreos? I swear, she hides them from me. I think she wants them for herself."

I stare at him, openmouthed.

"Jess?" He waves his hand side to side. "You're zoning out on me."

"N-no, I don't know what she did with them," I manage to answer.

He lets out a sigh. "Okay. Change of plans. Guess I'll make popcorn."

He goes back to rummaging, and I am frozen.

I cannot imagine Danny without his autism. It's as much a part of him as his brown hair or his love of video games. Part of me says I don't know this other guy, but I know I do.

I know he played football in high school, linebacker. He also sang in the chorus and had a solo in the final concert of his senior year that made everyone cry because it was so good. He works part-time at the loading dock of a manufacturing company across town, and he also goes to college. He's studying public relations.

He's Danny. My Danny, but not my Danny.

Suddenly, I'm frightened. I want to go back. But at the same time, I'm fascinated. I can have a conversation with Danny. One where I don't have to play word games to get information from him or hear him quote movie dialogue while I try to figure out how that applies to what he's really trying to say to me. He can just talk, and I can just listen.

"Lunch is out back, if you want it," he tells me over his shoulder. "Mom ordered from that new wings place."

I swallow my apprehension and decide I'm going to stay just a little longer. I open the sliding glass doors and stop dead in my tracks.

My parents are sitting together on side-by-side lounge chairs next to a moderate-sized pool.

We have a pool. And my parents are together.

"We've got wings!" my mom calls out.

I look at them, wide-eyed.

I realize that I'm blowing my cover here. I'd better act more . . . normal. But this does *not* feel normal.

"Hi," I manage to say.

"You hungry?" Dad asks, reaching out to offer me the bucket of wings.

"I don't think I can eat."

"Are you feeling sick?" Dad asks.

I take a moment and just look at them. They look like this is no big deal. Like the way we used to be. My parents divorced when I was nine and they're still civil with each other, but it would be a stretch to say they parted as friends. My dad still lives in town, and I see him one night a week and every other weekend, but I can't stop staring at him now.

They look content—with life, with each other. And I have a lump in my throat so big I know I can't speak. I shake my head no.

"It's because she came downstairs last night and ate a ton of snacks," Mom says, reaching for the wings bucket and heading back into the house. I give my dad an awkward smile and trail behind her, still feeling like my head is swimming.

"That's not healthy, you know," Mom scolds me as she puts the rest of the wings in a plastic container. "Missing sleep and loading up on junk is only going to make you sick."

"I know," I say. "I just couldn't sleep."

"If you had a date on a Saturday night, you wouldn't be home eating," Danny snarks from the living room.

My mother rolls her eyes. "Danny, that's enough."

"Just giving some free advice." He shrugs. "The girl needs a love life."

"Danny!" Mom objects.

"Just sayin'," he defends himself.

I look over at him sitting on the couch with a bowl of microwave popcorn balanced in his lap. I suppose some things are universal. He catches me staring and makes a face at Mom. I smile, unable to help myself.

"Jessa."

I turn to look at her again. "Yeah?"

"Just . . . take a multivitamin or something. Humor me."

"I will."

She steps back out the door, and I look over at the clock in the kitchen. I assume time runs concurrently—and if so, I really should get back.

I take one last look at my "normal" brother. I want to ask him a million questions. I want to sit and talk to him for hours. I mean, if I'm me, he's still him, right? He can tell me everything I really want to know.

Except it wouldn't really be him. Not the way I know him.

I move up the stairs to my bedroom. This time I make it through the mirror much more quickly, leaving my could-have-been life to another me.

I back slowly away from the mirror, not entirely sure about what I just experienced. Then I glance down at myself.

"Why am I wearing this?" I say aloud, and my eyes go to the mirror again. She changed me into a pair of jeans I had stuffed in the bottom of my closet because they're red. I went through a colored-jeans phase in ninth grade, but I wouldn't be caught dead in them now.

She added a bright-yellow-and-green flannel, layered over a blue-flowered T-shirt that's part of a sleepwear set. I look incredibly tacky. It only takes me a moment to get changed back into my T-shirt and sweatpants, and I wad up the other clothes, throwing them far back into my closet.

I can hear Danny downstairs, and he's shouting at someone—possibly the TV, since my mom is at work. I have an overwhelming urge to see him, so I race down the stairs and there he is . . . having an imaginary sword fight with Finn.

"Hey," I say.

They both stop to look at me. They're each clutching a cardboard tube from the center of a roll of paper towels—my mom collects them for craft projects at the retirement home where she and Danny work.

"Took you long enough," Finn says. "Weren't you changing your clothes?"

"I—uh . . . when did you get here? And why are you sword fighting?" This day is getting more and more bizarre.

"Jessa! You came back!" Danny smiles at me. "I'm giving Finn lessons."

"We were watching *The Princess Bride*," Finn explains. He looks at me oddly. "And you let me in. Then you ran out of here to change your clothes."

I'm still looking at Danny strangely, and I know it shows on my face. He's my Danny, and I didn't realize how glad I'd be to have him back, but . . . did he realize I had changed? I mean, not just my clothes?

"Jessa . . . ?"

Finn realizes something is wrong. "Danny, we'll do some more later, okay?" he promises. "I have to go help Jessa with her homework."

I feel Finn's hand on my arm as he leads me back up the stairs to my room.

"Okay," he says, shutting the door behind him. "What's wrong?"

"I . . . traveled."

He looks surprised. "By yourself?"

I nod. "And it was a lot like home, but my parents were still together."

His eyes soften. "Sometimes it's hard on the other side," he says. "You can't ever predict what it's going to be like, unless you've been there before. Sometimes, not even then."

"And Danny. He—he—" I stammer, trying to wrap my head around it. "He didn't have autism. How is that possible?"

"Who knows?" Finn shrugs. "They're not sure what causes autism, exactly, are they?"

"Not entirely, though they have found some genetic links."

"So his genes combined in a different way—maybe because of external factors, like your mom was exposed to something during pregnancy, or maybe it was just timing as he moved from one stage of development to another. It could have been any or all of that," Finn explains.

I sink down on my bed, still not sure how to process everything. As crazy as all that just was, I have a really weird feeling in my gut right now. Like there's a giant fist around my stomach. I think about my parents sitting there, side by side, and tears burn at my eyes again. I force my thoughts away from Danny, because I know I really will start crying if I think about all of it together.

"You okay?" Finn asks sympathetically. "It sounds like that was a lot to face."

"Yeah," I say quietly. That is a serious understatement. "Does that happen sometimes? Experiencing a reality that you kind of don't want to leave?"

He looks away from me.

"Yes, it happens. You'll learn to get over it."

I set my elbows on my knees and put my forehead in my hands. "I just want to write. That's all. I want to be a writer."

Finn sits down on the bed next to me.

"Nobody's stopping you. You've got an amazing gift. Take it as far as you want to go. None of that has to change."

"Everything's changed." I stand up and start walking for the door.

"Jessa, think about all this for a moment," he says, grabbing my shoulders and turning me to face him. "You've got something here that any writer would kill to have—unlimited worlds to explore, and all at the touch of your fingertips. How is that a bad thing?"

"How do you do it, Finn?" I ask him. "How do you keep from getting attached to people you know in these other realities?"

His hands are still on my shoulders, and they slide up to gently cup my face. "You don't. Not always." For a long moment, his eyes hold mine; then he drops his hands and shoves them in his pockets. "But it's better if you don't let yourself."

"I don't think I'm cut out for this."

"And Mario and I know for a fact that you are."

"So we're back to me having no choice in the matter," I say glumly. "Look, I appreciate that I have access to all this writing material. It's just everything that goes with it that I'm not so confident about."

"I know. But I'm not worried," Finn says.

"Why?" I ask, shaking my head. "What makes you all so sure about me? It's not like I've got superpowers or anything."

He pushes a strand of hair behind my ear.

"I'm always sure about you, Jessa," he says.

13

Possibilities

IT'S MONDAY, AND I'M BACK AT SCHOOL. SOMEHOW, THIS reality now seems surreal, and I'm living in some bizarre fantasy world in my head. I see the world around me with new eyes. Every nuance, every tiny decision falls like a rock hitting the surface of a frozen lake, causing cracks that spread, shattering the surface.

Do I want pizza or chicken noodle soup for lunch? Should I wear the blue hoodie or the gray one? What if my mom leaves five minutes late for work? What if Danny puts two packs of frosting on his Toaster Strudel?

The possibilities breed more possibilities, cycling on into infinity, and now I know there's a group of superpowered reality travelers who keep it moving smoothly. All these years I've been harvesting my dreams for story ideas and I never had an inkling that I was really experiencing any of it.

I certainly never, in my wildest dreams, thought I'd really be meeting Finn in the flesh or that he'd be trying to help me navigate this sea full of crazy. My mind is still whirling over all that

I've seen, and I've only been to two other realities. How many are there? Thousands? Millions?

I find Ben leaning on my locker right before history class, and I wonder for a moment what he would have been like in the reality I visited yesterday. The memories from the other me surface, and I sift through them.

There was no Finn in that reality. But there was a Ben. He and I traveled in different social circles, and we didn't speak much. But I did have a slight crush on him.

I let that sink in for a moment as I walk toward him in my reality, and to say this is a weird sensation would be a serious understatement.

It's not that I never considered Ben as romance material. I actually did at one time, when he first moved here from New Mexico a year ago. He was the focus of lots of female attention. Some of it was because he was new, from someplace most of the school considered to be "exotic," and this is a small, boring town. But he's also easy to look at.

We've only just gotten a class with each other this semester in AP Honors History, and then he joined Spanish Club. By the time we started hanging out, I'd begun dreaming of Finn on a nightly basis. How does anyone compete with your dream guy? It was a losing battle from the start, but I couldn't very well explain that to Ben without sounding like a complete head case.

I do like being around Ben, though. He makes me laugh, and he doesn't mind if we just hang out or occasionally do goofy stuff like playing Band Hero or binge-watching Netflix. Most of all, he's good with Danny, and not a lot of guys are. I think he makes people feel uncomfortable, and they don't know how to talk to him. Ben never worries about any of that. He just treats Danny like a normal person.

My mind flashes to Finn, pretending to sword fight with my brother, and I break into a wide grin as I reach for the handle on my locker.

"Do I have food on my shirt or something?" Ben asks.

I glance over at him. "Not that I can see. Why?"

"I figured you were smiling because you were fixing to bust on me for something. What's got you in such a good mood?"

"I was just remembering something funny," I reply. "How was your game yesterday?"

"We lost."

"Sorry." I grab my binder and my history book out of my locker, and he closes it for me before falling into step next to me.

"It's okay." He shrugs. "We suck."

"Go team," I snark. "That's the spirit!"

"I don't see you out on a field anywhere, St. Clair." He bumps me with his shoulder.

"Hey, how'd the diorama turn out?"

"It's done and it's good. Perfection."

"Ah," I say wisely. "The perfect partner project. I knew I could count on you."

We make our way into history class, where I put my pen on the paper and start working on my latest piece for creative writing class.

I listen to Mr. Draper drone on with half an ear as I start to form my story. My protagonist is a superhero guy who will appear to a person, and he's summoned there when they utter the phrase, "I'm all alone."

Once he's thrown there, face-to-face with the person he needs to help, he has only twenty-four hours to find them a friend. A true friend. Someone who can make a difference in that person's life.

It's a good premise. I can explore all the many reasons someone might feel alone, and Ms. Eversor is big on the humanity angle, too. She'll like that I've got people helping others. Too many kids in my class write horrible emo poetry and postapocalyptic zombie stories. She likes the upbeat stuff.

I flesh out the story a little more, concentrating on my supporting characters, and despite my efforts, the hero is shaping up to be exactly like Finn. Of course.

I stop gnawing on my pen and glance up at Mr. Draper, who hasn't moved from the position he took at the front of the class. I don't think he's changed the inflection in his voice, either.

I glance over at Ben so he can see me roll my eyes, but he is paying attention. More than that, he looks like he's enjoying this lecture. I've never considered the Prussian involvement during the Revolutionary War to be that exhilarating, but Ben is eating this stuff up, raising his hand a few times and really discussing the answers with Mr. Draper.

Finally, after what seems like an eternity, class is over. I'm distracted at school, and it's starting to show in my schoolwork. I had a C on my test in calculus and end up with a low B on my history pop quiz from last Thursday. I shove the paper into my messenger bag when Mr. Draper hands it to me, thoroughly disgusted with myself.

Ben holds the door for me as I exit the class.

"That was a rough one. You all right, St. Clair?"

"Yeah. I should have studied more." I make a face because I'm still mad about it. "How did you do?"

"I aced it." He shrugs. "But I always do. It's an easy class."

"Thanks." I give him a dirty look.

"It would have been easy if you'd studied," he chides. "What's up with you?"

"What are you? The nerd police?"

He raises his hands defensively. "Just being a friend. Sorry."

"No, I'm sorry. That was bitchy."

"Yep."

I give him a sideways glare as we walk down the hall. "I need to get my mind off things. My mom just bought that new space movie—the one with the airborne mutant virus and the scientists who get trapped on that planet."

"*Eosphere?*"

"Yeah, that's the one. We could watch it after school. Can we do it at your house, though?" I don't want Ben at my house, because I don't want to take a chance on Finn showing up to the party.

He looks uncomfortable for a moment. "I can't. I've got a date."

I stop in my tracks. "Really?"

"You don't have to sound so disbelieving, you know," he grumbles.

"I didn't mean it like that. It's just . . . it's Monday," I finish lamely.

"It's just a first-time get-to-know-you-over-coffee kinda thing after school. She lives in Manortown."

"Didn't they just beat your team in soccer?"

"Yup. Whupped our butts. She was there supporting her brother and came over to comfort me."

I raise a brow and make a tsk-ing sound. "Fraternizing with the enemy. What has our school come to?"

"I consider it good sportsmanship."

"I'll bet."

I try not to be disappointed, but I am. I'm just so used to having him as a fallback plan. I don't know who this girl is, but I instantly don't like her. And I also realize how completely petty that is, but I can't help it.

"Sorry," he says.

"It's okay." I wave him off. "I should be studying anyway, and Eversor wants me writing something about local ghost stories for the next installment of *The Articulator*. Maybe I'll go to the local historical society after school to research."

"Ghosts? In Ardenville?"

"They don't have ghosts in New Mexico?"

"Some. Mostly the things that go bump in the night are coyotes." He says it like a true westerner.

"Out here, that word has three syllables," I say primly. "You'd better learn that before they kick you out of the great state of New York."

"*Kigh*-oats," he repeats. "You're the one saying it wrong."

"At least I'm not a total suck-up," I say. "It must be nice to have a dad who's a history professor."

"Come on. I just asked about the Prussian helmet design and von Steuben's contributions to sanitation and their effect on lowering the rate of dysentery."

"Keep talking just like that. It's sure to get your new girl interested."

His eyes slide sideways to meet mine. "You jealous, St. Clair?"

"Of course I am. If you're out with someone else, who's going to discuss dysentery with me?"

I bump his shoulder with mine and head into creative writing class, uncomfortably aware that I am jealous. If Ben gets a girlfriend, he won't be hanging out with me anymore. That also leaves a lot more of my time free for Finn, and traveling, and all that comes with it.

I'm still not sure I'm ready for all that comes with it.

14

Unexpected

THE ARDENVILLE HISTORICAL SOCIETY IS HOUSED IN AN unassuming old stone farmhouse, on half an acre of what used to be a sprawling farm, before it got sold and developed into a community of town houses.

There's a woeful lack of ghost stories centered in or around Ardenville on the Internet, which is not surprising in the least, since there's a woeful lack of anything about Ardenville on the Internet. We're just not that exciting.

But since the local historical society is offering a ghost tour on Halloween night, I figure that's a good place to start with the research on my article. I push the door open, listening to it creak loudly. The wooden floorboards aren't any more forgiving, and I wince as I try to make my way silently into the room.

"Hello?" I look around, but there's nobody in sight. There's a light on in the next room, and the door is partially open. I make my way back to it.

"Hello?" I call again. "Are you open?"

The door swings open wider, and an older woman with a mop of unruly gray hair stuffed under a kerchief peeks her head out.

"Hello!" she calls out cheerfully. "Yes, yes, we're open. All the way to six. Sorry I didn't hear you. I'm trying to get this room sorted out. We've got a ghost tour coming up, you know."

"So I've heard," I remark, looking around. "I'm actually here to research that very subject."

"Oh, well, then," she says, brushing dust and cobwebs off her shirt and pants. "This is your lucky day! One of our volunteers organized it all into a collection, over there."

She gestures toward one corner of the room. "If you go behind those bookcases, there's a set of shelves on the wall and a small display of items from haunted houses in the area. You may take pictures, if you'd like."

I thank her warmly, and she heads back to her work, reassuring me that I only need to call for her if I have any questions. I make my way back to the corner, squeezing between packed bookcases and old, dusty cardboard boxes until I see what she was directing me toward. The shelves are small, and there can't be more than a half dozen or so books and a stack of yellowed newspapers a few inches high. I may not get much out of this, but I'm pretty sure I can stretch whatever I find into two pages of writing.

I carefully grab a couple of newspapers off the shelf and spy a weathered rocking chair across the room out of the corner of my eye. I make my way over to it as I skim the front page, and turn around to sit, laying the papers in my lap. I realize I'm too close to the wall behind me, because the chair makes a weird metallic thump against whatever the rockers have hit. I half stand so I can pull the chair out a bit more, and my eye catches a piece of my reflection when I glance behind me.

It's an enormous mirror with a very ornate frame, full of curlicues and scrollwork, and it's framed in pewter, so it must weigh a ton. It's propped up against the wall, and it's like something out of an old gothic novel or maybe some Jane Austen story. I'm fascinated by the intricate carvings in the metal, with roses and ribbons intertwining. It's just beautiful. The kind of mirror that would have hung in a grand parlor or a vaulted entryway somewhere in an opulent old estate. I stare at my reflection and smile, picturing the beginning of a story, of a girl in a high-necked dress, refined and genteel. I catch a glimpse of my reflection, and I smile as I reach out, putting my fingers against the glass.

Her eyes and my eyes lock, and she slowly stops smiling as the room behind me begins to change. The faded roses on the wallpaper give way to stripes, alternating crimson and gold. The arm of the rocking chair is against my leg, but before my eyes it becomes a leather-covered settee, also in a deep shade of crimson. I push my hand forward, and I am through.

I stop a moment to look around, and it's like I landed in some kind of weird Victorian fantasy. A music player that looks on the outside like an old Victrola, complete with the horn on top, sits on the rolltop desk in the corner, and on a table is a gadget with a hand crank and gears that powers what I know to be a projection screen, for watching movies.

I realize I'm having trouble breathing, and that's when I look down and see myself. Holy cow, I'm wearing a corset. I can feel it, binding my ribs and waist, under the mountains of fabric that make up my navy skirt and bustle and the smart navy short coat with brass buttons I'm wearing over it. A lacy white blouse with a high collar and a sapphire brooch at my throat round out the ensemble.

My hair is pulled to one side, hanging in artful curls over my shoulder. I pull my skirts back and take a look at my pointed navy shoes with a prominent brass buckle across the bridge and an inch-high heel. I pick up my foot to turn it this way and that as I stare at it.

I smile widely at myself now, taking it all in. I turn as far around as I can and crane my neck to see myself from the back. I look amazing! I wish I could take a picture of this, I really do.

I make my way over to the open window, and my senses register the sound of seagulls as I approach. I look out over the water and down at the docks off to the right. My house sits up on a small hill, overlooking it all, and it is spectacular. The ships at the dock are unlike anything I've seen before, bearing massive metallic sails that still manage to ripple and billow with the wind. A few are made of wood, but the rest are metal, sleek and shiny, with scroll-work figureheads and grand murals painted on the sides. It's like I've landed in some kind of steampunk reality.

I dash across the room, throw open the door, and push my way out into the hallway, nearly tripping on my skirts. I'd better slow down until I get used to this. Maybe I should go back and change into something easier to move in?

No, better not. Other me had a reason for putting this getup on. I'd better stick to her plan or people might get suspicious.

I grab the banister in one hand and pick up my skirts with the other as I slowly make my way down the winding staircase. It isn't until I step out the front door that I realize I live in a lighthouse.

I stare up at it in awe. It's whitewashed and red-trimmed, and the windows around the light gleam in the bright afternoon sunshine. I'm walking backward as I stare up at it, and give a violent start when I run smack into somebody.

"Easy there, my girl," says my father. "You tear that dress, and your mother will buy you another the color of dun."

"Oh, I couldn't bear it," I say, grinning mischievously. I am the apple of my father's eye. His darling girl. And I know it. He wouldn't have me seen in anything but the smartest clothes.

"I'm off to the docks," I tell him. I want to get a closer look at the amazing ships, but memory tells me that Daddy doesn't exactly like me wandering the docks.

"Mother said there was shipment of spices coming in today, and some perfumed oils," I improvise, pulling from a thread of memory.

"Don't be long," my father says sternly. "You've been spending a lot of time down at the docks. People will begin to talk." I answer with an indulgent smile. He worries too much.

My fiancé won't care a fig if I'm seen at the docks. My dowry will see to that.

Whoa. I'm engaged. His name is Boyce Hadley, and he's the son of a shipping tycoon here in New Devonshire. They're a respectable family but have recently found themselves a bit cash-strapped. My dowry will get them back on even footing again and elevate me into society, far above my current position as lighthouse keeper's daughter.

I search my brain, pulling the rest of the details together.

My mother is the sole heiress to her father's fortune due to the untimely passing of her elder brother five years before her father died. She married for love, never caring much about society. She and my father run the lighthouse because they enjoy it. My brother will be taking over someday.

And I will be marrying Boyce, in eight weeks' time, because it's what I'm supposed to do.

Wait . . . where in the world is New Devonshire? The UK? I pull from my memories here, and it starts flowing in. America never challenged the British. There was no Revolutionary War. We are part of the kingdom of Britain, and if my fuzzy memory is correct, New Devonshire is somewhere on the coast of what I know as South Carolina.

I'm nearly overwhelmed by all the sights and sounds and smells. High overhead, I can see a dirigible passing over, and I'm so excited to see it and the ships, I have to remind myself to slow down so I don't trip in these heels.

I make my way down the sandy pathway to the edge of the dock, stepping carefully and picking up my skirts in my fist so they won't catch any rough edges or nails on the boards. I make it about halfway down the dock when I see a familiar ship. The gangplank is extended, so I step carefully on and walk up it, reaching out for the bowline to steady myself as I step onto the deck. My skirt catches on the back of my heel, so I bend over, shaking it to pull it free. Just as I start to straighten up, I'm spun around and fall right into Finn's arms.

And he laughs as his lips come down upon mine.

15

The Other Finn

FINN'S MOUTH IS WARM AND HIS HANDS SLIDE AROUND my waist, pulling me in closer. He's moving his lips expertly on mine, giving me a series of soft, sucking kisses that deepen into something longer as his arms tighten around me.

"You're late," he murmurs against my lips, between kisses.

"Ummm . . ." I don't know what to say, but I'm also not sure I want to stop kissing him.

"Did your father suspect?" he asks. I pull back, looking at him curiously. He'd said *father* differently.

"Jessa? Is something wrong, love?"

I open my mouth and close it again, shaking my head. "You sound kind of . . . Irish."

"Well, how d'you expect me to sound?" he asks, confused.

"I—I don't know. I guess the Irish is fine." Actually, it was sexy and it made my stomach flutter, is what I really want to say to him, but maybe it's just the aftermath of those kisses.

I glance around. "Love the ship."

"Well, I would hope so. It'll be your home soon enough."

"But I'm en—" I break off as the rest of the memories fill my head. I'm not marrying Boyce. I'm running away. In three weeks, I'll be running away with Finn. He pulled into port four months ago and told me I was a Traveler. We'd become romantically involved shortly after. And we are leaving town, sailing away together.

Suddenly, entirely too many memories are filling my head, and I step back, putting a little room between us.

His eyes show his concern, and he steps forward.

"Jessa? Are you all right?"

I look up at him with entirely new eyes now that the memories are flooding in.

"Finn, I'm not—"

"Jessamyn!" a voice is calling loudly from the dock.

I look at Finn with wide eyes. *Jessamyn?* What sort of a name is that?

"Your father!" he says in an urgent whisper. "Here!" He pushes me behind him, motioning for me to head down the stairs to the crew quarters below. They're empty this time of day, and I press my back up against the wall in the corridor, straining to hear what Finn is saying to my father.

"Beg pardon?" Finn's voice carries to me. "Jessamyn? Blond hair, blue dress?"

"That's her," my father confirms.

"I've seen her around here before, never knew her name." Finn reassures him. "She passed by a few minutes ago, but I didn't see where she went after she turned off the dock. I was busy seeing to my cargo, mate."

"Spices?" my father asks suspiciously.

"'Fraid not. Gentlemen's trousers. Surplus load taken from a Dutch frigate in sovereign waters."

"Humph." My father sounds clearly disgruntled. "Did the spice merchant's load make port yet?"

"Hours ago," Finn informs him. "They've already offloaded and taken it into town."

"For your trouble," I hear my father say, and then I hear his boots ring out on the gangplank. A few moments later, Finn comes down the stairs, flipping a gold coin in the air and catching it.

"Not only did I drive him off your trail, but he paid me to do so. I call that a profitable day."

He grins a lopsided grin and reaches for me once more.

"Now," he says, maneuvering me gently back against the wall as his mouth hovers just above mine. "Where were we?"

He starts to lower his head again, and it takes a great deal of focus for me to push against his chest and back him up. He looks at me in confusion.

"Something wrong?"

"Finn," I say carefully. "Don't freak out, okay? I'm a different me."

He takes a step back. "Jessa?"

"Still Jessa, but not *your* Jessa. Sorry," I say apologetically. "If you'll give me ten minutes, I'll run home and get your girl back for you."

He looks concerned. "She's traveling without me? We agreed she wasn't going to do that."

"It's not her fault. I didn't agree."

"You wouldn't have been able to travel if she didn't want to as well. It seems she was looking for an adventure, just as you were, love."

I don't know why it makes me warm inside when he says that word, but it does. I'm getting way too comfortable with this Jessa's memories. It doesn't help that he's wearing black leather pants and a black shirt that clings to his arms and chest in a really distracting way. I tear my eyes away from him.

"Okay, then," I say. "Let's get her back so you can yell at her— or whatever."

"You're speaking differently as well, you know," he says. "Are you not living in New Devonshire, where you are?"

"No. I'm in a town called Ardenville. It's in New York State. Off the Hudson River." I glance down. "And we don't dress like this."

"How do you dress?" he asks, cocking his head to one side.

"Pants. T-shirts. It's a lot easier than all this stuff." I gesture down at my skirt, corset, and bustle.

"A woman in trousers." He gives me a speculative look. "Interesting. And I'm not from Greenore, I take it?"

"Is that in Ireland?" I ask, scrunching up my nose.

"Yes." A smile pulls at his lips. "So where am I from, then?"

I stare at him, thinking. "You know . . . I don't really know. You've been so annoying, I never got a straight answer."

He laughs lightly, chucking me under the chin. "You've got some backbone, love. I quite like it."

"Please don't tell me I'm some wilting hothouse flower over here."

He shakes his head. "Nothing of the sort. My Jessa has strength in her—it's just not so close to the surface as yours." He steps in closer again, invading my personal space to the point where I can feel his breath fan my lips.

"But I do love a woman with gumption," he adds.

I put my hand on his chest again. "Finn."

He lets out an exaggerated sigh. "Are you sure you need to go?"

I nod, trying really hard not to let him see how rattled he's got me. "You need your girl back," I remind him.

"You *are* my girl, or haven't you learned that yet?" he asks. "Wherever you go, you are who you are."

"Let's just say I don't have all the same experiences," I tell him, trying hard not to blush. I fail miserably, and he makes no effort to hide his answering grin.

"Really?"

My back stiffens. "I'm not sure I like that it surprises you."

He chuckles again. "I'm not casting aspersions, love. I just gave myself more credit in your reality."

"You only just showed up in my reality."

His eyes narrow thoughtfully. "Interesting."

"Anyway . . ." I look around. "You're a sailor?"

"I'm the captain," he says, sounding slightly offended.

"Sorry. That's right. Wasn't thinking." I feel really awkward now. "I'm new at this," I say.

"You'll figure it all out," he promises with a wink, and I'm staring at him—way too long.

"I'd better get back." I look toward the stairs, but he motions me farther down the corridor.

"Come along, then," he says.

He turns and walks to the end of the corridor and opens a door. It's the captain's cabin, and inside is a sleek four-poster bed that dominates the room. I try not to stare at it, and I wish I didn't remember it so well. I glance over at Finn, and I'm embarrassed to see that he's caught me doing so. He raises a brow, and his knowing grin makes it clear that he's figured out just what I'm remembering. I clear my throat, stepping around him.

"There you are, love." He points toward the mirror on the wall. "Bon voyage." He makes a grand, flowery gesture with his hand that almost makes me laugh out loud.

"Good meeting you, Finn. Again."

"You won't easily be forgotten, Jessa." He reaches for my hand, bringing it to his lips. I stare at him a moment, trying hard not to like him so much. He's entirely too charming, this Finn. And he knows it, too.

I shake my head to break his spell, and then I pull my hand from his and put it to the mirror, staring hard at the other Jessa. As my fingers push through, my mind can't help but say it:

Lucky girl.

16

On the Bridge

I SINK BACK INTO THE ROCKING CHAIR WITH A LONG, exaggerated sigh. Holy crap.

I take a deep breath in, grateful that I can do so without restriction. How in the world can women still be in corsets in a modern age? No wonder I was ready to run off. I still have a vague memory of my fiancé, with his pasty skin and receding hairline. He's nice enough, in a bland sort of way, but he's in his midthirties and nowhere near as exciting as Finn, who is my age.

Finn is very young for a ship's captain—he inherited the ship after his father's death, but he's already making a name for himself. He operates as a privateer, serving Her Majesty's interests and bearing a letter of marque and reprisal that allows him to board unregistered vessels, or those deemed to be carrying contraband cargo. His ship is one of the fastest solar schooners on the water.

In short, he's a pirate. A legal pirate, but a pirate all the same.

I can't help but laugh at myself, getting all fluttery over Pirate Finn. Good God.

I glance down at the papers on my lap and see that I've apparently gone shopping while I was away. There's a pink paper bag with raffia handles sitting on my lap from Baubles Ladies' Boutique on Main Street. I never shop there. I pretty much buy everything at the mall, but Baubles is only a few minutes' walk from here. It figures she'd go shopping.

My jaw drops as the memories rush in, and I reach into the bag.

Inside is the scantiest, laciest bra and underwear set I've ever seen, in a light shade of pink with darker pink ribbons. There's also a matching garter belt and pale-pink silk stockings.

The other Jessa had decided to do some exploring, reveling in the corset-less freedom of blue jeans and a comfy T-shirt. She'd stopped at the drugstore first, eager to try chewing gum, before she moved on to Baubles, fascinated by all the varieties of pants and short skirts. She'd discovered the scandalous lingerie section in the back, and once she'd overcome her initial shock, she brazenly thought she was doing me a favor. My mind floods again with some *very* specific memories of her Finn.

I hear the historical society lady in the other room on the phone and push everything back down in the bag, embarrassed to be seen with it. The receipt flutters to the floor, and I pick it up to put it in with the rest, but my jaw drops again.

"Eighty-four dollars!" I say in outrage. "You spent eighty-four dollars? On this?"

She'd even used the Visa gift card my dad gave me for my birthday! I had been saving that to use for Christmas!

Great. Now I'll have to stop there on the way home and return this crap. I wad the bag up, shove it down into my backpack, and pull out my notebook again.

I guess it was too much to hope she'd be sitting here taking notes while I was kissing her boyfriend. I wonder if she's mad at me. And I'm getting warm again remembering it all.

"Focus, Jessa." I shake my head at myself and reach down for the stack of papers that are now on the floor. I eventually find a story about a young girl who haunts the creek behind the public library, where she supposedly drowned herself over a hundred years ago after discovering she was going to have the mayor's illegitimate child.

My eyes slide back to the mirror.

I probably have enough information to write the article. I need to get out of here and away from this stupid mirror and its memories. I stand up, carefully placing the newspapers back on the shelf in a neat pile. Maybe I should head over to the library. I might be able to find more on this story, especially since a former mayor was involved. Then I can take some pictures of the creek behind it to add to the article. Danny normally volunteers on Saturday, but today is the library's birthday party, and he should be finishing up soon. I can walk him home.

I peek my head in the doorway to the adjoining room and thank the woman who helped me, assuring her that I have found what I need. She tells me to be sure and come back for the ghost tour, and I promise to spread the word about it.

It's a short walk over to the library, and I decide to get my pictures first before I go in. Knowing me, I'll get sucked into researching and forget that it's going to be dark in an hour.

I make my way out of the library, following the slope of the back lawn, and then I walk along the creek until it hits its deepest point, right around the old stone bridge. It was once used to connect Main Street to Greaver Avenue, but it was deemed unsound for regular vehicle traffic sometime in the seventies, because it floods when the creek gets high. You can walk on it, though, and people still fish off it from time to time.

I snap a few shots of the bridge before I walk up onto it, positioning myself at the center so I can get a couple of pictures of the creek's length. I've just stretched my phone out to set up the shot when I hear my name from up in the treetops.

"Jessa!"

I look up and to the left, and there, sitting in a tree, is Finn—and Danny is right next to him.

"What the—?" I shade my eyes with my hand so I can see them better in the late afternoon sun. "What are you two doing in a tree?" I yell.

"Ballooning!" Danny shouts back, full of glee. He's pointing up into the branches. A dozen feet above them is a Mylar balloon, stuck in the tree.

"I was on my way to Mugsy's and saw him out here chasing this thing down," Finn calls out.

"It's from the birthday party," Danny reminds me. "I lost my balloon."

Are they crazy? Danny can't be climbing trees!

"Get him out of there!" I shout back. "He's not good at climbing!"

Finn glances over at Danny, who grins back at him and shakes his head.

"I need to get the balloon." Danny is emphatic. "It's *littering*."

"We can't leave it there," Finn calls with a shrug.

"You get it, then!" I insist. "Danny, you stay put. Let Finn get the balloon, okay?"

"It's littering!" Danny repeats.

"Let Finn get it!" I throw my hands up in the air. "Finn!"

"I'm on it," he shouts good-naturedly. He starts to climb and his foot slips a little, making me yell, "Watch out! You need to—"

Before I can finish my sentence, two things happen simultaneously. First, I hear Finn scream, "No!" and second, I hear the unmistakable roar of a car engine as a blue sedan comes flying across the bridge. I have nowhere to go.

It only takes a split second, and I leap over the side, falling for what seems like an eternity before I hit the shallow but icy water below, slamming hard into the boulders and rocks just beneath the surface. I feel pain, and then I feel numb.

Then I feel nothing.

17

Saved

I AM REALLY, REALLY COLD.

I shake all over with it, and it only makes me ache more. I can feel hands roll me to the side and I cough several times, tasting the brackish water of the creek as it comes out. The hands are chafing my face, moving down to my arms, and then the pain becomes excruciating. I try to scream, but all that comes out is a watery cough and a long moan.

"Jessa? Jessa! Talk to me, please. Are you hurt?" Finn's voice reaches me through the fog of pain.

I manage to nod, but the shivers have turned into full-on convulsions now. I feel him wrapping his jacket around me, jostling my arm once more, and this time, I make plenty of sound.

"Sorry!" He moves more gently, tucking his jacket more tightly around me. "I think you might have broken your arm," he says.

"Jessa! Jessa!" Danny sounds frantic. "That car was killing you!"

I open my eyes finally and start to put out a hand to reassure him. The movement sends shafts of pain through my left arm, and I close my eyes again, feeling like I'm going to be sick.

"She's okay, Danny," Finn reassures him. "She's not going to die. She just hurt her arm a little. Let's call your mom, okay?"

I groan again as I realize I dropped my phone when I jumped. My mom is going to kill me, because my phone is probably at the bottom of the creek somewhere.

Danny pulls out his phone, but he's too upset to remember how to open the contacts and find our mom's number. Finn takes it from him and makes the call. I can hear my mother's voice on the other end. She's at work right now, but it's just a few minutes away from here. I won't have long to wait.

Finn pulls me up against him as gently as he can, trying to settle me into his warmth. I'm still shivering, and every shake of my body is agony. His legs are wet with creek water, so I burrow into his chest as best I can.

"You cut your head," he says, looking down at me with concern. "Did you hit it hard?"

"I d-don't th-think so," I stammer. "J-just m-my arm."

"Don't be hurt, Jessa," Danny says to me. "That car shouldn't have killed you."

I laugh, in spite of my pain. "I kn-know, Danny. I'll b-be okay."

"He's right," Finn says, glancing around. "What the hell was that all about?"

"S-some idiot," I manage to say.

"You really could have been killed."

"I would have seen them s-sooner if I wasn't l-looking at you c-clowns." I take a deep breath, and it hurts. A lot. "I think I m-might b-be sick."

114

"It's okay," Finn says. "I've got you. Just lie still." His voice is troubled, and his eyes won't stop shifting around. Danny is sitting on the ground next to us with his arms around his legs, rocking.

"D-Danny," I mumble.

Finn glances over at him. "You okay, Danny? Jessa's going to be fine, buddy. Really."

"My fault," he says loudly. "My fault. My fault. It's my balloon. My fault."

I try to shake my head, but that hurts, too. "No, Danny. N-not your f-fault."

"No, it's not," Finn reassures him. "It's mine." He says it grimly, like he believes it. I look up at him in confusion.

"Your fault?" Danny asks.

"Yes. My fault. I shouldn't have distracted Jessa."

Danny nods. "Your fault. Jessa shouldn't be killed by that car," he reiterates.

I hear a car horn in the distance. My mother has pulled into the library parking lot. Finn looks down at me.

"I'm going to have to pick you up. It's going to hurt."

"It h-hurts anyway," I tell him.

"Mom!" Danny is up and running, yelling out the details of our debacle as he streaks across the grass toward the parking lot. I feel Finn shift beneath me, and a few seconds later, he's picking me up in his arms. The world tilts as pain screams through every nerve ending in my body. I twist my head to the side and I am suddenly, spectacularly sick.

Somehow, Finn doesn't drop me, and lays me gently on the ground again.

"S-sorry," I mumble, trying to wipe my mouth with my good

arm. Even that hurts. I'm embarrassed beyond belief. My eyes fill up with tears, and they stream down my cheeks sideways, into my hair.

"Don't cry, Jessa," he says softly as he lifts me again. "Please don't cry."

He starts toward the car. My mother and Danny meet us halfway, and after a quick introduction and debriefing from Finn, she helps him settle me in the backseat of the car for the ride to the emergency room.

"Someone drove across the bridge?" my mom asks incredulously. "They've had that road closed off for forty years. There are signs all over the place! Who would do that?"

"S-some idiot," I say, keeping my eyes closed. The motion of the car is making me feel sick again.

"Someone in a blue sedan," Finn adds.

Danny reaches back from the front seat and pats my head.

"That car shouldn't have killed you, Jessa," he says.

18

Loopy

I LIE STILL, TRYING TO WRAP MY FUZZY MIND AROUND where I am.

I'm in a hospital bed, and Finn is sitting next to me. There's an IV in one arm, and a sling around the other. I think I've got a bandage on my forehead, too—I can feel it pull when I frown.

"Hey," Finn says, reaching out to touch my IV'd arm.

I close my eyes and smack my lips at the sticky feeling in my mouth.

"Why do I feel so weird?" I murmur sleepily.

"They've got you pretty drugged up." He moves his hand up to push my hair off my face, and I roll my cheek toward his hand.

"S'nice," I say. "Your hand is warm."

"You want to hear about the damage?"

"Sure. Lay it on me." I smile, totally loopy.

"Well . . . you've got a dislocated shoulder. That's why your arm hurts."

"It's not broken?"

"No. They reset it while you were under, but it'll be sore for a while," he explains. "Along with that, you've got assorted bumps, bruises, and scratches, and an IV pumping antibiotics into your arm because you got creek water in your lungs."

"Awesome," I say, closing my eyes again. "That's just awesome. I have to write now."

I can hear the smile in his voice. "No, Jessa. You have to rest. You can write later."

"No, I need to write it while it's fresh in my mind." I open my eyes and smile at him. "While you're fresh in my mind."

"Oh," he says, and I can tell he's pleased. "You're writing about me."

"I always do," I confess. "Well, almost always. Even before I knew you were you, I wrote about you."

I try to get up, but the movement makes the room spin madly and I slump back down.

"Whoa. Spinning."

"Would you like to sit up a little?" Finn asks. "I can raise the bed."

"Mmmm," I reply noncommittally. "Where's my mom?"

"Danny was hungry, so she took him down to the cafeteria. They'll be back soon."

"Oh." I close my eyes, and I think I may be dozing off again. I feel Finn straighten my covers, and then he kisses my forehead. I break into a loopy grin again.

"What?" he asks.

"You kissed me," I say, and then I giggle. I never giggle.

"It was just on the forehead," he protests. "I thought you were asleep again."

"You kissed me right on the mouth," I explain. I pull my IV'd arm up and put my fingers on my lips. "Right here."

"I did?"

"Other you did. And you were a *pirate*." I open my eyes, and he slowly comes into view. "You look good in black, you know."

He looks at me carefully, and then glances around the room before lowering his voice. "Jessa, did you travel without me somewhere?"

"Mm-hmm. It was easy this time. Piece of cake." I point at him with a crooked finger. "You didn't think I'd be good at this, did you?"

"I never said that."

"Well, other you seemed to think I was pretty awesome," I tell him, giving him a smug smile.

"Is that so," he answers drily.

"And boy, can he kiss," I add. My eyes slide closed, and I drift away again into a dreamless sleep.

When I wake, Finn is gone, and I can hear my mom talking quietly with Ben. My head is a little clearer, but now I can feel my shoulder a lot more.

I shift onto my side, to find the button that raises the bed up, but I groan as everything starts to hurt. My mom and Ben both turn at the sound.

"Looking pretty gnarly, St. Clair," Ben teases.

"Just out for an afternoon swim," I quip. My mom joins him

on the other side of my bed. She reaches down, taking my good hand.

"I'm just glad you're okay," she says. Tears start to fill her eyes, and she blinks them back before she leans down to smooth my hair off my forehead.

"They'll be bringing you more pain medicine soon. Your dad stopped by, but you were asleep and he didn't want to disturb you. He'll be back tomorrow."

I frown, and it pulls at my bandage again. "I have to stay here all night?"

Mom's hand gently strokes through my hair again. "You're hurt, honey. Are you hungry?" she asks. "Can I get you anything?"

I hadn't been, but now that she's said it, I am starving. "Yeah. I'll take whatever. You know what I like."

She glances toward the door. "I think they brought you soup, but you were still sleeping. They may still have it out there."

"Soup is fine," I say, clearing my throat. My voice is husky and my throat feels raw. I guess that's what happens when you swallow a creek.

"I'll be right back," she reassures me, kissing me again.

Ben takes her place, folding my good hand into his. "Hey, listen, St. Clair," he says. "Just because I'm dating another girl doesn't mean you have to throw yourself off a bridge."

I roll my eyes. "Please. How did it go?"

"How did what go?"

"The coffee date, stupid. What's her name, anyway?"

"Oh, the date," he remembers. "Didn't happen. My truck broke down on the way home from school, and Dad had his car at work."

"Better luck next time," I say.

"Right. So what were y'all doing, anyway?" he asks. "Danny said he was up a tree with your new boyfriend."

"My new . . . Danny said that?" That's not like Danny. He probably considers Finn to be more his friend than mine. They were climbing trees together, after all.

"Well, is he?" Ben doesn't realize he's squeezing my hand as hard as he is. I give it a tug, and he releases me.

"Sorry," he apologizes. "None of my business."

"No, it's okay. Finn's just a friend." I can't quite meet his eyes.

"Yeah. There's a lot of that going around," he mumbles. "Do you know anything about the person who almost hit you? Did you see who it was or anything?"

"There wasn't time. It all happened so fast."

"What about your *friend*?" He overemphasizes the word.

"Not that I know of. Maybe that's where he went—down to the police station or something."

"I told Finn to go home and clean up—he was soaked," my mother says, reentering the room. "He wants you to text him when you feel up to it. He's a nice guy. How come I haven't seen him around before?"

"We just met last week."

"Your brother certainly likes him." She slides a tray onto the bedside table, then turns the table to pull it across me. "Danny's pretty upset by all of this. I sent him down to the cafeteria to get ice cream."

"Well, I'm not too thrilled about this, either," I reply, raising my eyebrows.

"I know, sweetie. Here, try the soup. They said if your head isn't hurting, you can go home sometime tomorrow."

"When can I go back to school? I have a paper due."

"I'll call the school," she reassures me. "I'm sure Ben can turn in your work for you. The doctor wants you home until next week. Your dad and I are switching weekends so you don't have to be moved unnecessarily."

"Great." I sigh, trying to shift myself upright more so I can eat. Mom puffs up the pillow and slides it behind me, but it jostles my shoulder and I let out a groan.

"I think you're due for your medicine," she says with a frown. "They said it's better with food in your stomach. Let me go get the nurse."

She steps back out into the hallway, and I reach clumsily for the spoon and end up knocking it off the tray. Ben picks it up off the covers and puts it in my good hand.

"Do you need me to spoon-feed you?" he asks.

"I'm not that bad off," I say. "Just groggy."

"So what grade is Finn in?" he asks me nonchalantly, while he opens a pack of crackers.

"I'm not sure," I hedge, and really, it's the truth. "I just met him. He doesn't go to school here."

"Where'd you meet him?" he asks, raising a cracker to my lips. I turn my head away.

"I don't think I can eat that," I say with a grimace. "My throat feels like I swallowed rocks."

"You might have," he says, popping the cracker into his own mouth. He finishes chewing and looks at me thoughtfully.

"So . . . he's from Manortown? Or someplace else?"

He's not going to let up, and I really am not mentally up for

122

creating a backstory. I push the tray with the soup away and close my eyes.

"I don't know, Ben," I say. "I just met him. And I'm really tired and everything hurts."

"Sorry." He sounds chagrined. "Just looking out for you, St. Clair. Somebody's got to do it."

I don't have the heart to tell him the position is already taken.

19

Family

THE NEXT TWO DAYS GO BY IN A BLUR OF PAIN, THEN pain medication, then sleep. At least it was my left arm that caught the brunt of it. I can still type one-handed, so I do. I finish Ms. Eversor's ghost assignment. My mom dropped it by the school and returned with homework for English lit. My calculus homework sits on top of the pile by my bed, but I can't bring myself to do it yet.

Luckily, my phone somehow landed on the bridge and didn't get run over by the psychopath in the car, so I can at least play some games and surf the Internet. Mom is adamant about me not having visitors for a few days, so I'm starting to get really bored now that I'm awake more. It's only Wednesday and she wants me "quiet and resting" until Friday. My left shoulder is a sickly purple and green, and I can't move it much. We've cut back the medication, and now I'm only taking it at night, since my shoulder stiffens up while I sleep.

I finally get tired of lying in bed. I run a brush through my hair and walk downstairs in search of food.

"Danny, I mean it," my mother's voice warns from the kitchen. "You need to calm down."

I walk into the family room to see Danny standing with his hands in tight fists, making a face at my mother's back.

"What's going on?" I ask.

"Danny doesn't want chicken," Mom answers, running a hand across the back of her neck. "And I thought we had more macaroni, but we're out."

"*I want macaRONI!*" Danny shouts.

"We don't have any right now. I have to go to the store," my mom tries to explain, for what's probably the fifth or sixth time. She looks tired, and I realize very suddenly that she probably is.

"Hey, Danny," I say. "What if I make you a grilled cheese?"

"I want macaroni!" he repeats, refusing to budge an inch. Time to break out the psychological warfare.

"Fine. I'm going to make myself a grilled cheese and you don't get to have one." I stick my nose up in the air, and I walk toward the kitchen.

"No!" He tries to stop me. "I want a grilled cheese."

"I don't know . . . ," I say, as if I'm considering it.

"You make me a grilled cheese," he says emphatically. Then he remembers his manners. "Please, Jessa?"

I give him a begrudging look. "Okay. Just this once."

He leaves the room to go watch a DVD, and I saunter into the kitchen.

"Crisis averted." I open the cupboard, reaching in for the griddle.

"Let me do that," my mom says. "And what are you doing up?"

"I'm getting a backache from lying in bed all day." I lean

against the counter and look at her. "Have you even sat down since you got off work?"

She laughs. "No. When do I ever get to sit down?" She goes back to stirring her fry pan full of chicken and vegetables, and I reach across, taking the wooden spoon out of her hand.

"Since now. Go sit down and relax. I can stir chicken and make a grilled cheese."

"I don't want you hurting your arm," she says.

"I don't use my left arm to flip grilled cheese." I tilt my head toward the living room. "Sounds like Danny's watching *The Incredibles*."

She looks torn. "I love *The Incredibles*."

"I know you do. Go sit on the couch and watch the movie. Or open up a book for ten minutes. I've got this."

"Okay . . . if you say so."

"I say so." I point toward the couch with the wooden spoon.

She gives me a silly sort of half-smile and then hugs me carefully. Then she runs a hand over my hair.

"Why don't you call your friend Flynn?"

"Finn."

"Sorry. Why don't you tell him to come over? Or give Ben a call?"

"You mean it?" She nods and I perk up immediately, giving her a smile as I butter bread for Danny's grilled cheese. She peels the cheese slices from their plastic wrappers, laying them out for me.

"Enough, Mom. Go sit down."

"Okay. But watch that arm."

I plate up the stir-fry for Mom and me and deliver Danny's grilled cheese before settling between the two of them on the couch. I send Finn a quick text, telling him to come over, and I leave the phone in my lap as I eat. We watch the movie, and for a while it feels wonderful to be back in the normal world again. But I know there's no such thing. I don't get to be normal, ever again. Someone wants me dead.

Finn shows up halfway through the movie and watches it to the end with us. He's never seen a Pixar movie, and I have to remind myself that he's not from around here. After the movie, we go up to my room so I can tackle some homework.

"You seem like you're feeling better," he remarks as he sits down on the bed next to me.

"My shoulder still hurts, but it's not as bad as it was. It's a great shade of yellowish green. I only have to take my medicine at bedtime now."

"That's a shame," he says, and his mouth twitches into a smile. "You're awfully cute when you're medicated."

I put my hands over my face. "Oh God. What did I tell you?"

He's grinning widely now. "You met a certain pirate . . . ," he prods. "And I gather he—or should I say 'I'—got a little familiar."

"It all happened out of nowhere," I tell him. "I had no idea he was there until I ran into him. I was too busy noticing how weird everything was."

"It's all right," he says. "You're bound to run into me from time to time. It's just a little odd that you fell right into his arms like that. You've been so determined to run away from me."

He sounds almost . . . hurt. I owe him the truth.

"It's not you I'm running from, Finn. You come with a whole life I'm not sure I want for myself."

"Would it be so bad?" he asks softly. "Living that life? You're not alone in this."

His fingers come up to tuck my hair back behind my ear, and they linger, touching my face. "I'll take care of you, Jessa. You know that."

I give a little shiver as his fingers stroke my skin.

"You're cold," he says.

I try to get a grip on myself. "It's freezing in here."

"You think?" He shrugs. "Guess I'm used to the cold. I'm fine." He glances around, then finds my hoodie on the back of the chair by my desk. He hops off the bed and then helps me out of my sling and carefully into the sleeves.

Once I get my sling back on, I settle myself again, cross-legged. "So, where do you live that's so cold and has no Pixar movies?" I ask him. "Antarctica?"

He exhales, almost like a sigh but deeper, and I wonder if I shouldn't have asked that. Finally, he answers.

"My reality started out a lot like yours," he tells me. "We just got . . . derailed."

"By what?"

"Natural catastrophe, triggered by man. We'd been fracking and drilling all over Montana and Wyoming for decades, without a lot of regulation or oversight. Eventually, we triggered an earthquake cluster that kicked off the Yellowstone eruption. That led to global temperature drops, crop destruction, famine; all the rivers and streams were choked with ash. It happened when I was a little kid, but my mom used to tell me about what it was like before. It sounded a lot like your life."

"And now?" I'm almost afraid to ask.

"Widespread starvation and not a lot of natural resources. The government fell to a military coup, which led to a couple of short-lived wars in a battle for usable land that threw spots all over the world into anarchy. Now the few people who are left are running. Like me."

"From what?"

"From each other." He stops a moment. "There's no food where I live, Jessa. No animals, no plants, not even many living trees. It's all gone. The rest of the globe didn't fare much better, so aid has been extremely limited and without any kind of widespread distribution. In some places, humans are the easiest source of food."

I put my hand to my mouth. "That's horrible."

"You learn to sleep with one eye open. And you learn to avoid people when you do see them." He smiles faintly with a memory. "It took you and me a long time to trust each other."

I'm almost afraid to ask. "We didn't . . . eat people, did we?"

"No. But now you know why I'd rather be here with you," he explains. "And I never existed in your reality, so I wasn't sending anyone to a certain death when I came over."

"You never existed here? Really?"

"Not as far as I can tell. I tried to find my parents when I first got here, but no luck. And according to the census records at the town library, there's no record of me or anyone in my family anywhere in your reality."

"So how did you know to come here?"

"Rudy," he says. "Since I don't have a counterpart, he arranged everything through another Traveler—money, shelter, cell phone. I don't need much. I'm used to living with a lot less."

I reach for my notebook while my mind processes everything he just told me.

"No trees?" I ask. "At all?"

"Not many. A lot of the streams and creeks that fed their roots are gone. There were so many fires. They raged out of control with no one to stop them." He pauses a moment, and his eyes unfocus as he remembers.

"There was one big oak I found once," he continues. "It was on the bank of a river, so it was still alive. And green." His voice is wistful. "I hadn't seen green in a long, long time, so it was amazing when I saw it."

"Have you been back?"

"Back *there*? No way." His voice is emphatic.

"So you've never gone back home," I say. That just seems . . . impossibly sad somehow.

"It's not home," he says quietly. "Home is where your family is. There's no one there for me anymore."

He has no family. At least, not anymore. I think of my mom and Danny and Dad. What would it be like to lose them? To live in hunger and fear and cold every day? No wonder he travels. He's got nothing to lose.

But I do.

Oh, I do.

My mind starts to wander, and a scene begins to play in my head.

He stood sentinel in the doorway of what used to be their home. The picture she'd hung on the dirty wall had fallen, leaving a pile of glass and pieces of frame on the floor

*beneath it. He watched her pick it up, turning it over
carefully in her hand.*

"It's ruined," she said softly, her voice quavering a bit.

"I'm sorry."

*He looked like he wanted to comfort her, but the need to
protect her from whatever might be outside was stronger.*

"We can try to find another frame . . . ," he offered.

"No. It's ripped."

"Maybe we can fix it."

"No."

*She blinked back the tears because they were stupid.
Useless. "They weren't my family, anyway," she confessed.
"I just pretended they were."*

"I know."

*The kindness in his eyes was almost her undoing. "Let's
go. There's nothing here. They got it all."*

*She pushed past him, out the doorway, wiping her cheeks
as she went.*

I suck in a breath and Finn's voice breaks into my thoughts.
"What?"

"I just had a . . . a memory, I think. Something I dreamed
once. We were in a house with blue shutters. I think it had been
robbed or something. There was broken glass . . . and the door
was kicked in."

"We were only there for six days," he says quietly. "But it was
home while it lasted."

I slowly lay my pen on the page, then close the journal
over it.

"That was your world?"

He nods. "You and me and a handful of others, trying to find a safe place, scavenging for food. They got everyone else. Then it was just us."

"Who are *they*?"

His mouth turns down. "The bad guys. They're kind of the same everywhere you go—good versus evil. They were the evil, at least there, anyway."

"Wouldn't it be nice if evil stayed in one reality?"

He reaches for my hand. "It doesn't work that way. That's why I'm here."

And I know he's here because I'm no longer there.

20

No Rest for the Weary

THAT NIGHT, I TAKE A PAIN PILL AND DRIFT OFF TO SLEEP with my calculus homework still undone on my lap, and I find myself back in the classroom, staring at that red door.

"How are you feeling?" Mario asks, stepping forward to greet me.

"I feel great in here," I answer. "At home, not so much."

"Improving, though?"

"Yeah. Slowly but surely. I'm bored more than anything."

"Well, I can certainly take care of that," he says, gesturing to me to take a seat.

He leans back against his desk. "Tonight, we'll be laying some ground rules. I'm sure Finn has covered most of the basics, but I just want to reiterate."

"Do I need to take notes?" I realize how stupid that sounds the minute it comes out of my mouth. It's not like I'm going to wake up with a magical notebook in my hand.

"Sorry," I mumble. "Forgot where I was."

"It's okay," he reassures me. "And you can take notes if you think it'll help reinforce anything. Or if you're just more comfortable having a notebook in your hand." He smiles at me kindly.

"I'm okay. Sorry I interrupted."

He waves me off again like it's no big deal and turns to gesture to the whiteboard behind him.

"Rule number one," he says, and it appears in writing on the board, glowing a vibrant red. "Don't tell anybody what you are."

"Who'd believe me?"

"Exactly. It's just common sense. It's hard to travel when you're locked up in a padded room, and I can't exactly send someone to influence anything in your reality if you're in lockdown."

"No problem. I have a hard time believing it myself."

"Rule number two: Do the job you're assigned, do it quickly and simply, and then get out. Try to limit undue influence."

"Right."

"Rule number three is related," he says. "Be careful." The word *careful* is illuminated behind him, in letters much larger and bolder than the others.

"I don't mind you traveling recreationally because you need the practice, and so far you've kept everything nice and even," he explains. "Just be careful. You don't want to create a major ripple event that might take a lot of effort to undo."

I wince a little. "You know about my other traveling?"

Mario gives me a very knowing look. "I know everything about you, Jessa. And I know everything about *every* Jessa."

"You're not mad?"

He shrugs. "It's expected. Just be smart about it. Now . . ."

on to the next lesson," he says, walking over to the red door. "Come along."

He opens the door, and I get up from the desk to walk over.

"Where are we going this time? I ask.

"Back to the dreamscape," he says, opening the red door. "To the stadium. I set up a scenario for training purposes earlier today. We're going to watch a replay."

"What?"

"You'll see," he says. "Let's wait over here."

This time, Mario is a young, very attractive Latino with biceps to die for. He's wearing a tight muscle shirt and sunglasses, and women are glancing at him as they shuffle past.

"Nice look," I say.

"A favorite of mine," he replies, with a nod at an attractive redhead who stares a little too long.

Suddenly, the redhead plows into the man in front of her, because he plowed into the couple in front of him, and they stopped short because a middle-aged man with a ponytail and a team jersey has come to a dead halt, trying to scrape some gum off his shoe.

He doesn't seem to notice the furor he's caused, and a few of the people give him dirty looks as they make their way around him. He finally cleans his shoe off and everyone's moving smoothly again.

"For a minute there I thought she was stopping because of you," I said to Mario.

"She was—inadvertently."

Realization begins to dawn. "You set the guy up with the gum."

"That's right. See?" he says. "Simple. A piece of gum and wheels are set in motion. In and out and it's done."

He motions me over to the door, and we step back through, into the classroom.

"What was the point of that?" I ask. "How did it massively alter anybody's reality to be mildly inconvenienced for a couple of seconds?"

"It was long enough for the man in front of the redhead to reach into the purse of the woman in front of him," Mario says. "He stole her wallet."

My eyes widen. "You helped him steal a wallet?"

"I did," he says without remorse. "And if that were reality, it would set off an entire chain of events that would curb several dozen other events that would have splintered and formed over seventy new reality streams."

"So these . . . *corrections* keep things in check?"

"That's what most of our work is about. The realities keep expanding, and adjustments are a necessity."

"I don't even want to know how you manage to keep track of all this stuff." My mind is boggling at the thought of endless realities and endless possibilities. "Do you ever get any downtime? Ever?"

"Now you know why I try on new looks for entertainment," he remarks drily. "It's not like I can book a cruise."

"You need a spa day."

"Tell me about it," he sighs. "But I'll settle for getting you into a nice, mundane reality where no one's trying to kill you. How does that sound?"

"Sounds good to me," I say.

Well, the not-getting-killed part. I'm starting to get really tired of being mundane.

I'm beginning to think this traveling stuff might be the answer to my prayers—once it stops being such a curse.

Not long after I wake on Thursday, Finn is at the door with a scone and coffee from Mugsy's, hoping to cheer me up.

"Thank God you're here," I gripe. "Mom and Danny are out and I swear to God, there is nothing to watch on daytime TV."

"You're looking great," he remarks, setting my goodies down. "You look better rested, at least."

"No thanks to Mario. He started my classes last night."

"How'd it go?"

I shrug. "Fine, I guess. I was just getting rules and observing. He knows about my unauthorized travel, by the way."

"Of course he does," Finn says. "And as long as you're careful, it's not a big deal."

My eyes light up with a sudden idea. "Hey, can we . . . go somewhere?"

He considers a moment. "Do you have somewhere in mind?"

"It's too early for glitter mousse."

Finn raises his eyebrows. "It's *never* too early for glitter mousse."

"Somewhere new," I say. "Surprise me." I hold up a hand. "But in a good way."

"I have a few places in mind," he says. "Let's put in a call."

He tugs me to my feet by my good arm, and we head up to my bedroom. It takes a little longer this time—nearly ten minutes—before we get a response, and then we are through.

I am standing next to Finn, looking at myself in the side mirror of a van. Before us is a rocky cliff overlooking the ocean, and there are people about, but not many. We are both wearing wet suits.

"Looks like we might have another couple of hours at most before it rains," comes a voice from behind me. I look over my shoulder at my father, who is carrying equipment.

"Maisie had better be in a talkative mood today," he goes on. "Last time I didn't get anything I could use. It's like she's playing mind games with us, I swear."

"Do you need some help?" I ask.

My dad smiles. "You and Finn get the rest of the stuff," he calls over his shoulder as he heads back to the van.

"My father is a scientist," I murmur. That doesn't seem right, and yet I know it is. He doesn't work at a wastewater treatment facility. Here, he is a marine biologist and part of an ongoing dolphin study that maps their language and actually communicates with them.

"Yes, he is," says Finn. "And I'm interning with him. It's how we met."

We carry the equipment over to the edge of a short cliff that hangs out over the water, and Finn tells me he has to get the boat ready. I get the digital video camera out of the bag, setting it on the tripod as Dad puts on his headphones and tests out the sonar equipment. Then I reach for the sound sensors—these are attached to floating buoys. The dolphins are able to recognize them, and even approach to communicate on their own.

We've been talking to them for nearly eight years now, and what we've learned has helped us in so many ways—environmentally, scientifically . . . no one really thought it could be done, but my father was an important part of that breakthrough.

He studied marine biology on a full scholarship, instead of dropping out for two years and marrying my mom, then finishing an entirely different degree in night school after Danny was born.

I get the last sensor affixed to the buoy just as Finn pulls up in the boat. He's waiting just below where we stand on the top of the cliff face, about a half dozen feet above him.

"Drop the buoys!" he calls. I pick up a buoy each, and one at a time, we lower them down into Finn's hands so he can place them carefully in the boat. Then I give my dad a wave and leap into the water. Once I hit, I swim over to the boat, and Finn pulls me in.

"You ready?" he asks.

I give him a thumbs-up while I reach for a towel to dry off my face, and he starts up the motor and steers us back out into open water. I sit at the bow, holding the buoys steady until we reach the drop point. Once they're in place, I give Finn another thumbs-up and he takes the boat parallel to the coast, heading down toward the marina.

We pull up next to the dock, and he maneuvers us close enough for me to hop up and secure our mooring line to the post. He joins me on the dock a moment later, and we stand there, just looking at each other.

"So," he says.

"So . . . this is cool."

"I thought you might like it. Come on, I'll show you around."

I walk with him down the dock toward a row of shops set back off the marina.

"We can really travel anytime we want?" I ask. "I mean, every day if we wanted to? Dreamers don't get upset about it?"

"Think of it like a big football game," Finn replies. "Your Dreamer is your coach, and when it's game time, he pulls you onto the field. He tells you the play that's going to go down, and he tells you the part you're going to take in it, and you play the game. You may put your own variation on the play, adjusting for events on the field, but when the game is over—when you wake up—the coach doesn't follow you home to live with you."

He stops us both in front of the door to a small shop. The weathered plank sign announces the name: GRACIE'S CAFÉ.

"You have a life outside the game," he continues. "The coach might call to see how you're doing or even come by to drop something off every now and then, but your life is still yours. And if you want to play a friendly game of football at the park with a bunch of friends or a group of strangers, all your coach— your Dreamer—asks is that you be careful and not do anything that could wreck you for your next game."

"Believe me, I'm sticking to nice places like this if I can help it," I reply.

"You hungry?" Finn asks. "Gracie makes the best clam chowder around."

I make a face. "Ugh. I *hate* clam chowder."

He looks surprised. "Really? It's usually one of your favorites." He opens the door and I walk through.

"I got sick on it once when we were on vacation. I haven't been able to eat it since."

"Ah. Causality."

He nods his head as the hostess seats us. "It happens. One of the millions of little things that can alter a person in ways that can't always be immediately determined. Which explains the need for Travelers."

"Because of my aversion to clam chowder?" I ask skeptically.

"You never know. Maybe someday, some scientist in a lab will create a supervirus that wipes out most life on earth. Strangely enough, the cure resides in the chemical and organic combination of clams, potatoes, and cow's milk. Clam chowder is the salvation of mankind—all except for you."

He pauses a moment as the waitress hands us menus and takes our drink order. Once she's out of the way, he continues.

"And when you pass away due to your aversion to the cure, we will have also lost any contributions your descendants would have given us as well, including a new fusion drive that would have enabled space travel at far greater speeds than we travel at now. So that peaceful alien culture we could have discovered is ignored all because you got sick on clam chowder once."

The waitress takes our order as I mull all this over. I sip my Coke, trying to gather my thoughts.

"And Mario keeps track of all those repercussions?" I ask, finally.

"That's what Dreamers do."

I look around as the waitress puts our plates down in front of us. The other people in the restaurant seemed to be normal enough. Then I glanced down at my plate, and the bread on my sandwich is green.

"Yech!" I nudge the bread with my finger, almost afraid to touch it. "My bread is moldy."

"No, it's not," he says. "Think about it. You know it's fine."

He's right. It is fine. Bread is almost always this shade of green. They use a type of algae in it that's supposed to be really healthy, and it gained popularity a decade before my birth, when a huge blight wiped out most of the wheat in the country.

But I still don't want to eat it.

"Oh, go on," he prods.

"What if I get sick on it and we never go to Mars and discover fat-melting chocolate?"

He raises a brow and toasts me with his soda. "Here's to living dangerously," he says.

21

Recovery

I'M GETTING REALLY TIRED OF BEING AN INVALID. BY Saturday, I've finished all my homework and I'm rewriting one of my stories for the fifth time as Finn shows up, bearing my morning coffee from Mugsy's. "I'm *so* bored," I whine as he sits next to me on the couch.

He looks over his shoulder to make sure we're not overheard. "We could travel again," he says.

As much as I'd love to get out of the house, I shake my head no.

"I'd feel bad about it. When the other me got here, she really wasn't expecting me to be injured. There wasn't much she could do for fun. She ended up rearranging my room, remember?"

"We could watch a movie," he suggests. "Anything you want."

"*Donnie Darko?*"

He shrugs. "I don't know that one."

"Strangely enough, it's about a guy who can see shifts in reality and time. Everyone thinks he's crazy till the end, when you find out he's not."

"I can see the appeal." He grins.

"I feel so useless," I huff as I reach for the remote.

"I like you right here where you're safe."

His hand reaches out, and he twines his fingers with mine just as Danny's voice calls out from the front room.

"Jessa! Ben!"

"What about him?" I call back.

"His truck is here. I see his truck."

I pull my hand from Finn's, and a second later, the doorbell rings and Danny lets Ben in. He walks into the family room and does a subtle double take when he sees me on the couch with Finn.

"Oh. Sorry," he says uncomfortably. "I ran into your mom at the gas station and she said you could have visitors now. I can come back later."

"No!" I reassure him. "It's fine. Stay." I gesture to the empty chair across from the couch. "This is Finn. He's a friend. Finn, this is—"

"Ben," Finn finishes. "Jessa talks about you all the time."

I do? Since when? At least, not to Finn I don't.

"You're the guy who fished her out of the creek?" Ben asks.

"He's the one," I answer for Finn. "You want a soda or something?"

Ben takes his eyes off Finn long enough to roll them at me. "How many times do I have to tell you Yankees?" He asks as he roots through the fridge for his drink. "It's a Coke. Even if it's Dr Pepper, it's a Coke. I don't drink *soda*."

I give him a smirk. "Since when was New Mexico part of the south? It wasn't much more than a territory during the Civil War, and as I recall, both sides claimed it."

144

"That true enough," Ben says, finally taking a seat and popping the tab on the soda. "But they divided it, North and South. Under the terms of the Mesilla Convention, the southern half of the state joined the Arizona Territory as part of the Confederacy. I'm from Alamogordo, which would have been part of that agreement. That makes me technically southern."

"Southwestern," I correct. My eyes slide over to Finn, who's looking at both of us like we're talking Greek.

"Honors history," I explain. "Ben's kind of a prodigy."

"Really?" He looks at Ben and his eyes narrow slightly. "And how long have you lived here in Ardenville?"

"I moved here middle of last year," Ben answers. "My mom got a job up here."

"And how did you meet Jessa?"

"Finn," I say with a smile through gritted teeth. "Ben and I met in class. And didn't you promise Danny a game of Mario Kart?"

Finn raises his eyebrows. "I did." He nods to Ben as he stands. "Hate to meet and run, but I promised Danny."

"Are you sure you're ready to take him on?" I ask him.

"I've done it once or twice," he answers. "I'm sure I'll manage to keep up."

"Not with Danny," Ben and I chorus together.

Finn's eyes hold mine for a moment before he leaves the room. Ben watches him go.

"So what's his story?" he asks me quietly.

"What do you mean?"

"You meet this new guy and coincidentally, he's there when someone tries to run you over?"

Oh, for Pete's sake. "Ben." I can't keep the exasperation out of my voice. Honestly, between the two of them I'm ready to jump off the bridge again. "He pulled me out of the creek. He saved my life—I would have drowned."

"Well, that doesn't mean he owns you," Ben grumps.

I roll my eyes. "I didn't say that he did."

He gets up from the chair. "I need to get going."

"You just got here," I remind him. "You know you can stay awhile."

Ben's eyes move to the doorway Finn just passed through, then back again. "Can't," he says. "I just came by to see how you were holding up. I've got a game tonight to get ready for."

"Maybe your soccer honey will be there," I say hopefully.

"Nah. She's into somebody else already."

I raise my brows. "Great girl you almost had there."

"Tell me about it." He drains his soda, setting the can on the kitchen counter. "See ya Monday, St. Clair."

"See ya," I call after him. I hear Finn and Danny shout their good-byes, and as the door closes, I get up to go see how their game is going.

As expected, Danny is gleefully beating Finn, racing circles around him. It's not even close. As Baby Peach raises her trophy in the air, Danny jumps up to do a victory dance.

"Beat you!"

"And he did it in a stroller, even," I point out.

"I never stood a chance," Finn says, shaking his head. "He's a demon on wheels."

"Do I kill people with my car?" Danny asks.

"No, Danny," I affirm. "We don't kill people."

"Does Ben kill people?" he asks.

"What?" I look at him and shake my head. "No, Danny. Ben doesn't kill anybody. How can you say that? Ben is your friend."

"But when he doesn't drive his truck, does he kill them?" he insists. "When he's in his blue Dad car?"

I slide my eyes to Finn, who gets up from his chair slowly. "You saw Ben driving the car?" Finn asks. "The one that almost hit Jessa?"

"I didn't see. It was too fast. Too fast." Danny sits back down and reloads the game. "Let's race!" he says.

"I'm done for now, Danny," Finn says. "I have to go."

He walks with me into the other room, and then puts his hand on my arm. He lowers his voice and asks, "What was all that about?"

I sigh. "The car that almost hit me was a blue car," I say. "And he knows Ben's dad drives a blue car, because Ben's driven it here before. In his mind that means from now on, anyone with a blue car kills people."

"And Ben drives a truck."

"Yeah." I fold one leg under me as I start to sink down into the couch. I freeze halfway down and I'm sure I look comical for a moment, before I shake my head and finish sitting.

"What?" Finn's too clever to have missed that.

"It's nothing. Stupid." I paste a smile on my face, but my stomach is suddenly in a knot.

Finn crouches down in front of me, raising my chin with his fingers. "What, Jessa?"

I almost forget to answer him. His face is very close, and my eyes slide down to his lips, like they're beyond my control.

"Jessa—what?"

I take a deep breath. "Ben's truck broke down on Monday."

Finn's eyes widen. "So he could have been in his dad's car?"

I dismiss that outright. "No, he said his dad needed the car. He even canceled a date because of it. He couldn't have been driving—I would have seen him."

"It all happened very fast, Jessa," Finn points out.

"This is *Ben* we're talking about."

"I know. And you wouldn't necessarily have noticed him, because you weren't looking for him."

"What are you saying, Finn?"

"I'm saying, maybe he was looking for *you.*"

22

Accusations and Assignments

IT'S SATURDAY NIGHT, BUT I'M NOT OUT HAVING A social life. Instead, I took a pain pill for my shoulder that put me to sleep and now I'm sitting on the edge of Mario's desk in our classroom, swinging my legs back and forth and trying really hard not to roll my eyes as Finn speaks.

"Because of some new information," he says, "we think it might be Ben."

"Ben. Hmmm." Mario's eyes meet Rudy's, and they both look concerned. We're having a full meeting tonight, to consider what Finn calls *the new development*.

"*Finn* thinks it might be Ben," I correct him. "He potentially could have been driving a blue car on Monday, but that's pretty far-fetched."

"And he doesn't have an alibi," Finn supplies.

"Yes, he does," I refute. "He said his dad took the car to work."

"He *said*," Finn reminds me. "And we do know he's got motive," he continues. "I'm sure he's not exactly thrilled to have me here."

"No," Rudy agrees. "I would imagine he's not."

Mario taps his chin thoughtfully. "We can't rule him out as a possibility." His eyes are staring off somewhere in the distance, as if he can see all the multitude of unrolling possible futures branching off every choice and diverting factor.

"He wouldn't hurt anyone," I assert vehemently. "I know Ben. He's not like that."

"It's possible that Ben is being influenced," Mario says. "Travelers—particularly seasoned ones—know exactly how to set off a subtle chain of events to achieve a desired goal."

"Could someone influence him to borrow his father's car and drive across a bridge that's been closed for decades?" Finn asks.

"They couldn't," I answer through gritted teeth, "especially if he *wasn't in the car*."

"When I talk about influence, I mean that Ben might be unknowingly providing information to the Traveler who's targeting Jessa," Mario says. "Someone does seem to have information regarding her whereabouts."

"Is it possible that Ben is the Traveler?" Finn asks.

"I've already looked into anyone who deals with Jessa on a day-to-day basis," Rudy explains. "If there were another Traveler among them, I would have been informed. We've put the word out and so far, no Dreamer has claimed ownership of a rogue Traveler."

"You all need to get this out of your heads," I say. "Ben's not a Traveler, and he's not a killer."

"You trust him." Mario makes it a statement, not a question.

"Yes." I am firm on this. But a look at Finn says he's not so sure.

"Perhaps Finn isn't being entirely unbiased," Rudy says, eyeing him shrewdly.

"Ya think?" I snark.

Finn glares at me in response. "I'm looking at every option, Jessa." He leans sullenly against the wall.

"We should investigate a little more thoroughly," Rudy suggests.

Mario nods. "Agreed."

"She needs someone closer at hand," Rudy says thoughtfully. "Perhaps I should make accommodations for Finn to join her at school."

"You can do that?" I ask.

"We can set events into motion and arrange it," Rudy says. "Just as I arranged his arrival here in the first place."

"Then I can keep a closer eye on you," Finn says. "And Ben, too."

"You're wasting your time with Ben," I say again.

"We just want to observe the situation," Mario says placatingly. "In the meantime, I've got your first assignment."

"Really?" I brighten instantly.

"She's not really at the top of her game," Finn says, frowning.

"This is an easy one," Mario assures him. "A minor adjustment. She won't be gone more than ten minutes."

"It's just as well," Rudy says. "Finn, you and I have some follow-up to discuss."

Finn's not listening, so Rudy gently clears his throat.

"Sorry," Finn mumbles, pushing off the wall where he'd been

leaning. He gives me one last look over his shoulder before he follows Rudy out the red door.

Mario gestures for me to take a seat at a desk as the whiteboard shimmers to life behind him. A scene appears—like I'm watching a movie. It's a park with lots of grass and benches, walking trails, and a fountain in the background.

"Where is that?" I ask.

"Arizona again," he says.

"Arizona has grass?"

"In places. It's not all desert, you know." He leans back against his desk. "So, Jessa, are you ready for your first assignment?"

"I guess. You said it won't take long, right?"

"It's not difficult. Just a routine reroute."

"So what do I do?"

He turns back to the scene to gesture toward a girl with curly brown hair, sitting alone on a bench near the far side of the open field.

"See her? Go over there, and recommend the book that's on the bench next to her."

I look at the girl. "That's it?" It certainly doesn't seem difficult.

"That's it," he affirms.

"That doesn't seem life-altering."

He shrugs. "This is typical, Jessa. You seem to think we're going to send you on epic quests, but a lot of what we have you do is pretty minimal."

"Okay," I say. "I'll give it a try."

"You'll need to make the transfer at seven thirteen tomorrow morning," Mario instructs. "Go straight over to her and find a way to talk about the book. Then get right out of there."

"What am I using for a mirror over there?"

Mario smiles. "There's a public restroom just behind us." He waves a hand and the scene behind him changes to show me the location. "Just follow the running trail back around to it. It loops the field."

"Sounds easy enough."

"It usually is."

"Usually?"

"If it's done right." He waves his hand and the scene changes again. "Here's the inside of the restroom, so you know what to look for. Once you've been somewhere, you can just think of the place, but early on you might need more visual cues. Like land-marks versus street directions when you drive."

I study the scene, focusing on a bit of graffiti on one wall. I should be able to remember that. Once I'm satisfied I've gotten a good look, I turn back to Mario and give him a thumbs-up.

"We'll work up to more. But this is a good start," he says, striding over to the red door. I follow him, glancing back one last time at the scene on the board.

"Remember, Jessa—do the job and keep it simple."

"Simple. Got it."

He opens the door for me to step through. A moment later I'm in bed, staring blearily at my alarm clock, and it's 7:05.

"Crap!"

I hastily brush my teeth and pull on some clothes.

"A little more notice would be appreciated," I grumble aloud, in case Mario can hear me. I know I don't have to worry about how I look, since I'm changing bodies, but I don't want her coming over to my morning breath and ratty pajamas.

At 7:13 exactly, I touch my hand to the mirror, and away I go.

I'm in the bathroom, and once again, I'm finding it hard to breathe in my new body.

"You've got to be kidding me," I moan. Ugh. This Jessa is a runner. Who gets up this early in the morning to run without rabid animals chasing them or something? I'm coated in a thin film of sweat, and it's clear I've been running for a while. I run track at school here, and I'm training for a 10K next month.

"Okay," I say, giving myself a pep talk as I jog in place. "I can do this."

I jog through the door and out onto the trail, circling around the path on the far side until I come up behind the girl on the bench. She has a pile of papers sitting next to her, and the book is perched on top of them. She's staring at her phone, and she doesn't even know I exist. I run by, bump into the bench, and knock the book off the pile onto the ground.

"Oh my gosh!" I say, trying to sound convincing. "I'm so sorry! There was a squirrel—it ran right in front of me!"

"Oh, it's okay," she reassures me. "I don't like this book anyway."

I crouch down, picking it up off the ground. I don't recognize the title, and I know nothing about it.

"Yeah, it starts a little slow," I improvise.

"You're telling me." She rolls her eyes. "Everybody loves it, but I just couldn't get past that first chapter."

"You need to!" I say with conviction. "Seriously. It's so worth it. Don't let the first chapter throw you."

"Really?" she says skeptically.

"Really. It's one of the best reads I've had in a long time."

She takes the book from me. "Thanks. I guess I'll give it another shot."

"You won't regret it," I assure her. Then I take off jogging.

I'm jogging, I think. I can feel my legs stretching and the blood pumping in my veins. I'm moving at a pretty good clip, and the wind is rushing past my face. I feel like I could run for hours. This is amazing!

I loop the path twice more before I reluctantly head back toward the restroom. I can't risk stomping a butterfly or something and wrecking things over here, but at the same time . . . I've never been an athlete before. Not that I'm horribly out of shape, but I'm also not the most coordinated person I know. And I don't just run here . . . I dance. Oh, wow. I *dance.*

The memories burst inside me of recitals and competitions, spinning and flying through the air as my partners lift me or I leap impossibly high. I've got a performance next weekend, as a matter of fact.

I hesitate outside the restroom, and then I get a grip on myself and force myself to go back inside. There's a woman there with a toddler, and I grab some paper towels, wet them down, and dab them to my face while I'm waiting. They finally clear out. I start to put my hand to the mirror, but I pause.

"Hold on," I tell her. "Do you mind?"

She doesn't seem to object, so I step back and kick off my shoes.

I give one more glance at the door, and then I spread my arms wide. I set my feet apart, and with one strong kick off my right leg, I am turning. My head snaps around, and I spot perfectly as my body spins almost effortlessly on the tiled bathroom floor. Oh, I could do this all day. . . .

I snap to a stop, panting, red-faced, and exhilarated. I throw my arms around myself and laugh out loud. "Oh my God!" I say. "I can dance!"

I look at myself in the mirror.

"I can't dance," I say with a sigh. "*You* can dance. I get to sit on a couch with a bruised shoulder."

Now I feel guilty. She's probably miserable in my body. I touch my hand to the glass, and she does as well, but before we push through, I see her glance back one last time.

I'm standing in my mom's room. She only works one job on Sundays, and today she doesn't go in until later. She's asleep in bed, and the covers are pulled down on one side. The other me had been lying there next to her, just watching her sleep. I'd curved myself into her, and she'd pulled me close, just like when I was little.

I shove my fist to my mouth, and tears blur my vision as the memories of another life fill my head.

My mom died four years ago in a car accident. Dad says if she'd been two minutes earlier getting onto the interstate, she would never have been part of the pileup.

I often picture her stopping at the end of the block that day because she forgot her purse, and turning around to go home and get it. Or hitting snooze one extra time on the alarm clock that morning. Who knows what choice she made that did it? And it doesn't matter if I do know or not. It's done. There, it's done, and everyone has had to live with it.

Other me has seen her many times while traveling. And every time, every single time, all I want to do is just be there, normal and ordinary. Just living a life with her in it. I only wish she could have seen me dance just once.

I step through the doorway to the hall bathroom and blow my nose before I splash some water on my face and pull myself together. Then I go in and lie back down next to my mom.

"Hey," she says sleepily. "Is your shoulder hurting?"

"No, not really. I had a bad dream." *That wasn't really a dream.*

She gives me a sympathetic look. "What time is it?"

"It's almost nine."

She stretches and gives a yawn. "I'd better get started on break-fast," she says, sitting up. "Danny will be up soon."

"Mom?"

"Yeah, honey?"

"Do you think . . . could I maybe try dance lessons?"

She looks over her shoulder at me. "Dance lessons?"

"I can pay for them," I say hurriedly. "I just think I might want to try it."

She gives a shrug. "Sure. We have a lady who teaches classes at the retirement home—she runs the dance studio here in town. I could ask her for the information."

"Would you, please?"

"I'll be tossing roses at your first performance," she says with a grin. "Promise."

My eyes shift to the mirror over the dresser. And I think that smile may not only be mine.

23

The Man with the Secret Past

WHEN I GET TO SCHOOL ON MONDAY, I DISCOVER THAT just this morning, through a series of coincidences, Finn's paperwork arrived at the school and he was admitted as a transfer student, despite the fact that a parent wasn't with him and he didn't come from whatever school they put down on the paperwork. Everyone in the office remembers meeting Finn's mother, though, so they're sure she must've stopped in and filled out everything that needed to be signed.

The coincidences continue as Finn shares my schedule exactly, even lunch period and electives. I don't know if this is good or bad. On the one hand, he can keep an eye on me, but on the other hand, I'm finding it hard to concentrate.

Seeing him in the office as I walked into school this morning was a wonderful and unexpected surprise that I plan to take full advantage of. I gallantly offered to show him where his calculus class was, since I have the same class, too. Mrs. Cerino in the office gave me a smile and shooed us along, out into the hallway.

The morning passes uneventfully until we encounter history class, and by default, Ben. To say he is less than thrilled to see Finn would be a serious understatement.

"What's he doing here?' he asks bluntly.

"I transferred in," Finn replies. "Just today."

"You knew about this?" Ben asks me.

"Of course she did," Finn says, before I can get my mouth open. "And as luck would have it, our class schedules are the same." He says it with a smile, but even I can read the warning in his eyes. He's as much as telling Ben that I'm under surveillance. Ben seems to bristle.

"Great," he says through his teeth, and then he stomps over to take his seat.

He sits next to me like there's a storm cloud over his head, and it gets darker the more my gaze strays across the room to where Finn is sitting. I don't suppose I could ask Ben if he'd change seats with him—that definitely wouldn't go over well.

When the bell rings for the next period, Ben is out of his seat and gone before it even finishes echoing down the hallway. I wait by the door for Finn to join me.

"He was a ray of sunshine," Finn points out. "Did he even say a word to you during class?"

"No." I glance out the doorway, hoping to catch a glimpse of Ben at his locker. Suddenly, I'm feeling kind of bad. I miss my friend, and I'm obviously hurting his feelings, but there's not much I can do about it. Not while somebody's trying to kill me, anyway.

"I'll text him later," I say, biting my lip.

We turn the corner and walk into creative writing, where Ms. Eversor's eyes light up as she gets an eyeful of her newest student.

"Hello!" she calls out gaily. "But who is this? Are you my new pupil?"

"I'm Finn," he says, extending his hand.

"Finn!" Her French accent makes her pronounce it funny. Like she's saying *Feen*. "I am Ms. Eversor, and this is *l'écriture créative*—creative writing! Oh, we have such fun!"

She claps her hands, and the multitude of jangling bracelets she always wears sounds a loud cacophony that gets everyone's attention.

"Class! This is Finn!" He flushes, a little embarrassed at all the attention.

"You must forgive us, Finn," she explains. "It is so rare that we have anyone new, you see. So we make the most of it when it happens." She gestures him over to the empty desk next to mine, and then she moves to the whiteboard as he takes his seat.

"Today," she begins, "we play a game! When I was a young girl, growing up in Côte d'Ivoire, the Ivory Coast, we played a game to pass the time. We would tell each other stories about our lives, but they would be fanciful, you know? Not true, but maybe more like wishes. Some good, some bad. And when a stranger came to town, it was delicious! We could make up such stories about them, you see, because we didn't really know them. And because we didn't really know them, the stories just *might* be true. So to honor our new friend Finn, we tell his story today, in five hundred words. And Finn, you tell us your own story, and we will compare. Your story, of course, can be anything! Real or fanciful, you choose."

She puts the marker to the whiteboard and writes *Finn's Story*.

"So," she says. "Finn's story. Begin!"

I look over at him conspiratorially, wondering just which Finn he's going to pick to be. He gives me a sly look, and then he cups his hand around the corner of his paper so I can't see what he's doing. I shoot him a mean look in return, and I write.

His name was Finn, and he was known far and wide for his elegant cheese soufflé. He arrived in the small town bearing a whisk and an attitude, and no one knew quite what to make of him. He was as cool as a cucumber under pressure, which seemed at odds with the usual passionate temperament of the average egomaniacal chef. What no one knew was that under that calm exterior was a secret.

Finn was a double agent. Sent by spies from the most famous waffle chain in the south, Finn had a mission: Get that recipe for apple spice pancakes, or die trying.

Good God. That was awful. Let's try that again.

The stranger found a home in the trunk of a giant oak tree. She didn't notice him at first, which shouldn't come as a surprise to anyone, since he was barely a foot in height. It wasn't until she poked her toe at the strange mound of dirt covering the pot of gold behind the tree that she realized who she was dealing with, or rather, what.

"A leprechaun?" Finn hisses, apparently having poked his nosy nose over toward my paper. "You're making me a *leprechaun?*"

"You have a problem with the Irish?" I ask, looking innocent.

He shakes his head and rolls his eyes at me simultaneously. "Write whatever you want," he says in a low voice.

"Thank you," I whisper sarcastically. "I'll do that."

"Just know that there will be repercussions . . . *Emeline*."

I shoot him another dirty look. I thought the leprechaun thing was genius, personally. I've got a magical creature, the whole angle of the wishes to play on, and I was going to give him a cute little Irish accent, too.

My pen stops on the paper as a voice echoes in my memory. *I do love a woman with gumption*, he'd said, in that sexy Irish lilt.

My pen starts to move, and I lose myself in the telling of his story.

He was only sixteen the night his father died, leaving him alone with the ship. His mother had gone long before, never caring for a life on the water as her men did. He was born with the sea in his veins and the smell of the salt in his hair. There was no place to call home now but the ship that was his birthright, and the crew that followed him as easily as they'd followed the man who left it to him.

His status as a privateer opened doors for him around the globe, but the people he met were the real reason he made the trip. So many stories. So many far-off lands and delicious foods. So many blazing sunsets and glorious sunrises viewed from a rooftop, a garden, a mountain, or the deck of a dipping and cresting ship. His life was out there, and he reveled in it. Nothing could match the freedom of the open sea and the sun on his sails.

I look up a moment, with the top of my pen sliding back and forth across my lower lip as I think. I realize a startled second later that Finn is not only looking at me—or should I say, at my mouth—he's glaring.

He starts writing, and I lean over to look.

"Uh-uh," he says. "It's a surprise."

He shifts in his seat so he's practically got his back to me, balances his notebook on his lap, and starts to write.

"Fine," I whisper. "Be that way."

"Fine," he answers, over his shoulder.

"Fine," I say again, just so I can have the last word.

And I wonder what he's going to do to get back at me. I catch myself rubbing my pen against my lips again, and I blush before I put my pen back down on my paper and finish my story.

24

The Setup

"I THOUGHT I WOULD HAVE SEEN YOU LAST NIGHT," I SAY to Mario, who has just entered the classroom and taken his seat at his desk.

"You needed the rest," he said. "I sent you that great dream about the beach instead."

"Thanks. So . . . how was my first job?"

"I'll let you know," Mario replies, smiling at me. "So far, so good."

I have to know. "What's so great about that book? It looked like a trashy romance novel or something."

"Oh, it is," Mario says matter-of-factly. "But if she reads it, she'll relate to the main character, who has a sister who means the world to her. She'll decide that she needs to call her sister, who she hasn't talked to in a long while. And that needs to happen."

"Why?" I ask.

Mario shrugs. "It just does."

"Well, that's . . . cryptic."

"Don't try to figure it out," Mario advises. "It'll just make your head hurt. Leave that stuff to me."

I'm not so sure about this blindly-following-orders stuff. How do I even know what my actions have done, really?

"You're asking for a lot of trust here," I point out. "How do I know I didn't just start World War III or something?"

"It is a lot of trust," he agrees. "But I've been doing this a very, very long time. And I have no reason to try to bring about an apocalypse. If you're ever uncomfortable with an assignment, you only have to discuss it with me. I'll do my best to allay your concerns."

My fingers trace the edge of my desk, and my voice is quiet—and maybe a little accusing. "You didn't warn me that my mom would be dead—in the other reality, I mean."

"You weren't supposed to be there very long," he says, crossing his arms and giving me a pointed look. "I didn't think it would come up."

"It came up the minute I got back and felt everything she was feeling. A little warning would have been nice."

"You have to be prepared for absolutely anything," Mario reminds me. "And you have to keep going, no matter what gets thrown at you."

I lift my chin and glare at him. "So I can expect more of this kind of stuff?"

"You can expect nothing but this kind of stuff. You're dealing with realities forged by choices that were never made in your world." His voice softens. "Every choice comes with consequences, Jessa. Every choice."

I lean back in my chair. "Speaking of consequences . . . what about accidents? If a truck decides to plow me down on a cross-walk while I'm in another reality, what happens to the other me? I mean, who dies? Her or me?"

"*You* die, in her body."

"And the other Jessa comes back to her reality?" This is seriously confusing.

"No. Once you've physically died in your reality of origin—no matter where you were when it happened—you can't get yourself back there again," he says. "Which highlights again the need for caution when traveling."

"What about a reality that I don't exist in? We can go to those like Finn does, right?"

"There's an important distinction here that needs clarification," Mario says. "You can go into a reality that you've never existed in, but you can't go to a reality that you've died in. It causes too many ripple effects."

"So if I'm out traveling and the other me jaywalks in front of a bus or something, I'm just stuck?"

"You're a Traveler," Mario reminds me. "You're not 'stuck' anywhere. You'll still be able to shift; it just alters your origin. Can't have you roaming around someplace where you're supposed to be dead. Not that some Travelers haven't tried."

"Really?" I lean forward, fascinated.

Mario shrugs. "It's happened on occasion. You have to enlist another Traveler to pull you through if it's a reality you're blocked from. Then people write up ghost stories and your Dreamer has to do damage control."

"What if it's nothing serious? What if other me just likes it better at my house and won't trade back?"

166

"Sometimes a Dreamer has to give somebody a nudge, but it would be useless to argue. Your Dreamer would just read you the riot act when they see you. You can't stay awake forever."

"You'd give us *nightmares?*"

"We've got power over your subconscious mind, Jessa. You cannot imagine the havoc we could wreak if we wanted to."

I'm really starting to grasp how primitive people considered the Dreamers to be gods. He's right—their kind of power could be a really terrible thing in the wrong hands. I don't plan on breaking any rules if I can help it.

"I'm going to have Finn working with you on refining your transfers," Mario says, pushing out from behind the desk. "I can give you all the theory and the rules behind it, but he's got the practical know-how that will help you sharpen your skills."

He waves his hand, and the whiteboard behind him comes to life.

"Are you ready for your next assignment?"

"Go ahead," I sigh.

The scene is an unfamiliar pizza parlor. The place is enormous, with two levels of seating and a stage for a live band to play in the corner. There is even a bar. It couldn't possibly be in Ardenville. We're too small for a place like this.

"Where is that?" I ask Mario. "It can't be in my town."

"It's your town, but it's called Greaverville. The Greaver family is very prominent and owns most of the town, including this place. By the way—the drinking age was reduced to sixteen here sometime back in the forties."

"So they funnel their money into pizza parlors?" I still can't believe this place. There's an arcade room off to the side, an entire sports-bar area with pool tables and dartboards and big-screen TVs, and what looks like an enclosed ball pit and play area for kids, too.

"Greaverville is five times the size you know Ardenville to be," Mario says. "The Greavers worked hard to put this place on the map and are known for their shrewd but ethical business practices. They're a far cry from the Greaver family as they were in your history."

"The name is familiar," I admit. "Greaver's Mill Road is where I used to go for piano lessons before I told my mom I was quitting. And I think there was a Greaver's store or something, wasn't there?"

"There was a Greaver everything in your town at one point," he tells me, leaning back against his desk. "They owned the local mercantile, the lumber mill, the zinc mine, the racetrack, the waterworks, and according to some scandalous newspaper articles, they owned the mayor and half the judges in the area as well—that is, until the empire crumbled around them."

"What brought them down?"

"Shoddy construction. Bad labor policies. Too many payoffs changing hands. That kind of stuff." He gestures at the board again. "They were a little better at business in this reality."

"So why here? What's the job?"

"Another easy one," he says, "piece of cake. You see that woman with the two young boys over there?" He gestures toward their table. "I need you to spill your drink on the youngest boy."

"Just . . . walk over there and dump a drink on him?" I clarify.

"Not like that." He looks annoyed. "Make it believable. Trip or something. But make sure it hits the kid full-on in the chest."

I feel kind of bad about this one. The poor kid's going to get soaked, and his mother is going to have to deal with it. I watch them and my face must show my reluctance, because Mario makes a tsk-ing sound and shakes a finger at me.

"Remember the greater good," he says. "I wouldn't have you do it just to do it."

"I would hope not."

"Now let me show you the bathroom, so you know what to look for in the mirror."

"When do I go?"

"Tomorrow after school. Go straight home, make the transfer."

"No surprises this time," I warn him. "Is everybody alive and well over there?"

He thinks a moment. "Yes. But I meant what I said earlier, Jessa. You have to learn to roll with whatever you get handed."

"Whether I like it or not?"

He gives me a noncommittal shrug as I walk over to the red door.

"Keep it simple," he reminds me.

I step through the door, and when I wake, I wonder how he can ever think that a life like this is simple.

25

Dirty Job

I STARE AT MYSELF IN THE MIRROR AND WATCH AS MY face changes slightly—the makeup gets heavy and turns very goth-looking, with a lot of black eyeliner. I have an eyebrow piercing. And bangs—ugh! I step through into the bathroom at the pizza parlor.

I give myself one more glance in the mirror, shaking my head, especially when I remember the entire notebook full of sad, death-related emo poetry that's in my bag. I wrinkle my nose and step out of the bathroom.

I'm early, so I kill some time by ordering a slice of pizza to go with my soda. I toy with the idea of getting a beer or a glass of wine since I can, but I decide I'd better keep my wits about me.

It's been at least three-quarters of an hour, and I'm about to call it quits when they finally walk in. The mom looks nice enough, and the boys look about ten and six. The younger one is sitting on the outside, making my job easier.

"Right. I can do this," I tell myself.

I stand up, grab my soda, and walk like I'm heading for the bathrooms, with a slight detour by their table. I do a pretty credible job tripping—mainly because I really do start to trip once I try to fake it—and I end up throwing not only my soda at the kid, but my whole self as well, knocking him over in his chair as I go staggering.

He starts shrieking almost immediately, and it's a horrible sound, like I've seriously injured him, and I am terrified. I run back to him immediately and his mother is right next to me, pulling him up and into her arms.

"It's okay, it's okay, it's okay . . ." She's rocking him back and forth as she repeats it over and over again, and I see him desperately pulling at his shirt, trying to get the wetness of it away from his body as he continues to shriek.

Something in the way she's soothing him, the dirty look his brother is giving me, and the child's overblown response clicks, and I crouch down next to him, completely horrified. I look at the mother.

"I'm so sorry. Listen, I have a tank top on under this." I lift up my shirt to show her. "Can I give him my shirt? It's dry. He won't notice the wetness that way."

She looks at me gratefully. "Are you sure?"

"Yes. I feel terrible about this." I yank off my T-shirt and hand it to her.

"It's okay," she reassures me, as her eyes dart around to all the people staring her down. I watch one woman in the booth next to us mouth the word *brat*, and I am suddenly on my feet.

"He's a little boy!" I say to the woman in the booth. "I just startled him badly and his shirt is soaked through, making his skin cold and wet. He's having a hard time processing all of it at once, okay?"

The booth woman looks at me like I'm crazy, but she's smart enough to mumble "sorry" to the mother, who is wriggling her son into my shirt. He begins to calm and I squat down, getting on eye level with him.

"I'm sorry I knocked you over. It was an accident. I'm sorry." I smile at him, and he's still clinging to his mother, but he's not crying or shrieking anymore.

"He doesn't talk much yet," his mother says to me. Her eyes shift to the woman in the booth. "Thanks for sticking up for him."

"I have a brother who's a lot like him," I say.

This is how we talk, when we meet someone who has a kid or a brother or a sister like ours. We won't say the word for fear that we use the wrong one, or we've found an undiagnosed kid, or a parent who just plain hates to hear the word. But we all know. We can recognize it from across a room.

"I need an address, so I can mail your shirt back," she says to me.

"No, keep it. I don't like the band anymore, anyway."

She gives me another grateful smile as she guides her son to his feet. He stands, tracing the words and designs on the oversized shirt with his finger while she wipes off his chair. One of the workers helps her, asking her if she needs anything else or if her son was hurt. She thanks him and tells him they're fine, and the worker hurries off.

"I'm really sorry," I say again.

"Oh, it's okay. It was worth it to hear you take that woman

down." She gives me a conspiratorial grin. "We're all in this together, right?"

I nod. "Right. Anyway, it was nice meeting you . . ." I look at the little boy.

"Mark," she prompts.

I squat back down, looking him in the eye. "Mark. It was nice to meet you." I put out my hand and he looks at it a moment. Finally, he takes it, shaking it twice.

"Bye," I say, straightening up. I look back over my shoulder as I walk away, and Mark is still standing by the table. He is waving at me. I wave back and then rush to the bathroom, so I can get myself home.

When I come through, I am fuming. I am so angry at Mario, I'm practically vibrating with it.

That gives way to shock as I stare at my new reflection in the mirror.

"You cut my hair?" I say in disbelief. "You cut my *hair!*"

I stare in dismay at my new bangs, hanging just at my brow line. I haven't had bangs since sixth grade, and it's taken me all those years to grow them out again. She—I—up and decided to do myself a favor and give me bangs again. She also ate almost an entire box of crackers while lying in my bed. Ugh!

My fingers poke and shove at my bangs, but there's no way to change this. They're even a little crooked. I look down at the scissors lying on my dresser, and the locks of hair tossed into my trash can.

"Why would you do something like that?" I demand, looking in the mirror again. Great. Now I have to stop at the haircut place by Wickley's and get these things straightened out. And spend another six years growing them out again.

As I'm heading out the door, Danny calls out after me.

"Are you coming back, Jessa?"

I stop in the doorway to reassure him. "Yes, Danny. I just have to run an errand, okay?"

"Are *you* coming back?" he clarifies.

It's spooky how he knows this. His brain doesn't work like ours, I know, but it's spooky and comforting at the same time. Danny will always know the real me, I guess.

"Yes, Danny. I'll be back, just like this."

"With your new hair?"

I grit my teeth. "Yes, Danny. With my new hair."

My hair gets fixed—well, as fixed as it can get—and after dinner I get involved in writing a new story. Eventually, I make myself go to bed because I've got a lot I want to say to a certain Dreamer.

He's waiting for me in the classroom, sitting behind the teacher's desk and tapping a pen against the desktop.

"What the hell!" I round on him. "You made me throw a soda on a kid who was . . . you know!"

"Yes," he says, more than a bit perturbed. "And you just wrecked the whole scenario."

"What? You're mad at *me*?" I sputter. "I terrified that kid!"

"I didn't ask you to flatten him," Mario points out, standing up and coming around the desk. "Just spill on him. You went overboard."

"I didn't mean to. And how could it be helping anyone to have me drown him with my soda?"

"Well, if you had done what I *told you*," Mario says, "everything would have worked out fine. The kid would have been upset, the worker would have rushed out, and he would have offered to let the kid have an official Greaver's Pizza apron to wear. He would have taken care to tie the ties so it covered the kid just right, and he would have written the kid's name on it with the green marker, because green is the kid's favorite color. And the mother—who's single, by the way—would have noticed all of this and thanked him and blushed when he told her it was fine, and starting next week, they'd be back to dine every Friday night, until he finally asked her out."

"Oh."

"Yes. Oh." Mario glares, obviously pissed at me. "He's going to make a great stepfather, by the way. Only now I have to find some other way to get them back on track, all because you couldn't do what you were asked."

"Was I supposed to just let him scream?"

"*Yes.* Do what I ask you and don't get crazy embellishing things." He sits back down behind the desk and laces his fingers together, eyeing me. "Incidentally, your words to the other woman created some ripples, too, but they're nothing bad, as far as I can tell. They just . . . alter some things."

"Doesn't everything alter something?" I grumble.

"Yes. But not everything altered is terribly important. We all live a lot of boring lives, believe it or not. So many of the decisions we think are very important are really only that way to us. They don't always impact ourselves and others in a truly life-changing way and therefore . . . no ripple."

I wish for a moment I could travel back to the pizza parlor and get myself an underage drink.

"Well, if you're going to use me for this stuff, you're going to have to know that I'm going to react sometimes. I couldn't just walk away," I snap at him.

"Travelers have to learn to be unbiased, Jessa," he reminds me firmly. "If you let yourself get too involved in the other realities, you won't be able to do the job correctly. And that could have big repercussions. That's why we send you out. Making changes in your own reality is hard to do without feeling invested."

"I can't be unbiased about everything! And definitely not about this!"

"You're going to have to learn to be."

"So . . . what? I lose all my empathy? I don't care who I'm screwing with or what I do to them? Are you going to have me pushing people into traffic next?"

"You need to calm down."

"The hell with that!" I shout. "And to hell with you! I'm done here!" I stomp out of the classroom and through the red door to find myself staring at the alarm clock, lying in bed, with my hands still clenched into fists.

26

The Enchanted Pirate

I'M STILL GLOWERING AS I SIT IN HISTORY LISTENING TO Mr. Draper drone on about the Gadsden Purchase and Manifest Destiny, and I'm writing stray thoughts down in my journal, looking across the room at Finn when I can and trying not to zone out too much.

"St. Clair."

I look over at Ben, who just whispered my name.

He points down at his phone, and I very carefully pull mine out, half hiding it under my journal.

I make sure the ringer is off and check my texts.

> Can we talk?

> Sure. What's up?

> Alone

> **Oh**

I see his jaw tighten as he reads my message.

> **I guess that's a no**

> **No, that's a yes**
> **Is everything okay?**

> **I don't know**

He pockets his phone and I slide mine out from under my journal and put it away. I look over at him, but he's looking at Mr. Draper and not at me. He's probably just making sure I'm okay after my near-death experience. Whatever it is, I'm just glad to be communicated with. He hasn't said two words to me in the two days since Finn showed up at school.

Ben says nothing to me for the rest of class, even when he and I are assigned to the same four-person group for a project. When the bell rings, he lingers as I gather up my notebook and my backpack.

"Can I walk you to class?" he asks. "I promise not to make fun of your hair."

I look up with a begrudging smile, glad to have him talking to me again. "Sure."

"We can both walk you to class," Finn suggests, coming up behind him. He's not going to let me out of his sight, and the look on his face tells me he's definitely not going to let me out of sight with Ben.

And Ben has had enough. He rounds on Finn. "We're trying to have a conversation here."

"So have it," Finn says. "I'll wait."

"A *private* conversation," Ben stresses. "That means you can find something else to do."

"Finn . . ." I start to ease my way into the conversation, but the testosterone pushes me back out again.

"I've got a pretty boring life," Finn retorts. "I don't really have anything else to do."

Ben steps forward, getting in Finn's face. "I'm fixing to give you something to do."

"Ben!"

"Who the hell does he think he is?" Ben demands, gesturing at Finn. "And since when did you decide he's your babysitter?"

"I didn't see you by her side last week much," Finn says.

"Because she'd have to make room for me on the couch next to you!" Ben throws back.

Mr. Draper has finally figured out that there's about to be blood splashed on his classroom walls, and he hurries over to remind us that it's time to get to our next class. We step out into the hallway, and I turn to Ben.

"Let's finish this conversation at lunch," I tell him, giving Finn a look. "Alone."

Finn does not like the sound of that. "Jessa—"

"Lunch, Ben," I reiterate, and he gives me a stiff nod before he stalks off.

Finn glowers as we walk toward our next class. "Are you sure that's wise?"

"He's not a threat. He's my friend, Finn. And you're only a text message away," I remind him.

"So what am I supposed to do for lunch?" he gripes.

"You'll survive." I push past him and he follows me into the classroom.

"Finn!" Ms. Eversor comes up behind us and puts her hand on his back, making her bracelets jangle noisily. "I must tell you how I loved your story! It was inspired! To have yourself as a fat, ugly pirate disguised by a magician's spell—so creative!"

My lips twitch. "That was your backstory? An ugly pirate?"

He shrugs, but Ms. Eversor isn't done singing his charms. "Yes, it was! Just as yours was, Jessa, though your pirate was much more dashing. Finn's story had such a good plot device," she bubbles. "His pirate's spell was discovered when he got too close to the girl he was trying to woo and she *smelled* him!" She claps her hands together with pleasure, as she heads up to the front of the room to start class.

"The odor shattered the illusion and broke the spell," Finn supplies.

I give him a look. "An ugly, malodorous pirate? Really?"

"And fat," he adds. "Really morbidly obese. I thought about giving him a clubbed foot, but decided it was a bit of a stretch."

"A bit," I deadpan. I slide into my seat and he takes his place next to me.

We spend the next half hour working with Chloe Merrick to craft a group poem, utilizing words that begin with the first eight letters of the alphabet. I hate assignments like this, since the structure is so confining, but I think we do a pretty good job of it. We finish early and we're just sort of talking when Chloe turns toward Finn.

"Hey," she says. "Did I hear you say you have nothing to do for lunch?" She gives him a megawatt smile, and I find myself sitting up in my chair from my former slouched position.

"As a matter of fact, I don't," he says, and his eyes shift to me briefly before he gives her his full attention.

"Well, I'm, like, in the drama club and we're supposed to do this show tonight?" It's not a question, but the way she talks, it sounds like it. "It's a really boring show," she goes on. "About some stupid judge here in town and a big trial or something. The lady from the historical society wrote it. Anyway, we haven't finished painting the set and we could really use a hand."

"Sure," he says. "Where do I go?"

"I'll walk you there." She leans in, putting her hand on his arm.

We don't say another word to each other until the bell rings, and as he follows Chloe out the door, he turns back to me.

"Maybe she has a thing for enchanted pirates," he says.

I press my lips together and glare at him. "Maybe she hasn't noticed your smell yet."

27

Tug-of-War

I FIND BEN WAITING FOR ME OUTSIDE THE DOORWAY to the cafeteria. He's leaning against the wall, with one foot up against it, and he looks like he wants to be anywhere but there waiting for me.

"What's up?" I grab a tray as we file through the door and head up to the line.

"So he let you off the leash?" Ben says snidely.

I raise my brows. "We're talking about Finn?"

"My favorite subject," he says. "You two are joined at the hip lately. I couldn't get a word in if I tried."

I put an order of french fries and a bottle of water on my tray and give him a glare.

"Last time I checked, I don't have to report to you," I say.

He grabs a slice of pizza for himself, shoving it next to my food on the tray, and we make our way to the cashier.

"I got this," he says, reaching for his wallet.

"Don't do me any favors," I say, pushing his hand away.

"Don't be like that."

"Then you don't be like *that*."

He throws a twenty down before I can dig in my bag, and we take our stuff over to a table and sit.

I grab my food, shoving a fry in my mouth and looking pointedly away from him. I hear him let out a sigh as he shoves his pizza away.

"I hate this. What are we doing, St. Clair?"

I look at him with chagrin. "I hate this, too. I miss you."

He leans across the table. "I miss you, too. I miss hanging out. I miss talking in class. I miss all our dumb nerd humor."

"Well, you're the one who's shutting me out," I say crossly.

"I can't get anywhere near you without him in the way. Are you two officially dating, or what?"

"It's complicated," I sigh. "Seriously. You can't begin to know."

He leans forward, crossing his arms on the table. "Listen, I'm worried about him. He just shows up here out of nowhere and suddenly he's signed up for school and acting like your shadow. What do you really know about this guy?"

I look at the situation from Ben's point of view. He's right. All he knows is that Finn is practically a stranger and I almost died on a bridge with him nearby. He probably thinks Finn is dangerous, and he's not entirely wrong.

"I know you don't trust him," I say. "But he's a good guy. I know more about him than you think."

"And is he going to be okay with you still hanging out with me sometimes? Maybe without him there? Or are we not allowed to be friends?"

I consider that for a moment. "He's going to have to be okay with it. Because I say it's okay."

He bites his lip. "You mean that?"

"I do."

I do mean it. Finn is going to have to get a grip. I can travel all over multiple realities ending up who knows where and dealing with who knows what, but I can't hang with my best friend? He's going to have to trust me on this.

"Can we hang out tomorrow for a while?" Ben suggests. "I don't have practice."

"Sure." My mind works to find a suitable meeting place. Normally we'd go to Mugsy's, but it just seems weird going there now without Finn.

"We can go to that new ice cream place on Fifth," I suggest.

"I guess. Or we could just hang at your house, if you want," he says. I think about that for a moment, but discard it instantly. If there's any place Finn will be sure to hang around waiting, it'll be my house.

"No, I really want ice cream," I say firmly. Lucky for me, I don't have to try to convince him. He knows how much I love ice cream.

"You're on," he says.

"Do they even have ice cream in your country?" I tease. "Or refrigeration?"

He rolls his eyes. "Even if I did live in Mexico instead of New Mexico, it's not the middle of the Sahara. And it pains me that someone did actually ask me if I grew up with running water."

"No!" I can't help it. I have to laugh. People are really, really stupid sometimes.

"Did you enlighten them about all the historical advancements and interesting facts you probably know about the country?" I ask. "Or did you just remind them again that you used to live in the United States before you came to live in the United States?"

"Neither. It's useless to try to cram knowledge into a brain that's not big enough to hold it," he scoffs. "Would you like me to teach you how to spell Albuquerque?"

I eat another french fry. "I have to reserve my brainpower for calculus."

He laughs, and I realize how much I missed his laugh. It's good to have my friend back again.

"So, I'll meet you at your locker after school?" he asks.

I feel my phone buzz in my pocket, and I pull it out, giving him a nod to answer his question.

"It's Finn," I say.

Ben rolls his eyes. "Surprise, surprise. His Spidey sense must have been tingling."

I hit the answer button as I mouth *nerd* at Ben.

"Hey."

"Hey. I'm just finishing up," Finn says. "You want to come see my handiwork?"

I check the time, and I still have twelve minutes of lunch left.

"Sure. I'll be right there." I pick up my tray and stand up. "I have to go to the auditorium."

"What a coincidence," Ben says. "I'm fixing to walk right by there."

I crinkle my nose as we toss our trash, then walk through the doors and out into the hallway. "Why do you say that?"

"What?"

"That you're 'fixing' to do something. Is that a New Mexico thing?"

"I think it's actually a Texas colloquialism that manifests itself throughout the Southwest."

"Ooh." I raise my brows. "Bonus Scrabble points for two big words in a sentence."

"I even used a Q," he jokes back.

Ben opens the door to the auditorium for me and I walk down the center aisle, looking for Finn. There's a group of people painting backdrops, so I climb the stairs at the side and step up onto the stage. I see Finn on the other side in the wings and start toward him.

And then I'm pulled violently backward as a heavy steel bar full of lights crashes from the ceiling to the stage right in front of me and shatters, spraying me with flying glass.

28

Near Miss

"ST. CLAIR!"

"Jessa!"

Ben and Finn shout my name at the same time, but I'm lying on my back and I have the wind knocked out of me. I couldn't answer them even if I wanted to.

Ben gets to me first, since he was the one who pulled me out of the way. I look up at him with startled, slightly unfocused eyes.

"You okay?" He's running his hands all over me, swiping off chunks of glass.

I nod because I'm still winded.

He glances down and makes a face. "Does it hurt anywhere?"

I push myself up on my elbows. "No." My head drops back and I suck in a big lungful of air. By now Finn has reached us, and he kneels down next to me, kicking some glass out of the way before he does.

"Did you hit your head?" he asks, cradling it in his hand.

"No. Ben pulled me flat on my back."

He looks over at Ben. "Thank you," he says.

"You saved my life," I add. "If that bar had hit my head, I'd be a goner."

Ben makes a waving motion with his hand, like it's no big deal.

"She's right," Finn says. His mouth turns down in a frown.

I waggle my brows at Ben. "Now who's got the Spidey sense?"

He sits back on his heels, letting out a sigh of relief. "You must be all right if you're making nerd jokes."

"To tell you the truth, now that the adrenaline is leaving my system, I'm feeling kind of faint." I look up at all the other students and adults who are now gathered around me. Mr. Green, the drama teacher, has come running from the back of the auditorium, along with the lady from the historical society, who was watching a scene rehearsal at the back of the stage.

"Oh, my dear!" she frets. "Goodness! Are you hurt?"

"No, I'm okay," I reassure her.

"How did that happen?" Mr. Green asks. "Who was up there last?"

Finn makes a grim face. "I was. Chloe needed the lights adjusted, but she's afraid of heights and asked me to do it. I thought they were secure when I moved them."

"You have to retighten the bolts on the bar with a wrench if you've been moving them around and adjusting them," Ben explains. "I worked lights for the last show. The mounting brackets on a lot of those are stripped. They can come loose if you don't tighten them back down."

Finn looks down at me, his face full of concern. "Are you sure you're okay?"

I sit up completely, rolling myself carefully onto my knees away from the pile of broken glass. "I'm okay. Really."

"I'll grab a broom," Ben says, jogging over to the cabinet backstage.

Mr. Green shakes his head, still not over this. "You got cut," he says. "Your palm is bleeding."

I look down, and he's right. "I put my hand up in front of my face when the glass started flying," I say. "It's just a nick."

"I want you to go to the nurse." Mr. Green is adamant. "She needs to look you over."

"All right."

He helps me up to my feet, and Finn reaches out, gently grasping my hand and flipping it over to look at my palm. Then his eyes meet mine.

"I'm sorry, Jessa."

"I can walk her to the nurse," Ben volunteers quickly. "She's still not too steady on her feet."

He hands Finn the broom, and Finn looks like he wants to object, but I let Ben wrap an arm around my shoulders and off we go.

"That was freaky," Ben says as he leads me out the door. "You really should take it easy. You might have shaken something loose in that nerd brain of yours."

I look up at him. "I didn't know you ran lights for the last school play."

"It was last semester," he says. "Somebody got sick, so I was just helping out."

"You can let go of me now," I say. "I can walk fine."

"Just making sure." He frowns at me, and then his face brightens. "Hey, the lady from the historical society remembers you. Eversor showed her your ghost story, and she wants to use it on her ghost tour."

"Really?" I know it's not huge, but I'm stupidly pleased all the same.

"Really. She's even giving you credit for it, too. She gave me free passes, if you want to go."

"That's this Friday, right? I can't imagine it'll be a problem. I'll run it by my mom and let you know."

"Good." He opens the door to the nurse's office. "If she clears you, I'll pick you up at six. We can hit dinner before."

"Okay." My forehead creases as I realize I just got maneuvered into a date. Ben is looking entirely too pleased with himself.

"Take it easy, St. Clair," he says, putting his hands on my shoulders. "I mean it."

"I'll do my best," I promise.

But I wonder how long that'll last. Whoever is after me is getting braver—and closer.

The nurse lets me go with a Band-Aid, and Finn beats me to the doorway when our last class is done. He pulls me down the hall, out the doors and down the street to Mugsy's, not even letting me stop at my locker.

He holds the door for me as we go in, and then he leans in and says, "You want to go someplace a little more . . . sparkly?"

I give an affirmative nod, and soon enough, we're sliding into a high-polished chrome booth with cupcakes and glitter mousse on the table before us.

"Are you feeling all right?" he asks with concern. "That was another close call. Obviously our rogue Traveler is a lot closer to you than we think."

"You think it's someone in the school?" I ask.

"Possibly. Someone who could have maneuvered me into fixing that light bar."

"Chloe?" I ask incredulously. "She doesn't have a brain in her head."

"Don't judge a book by its cover."

I load a spoonful of glitter mousse in my mouth so I won't make a snarky remark about Chloe's tight-T-shirt-too-much-makeup cover. Finn gives me a look that says he knew I wanted to say it anyway as he leans back in the booth.

"Chloe did suggest I call you," he says. "She and her friends were arguing over who the original Avengers were. I told her if it was a nerd question, you could answer it."

"Movie? Or comic book?" I ask.

"I don't know. I just know I called you and because of that, you stepped onto the stage, right after Chloe sent me up to adjust the lights."

"You could have texted me the question, you know," I point out. "Why didn't you just ask me when you had me on the phone?"

He looks embarrassed. "Because I wanted to pull you away from your lunch date."

I roll my eyes at him. "And look where it got you."

"Even if she isn't the Traveler, Chloe could be the influential factor that pushed me into my normal position of having a hand in your demise. Anyone could have influenced her to suggest I go

191

up there. Whoever set that in motion just didn't count on Ben tagging along."

"Ah, so you believe Ben is innocent now?"

"Not necessarily. He seemed to know an awful lot about those lights, didn't he?" Finn reaches for a cupcake and starts peeling off the wrapper.

"He saved me, Finn."

"There were too many witnesses," he said. "Maybe he suddenly realized someone else could get hurt."

"You're grasping at straws."

"Maybe," he admits grudgingly. "I just think we have to carefully consider every single option. That's all."

I stick my finger in the frosting on one of the cupcakes. I'm not really hungry, even though it looks delicious. Besides, other me has worked so hard to stick to her diet. I'm looking really good.

"So let me get this straight," I review. "Whoever is trying to kill me is a classmate. Or a teacher."

"Or a lunch lady, or a janitor, or guidance counselor, or the guy who delivers the office supplies—who knows?" Finn expounds. "But they've got a way into the school now, so we need to be even more careful."

"How can you watch out for somebody who could be anybody?" I ask.

"I don't," he says. "I just keep watching out for you."

29

Hiding Out

IT'S 5:40 ON FRIDAY AND I REALLY, REALLY DON'T WANT to do the ghost tour tonight. I have a feeling all Ben will want to talk about is Finn, and once I get back, all Finn will want to talk about is my night with Ben—especially since he's still not entirely convinced about Ben even after he saved my life right in front of him.

I catch a glimpse of myself in the mirror over my dresser, and I make a face.

"I don't suppose you'd like to go out to dinner and take the ghost tour, would you?" I ask in a disgusted voice.

And as I stare just a little too long, I swear I see her—my—head nod, ever so slightly.

"Oh, it can't be that easy," I murmur. I've got a way out of this. I'll go hang someplace else for a little while, until the evening is over. And it's not like she'd have it bad—my arm is mostly healed and I'm out of my sling now.

I haven't traveled anywhere since the soda-spilling debacle.

Mario seems to have backed off and let me cool down—I don't really harbor any hope that he's letting me out of my job entirely. So I haven't traveled and no one's tried to kill me in two days.

In short, I've been living a plain old normal life. I look at myself in the mirror again.

I know I shouldn't do it, but I put my hand to the glass anyway.

A moment later I am through, and my mother bustles into the room behind me.

"Are you still standing there?" she huffs.

"What's going on?" I ask, turning to greet her.

"It's time to get ready!"

My eyes widen as I take in the room around me, the striped wallpaper and the wainscoting.

"Jessamyn! Now! It's nearly six!"

She stands imperiously at the foot of my bed, tapping her foot on the hardwood floor. My mother looks every inch the elegant Victorian woman—one who's got an agenda. I look at her and can't help but break into a wide grin.

I've seen my mom in work clothes, of course, but she has more of a dress-slacks-and-blouses kind of wardrobe. She might toss on the occasional sundress in the summer, but to see her all decked out in a fancy dress and lacy blouse is beyond surreal.

"Are we going somewhere?" I ask.

"Oh, for heaven's sake! You have to start getting ready." She throws a pile of undergarments on the bed. "Get your bath and then get all this on. Eleanor will be in to help you with the corset. We leave in an hour."

"Where are we going?"

"Jessamyn! Are you awake?" She snaps her fingers in front of my face.

"The Bradleys' ball is tonight," she informs me. "Boyce will be around to collect us, and you had better be ready. You know how he hates to be kept waiting."

I finally pull my thoughts together. Tonight there's a ball celebrating the birthday of Elmira Bradley, the wife of a local barrister, and my fiancé and I will be attending. Mother had the dress brought in all the way from Charlotte, and everyone who is anyone in local society will be there. I planned to be bored out of my mind and counting the hours until I could sneak out of my house and meet up with Finn. No wonder I was eager to trade off. It's a win for both of us, because I get to go to my very first steampunk ball.

I follow my maid, Eleanor, with a sigh and climb dutifully into the bath. Then afterward I take entirely too long to get into all the undergarments in front of me on the bed. Between all these pieces of clothing, plus a corset, plus a mountain of skirts, how did Finn and I ever become intimate? It must've been a monumental undertaking.

And I've done it again. Now I remember exactly how monumental it was. Pirate Finn was a determined man and I was an enthusiastic accomplice, on numerous occasions. I shake my head, trying to lose those memories so I can concentrate on getting all this stuff on my body the right way.

My mother arrives with an enormous box a few minutes later, laying it carefully on my coverlet. Eleanor has me brace myself against the post of my bed as she laces my corset so tight, I swear the blood vessels are bursting in my eyes.

"Mother?"

"What, Jessamyn?" She's rooting through the drawer of my vanity, pulling out cosmetics.

"Can we loosen this a little? My stomach isn't feeling well, and I'd hate to get sick all over Boyce."

She steps over to me, pressing the back of her hand against my head. "You feel a little warm," she worries. "But we really should go. If we decline now, the Bradleys will think we've snubbed them."

Eleanor loosens my corset strings a bare millimeter and I can breathe better—marginally. I turn so that she can lower the ball gown over my head. She shakes it into place, and then moves behind me to fasten the buttons up the back. I stand before the full-length mirror and gasp aloud at my reflection.

The gown is beautiful. It's long-sleeved, a deep-blue satin with gathers at the bottom to display the black ruffled lace underskirt. Another line of black lace lines the décolletage, and a blue satin choker with black lace trim completes the ensemble. Once everything is in place, Mother leads me over to the vanity and drapes me with a linen cloth to keep the cosmetics off my dress as Eleanor applies my makeup. She finishes off by dusting me lightly with a shimmering powder across my chest and face.

After, she gets my hair loosely curled and pushed up into a big, pouffy pile on top of my head, with a few artfully curled tendrils falling around my shoulders. One more dusting of powder and my mother pronounces me perfect.

Boyce arrives a short time later, and I grin widely when I see what we're riding in. It's a hydrogen carriage—and it really does look almost like a carriage, but horseless, of course. It's a large, ornate, ungainly thing, suited only for short rides around town.

He has another vehicle for longer trips, but this one is the status symbol, and it's garish in the extreme.

Boyce tries to make conversation with me, but my thoughts are a million miles—or one reality—away right now. My mother ends up talking to him most of the way to the Bradleys' house, and it isn't until after the dinner is finished that Boyce and I find a moment to speak.

"I'd like to apologize," he says. "It really was unavoidable."

"What?" I take my eyes off the couples who are making their way to the ballroom and try to look interested. I can't be blowing this Jessa's cover.

"I want to apologize again," he repeats. "For having to leave the ball early this evening."

"Oh. I completely understand," I say with a forced smile. "You do what you have to do."

He looks at me curiously. "You're not angry, then?"

"No, of course not. I'm sure you have a good reason."

"I need to be in Savannah by morning or we'll lose the deal on the new carriage engines. It can't be helped." He shrugs apologetically.

I try to look interested. "You're working hard to secure the future of your business, Boyce. How can I be angry about that?"

He gives me a tepid smile in return. "Well then, I suppose I should have my dance before I take my leave."

He leads me onto the dance floor, and luckily, although the dance is fairly complicated, involving clapping and circling and partner changes, I remember it well enough that I can hold my own. Boyce is not very talkative. He looks as bored with me as I am with him, and I realize that he always is. He's only marrying me for my money, after all. I get the feeling he wouldn't marry at all, if he had his choice. I feel sorry for him.

He returns me to my mother's side, and with a short bow in her direction and a light kiss on the back of my gloved hand, he leaves. I turn to my mother.

"How much longer before we go?"

"Go? We just got here," she says, surprised.

I glance over at the grandfather clock in the corner of the room. "It's been nearly two hours," I complain.

Her face is sympathetic. "Are you still feeling unwell?"

I nod. Really, I just want to grab a pen and paper and write all of this down—I swear a thousand stories are swirling in my head—but I can't very well tell her that.

"Bear up, darling," she says, straightening my satin choker. "Only a few more hours and we'll be on our way."

I stifle a groan, and I've made up my mind to get off my feet when someone taps my shoulder.

"May I have this dance?"

I turn at the familiar sound of that voice, and I almost start laughing. Holy cow. Would you look at Ben!

He's dressed in a severe black greatcoat, a green-and-gold waist-coat, and a top hat with a really tacky hatband to match the busy pattern on the vest. He even has a lacy cravat to complete the look, and the overall effect is like some sort of elegant peacock. This is so far from the nerdy, joking jock I know. I take his hand and can't help but smile.

"Hello, Miss St. Clair," he says, moving smoothly through the dance. "I do hope you remember me."

I do. His family moved into town just a few months ago. I'm

taught by a governess in this reality, so instead of attending school together, he and I were introduced at a cotillion last summer.

"Of course I do, Mr. Hastings. It's nice to see you again."

"May I offer my congratulations upon the happy occasion of your engagement?"

I smile even bigger. He's so . . . formal. It sounds ridiculous.

"You may. And thank you."

"I had hoped you might wait a little longer and choose your intended with more care," he offers. "Since money is not a concern for you."

What's that supposed to mean? I stop paying attention to the dance steps and look up at him, and he looks kind of . . . sad.

"My parents thought it was best to have the matter resolved." I try to keep the tone of my voice pleasant, but it's hard. I still have a hard time understanding how parents can support their child marrying a stranger. It's just crazy to me. Apparently, I'm not alone in that sentiment.

"I see," Ben says carefully. He gives a slight bow over my hand as the music comes to a stop, and then he turns on his heel and strides out of the room, oblivious to the crowd of young ladies who are giggling as he passes. One of them peels off to come over to me.

"You're Jessamyn, aren't you?" she asks, waving her lacy fan against the heat of the ballroom.

"Yes. I believe we've met," I say, remembering. "Olivia, right?"

"That's right. And now that you're engaged, I can finally stop hating you quite so much," she says with an impish smile.

I give her a startled look. "Hating me?" What did I ever do to her? I search my memories, but nothing comes to mind.

"I'm teasing, of course." She swats me playfully with her fan. "I'm just relieved to see you safely on the shelf, leaving room for the rest of us to pursue our dear Mr. Hastings. I've been swooning over him ever since he arrived in town, but he's only had eyes for you."

"Oh, I'm sure that's an exaggeration," I say awkwardly. "He and I are simply acquaintances."

She stares off toward the doorway, as if hoping for one more glimpse of Ben's retreating back. "You will do me the favor of an introduction the next time he's about, won't you?" She turns pleading eyes up at me, and I shrug.

"Sure. Happy to help."

"Oh, they're starting another waltz," Olivia notes breathlessly. "Mother considers them a scandal, but how else is girl going to get close enough to a man to really get to know him?"

"How, indeed," I improvise, hoping I sound Victorian enough. I think I've got most of the lingo down around here, but I can't even begin to copy the accent.

Olivia shuffles off with a wave of her fan, and I decide I'm going to try to find somewhere to sit down in this crush of people. It's warm in here, too. How do women do this stuff in all this clothing? It's crazy.

I walk along the outside edge of the crowd, sticking close to the wall as I spy the open French doors leading out to the gardens on the other side of the room. I make my way over to them, stepping out into the cool night air with a sigh of relief.

They have the pathway to the gardens lit with gas lanterns, and the smell of magnolia and jasmine mixes with the breeze off the water. It's just beautiful, and I'm honestly enjoying myself until some semi-drunken dandy stumbles down the path and comes to a screeching halt in front of me.

"Well, look at what we have here," he says, smiling widely. "Were you waiting for me?"

I actually look behind me to see who he's talking to, and that's my mistake—I should never have turned my back on him. He's got his arms around me in an instant, and his alcohol-fueled breath is making me sick as he tries to press wet kisses all over my face and neck. I start to scream, but his hand clamps over my mouth. I struggle madly, my fingers clawing at him. I'm just about to rip out a handful of his hair when I feel him go flying, knocking me off-balance and sending me staggering down the graveled path. I barely have time to right myself before someone's hand clamps down on mine and I'm pulled along the path and then out of sight through the middle of a bunch of bushes that snag at my skirts. I'm about to try to scream again, but as I'm pulled up against another hard body, a voice murmurs low in my ear.

"Easy, love. Didn't mean to frighten you."

I relax, sagging in relief.

"Finn," I say, when I can get my breath again. "What are you doing here?"

"I saw your lump of a fiancé take himself off, and thought I'd step in to entertain you," he says with a grimace. "I had no idea someone else had the same plan. Are you all right? Did he hurt you?"

"No," I reassure him. "I am just *really* freaking tired." I sink onto a bench nearby, taking my weight off my aching feet. These high-heeled buttoned boots are torturous. I look up and he's staring at me with his arms crossed, and his hand is stroking his chin thoughtfully.

"Well, hello there, love," he says huskily. "What brings you back again?"

30

Here I Go Again

I PULL MY GLOVES OFF AND WAVE MY SWEATY HANDS IN the air. "I'm trying to avoid someone," I tell him.

"You're not here on an assignment, then?"

"No. I sort of . . . quit."

He looks amused. "Did you now? How'd that go over?"

I make a face. "I'm sure I'll hear about it."

"So this is a social visit?" His eyes brighten, and something in my stomach tightens in response.

"Uh . . . I'm supposed to be out with someone."

He takes a seat next to me. "It isn't me you're dodging, is it?"

I smile. "No, it isn't you."

"Well, that's a relief. It'd be a bloody shame to have you avoiding me anywhere."

"I'm not allowed to avoid you," I say. "You're training me. At least, over there you are."

"Whatever you need to learn, I'll be happy to tutor, as needed."

A devilish gleam lights his eyes, and I flush under his regard. "I think you've tutored this Jessa enough."

"Apparently not," he disagrees. "You need to learn how to fight dirty, love. If you were going to be living a life with a privateer, you'd be spending a lot of time at the docks—which are not always the most savory of locations, unfortunately." He pulls me up to my feet. "Here. Let me show you something."

He spins me around, knocking me off-balance again, and wraps his arms around me. I'm still out of breath, and I try my best to calm my breathing down. It must be the corset.

Sure it is, Jessa.

"The key to getting a man off you when he's already got you in a stranglehold is creating some space," Finn goes on. "This is best done with the element of surprise."

He reaches out, taking both my hands in his, and sets his chin down on my shoulder as he instructs me. I can feel his cheek rubbing against mine, the stubble of the slight beard he has here. It feels incredible. And I have to remember to breathe.

He takes my left hand, curling it into a fist, and places it in the palm of my right hand.

"There now," he says. "Wriggle your hands free any way you can, and get your fist braced in your other hand. Then use the added push from the fist into the open hand to propel your elbow back into his ribs or stomach. Aim lower, if you can. Go ahead," he urges. "Give it a try."

I turn my head, and I'm a hairbreadth from his lips. "I don't want to hurt you."

"Well, keep it gentle and keep it above the belt, then, if you please."

He gives me a wink, and I can't help but smile. I push with my right hand and drive my left elbow into his stomach, hearing the whoosh of his breath leaving him.

"Gads!" he complains. "You call that gentle?"

"Sorry," I say sheepishly. "Now what?"

He straightens back up, rubbing his stomach. "Now that you've got him bent over, you can give him a knee to the head or slam your reticule down across his neck, provided you're like most women and carry an arsenal in yours."

I laugh. "I really have no idea," I say. "Do I even know what a reticule *is*?" I wonder aloud. It's coming to me.

"Your handbag." He points at the bag lying on the bench next to my gloves. "With all that beading, you could have hit the cad in the eyes and blinded him for life."

I look down at myself, raising my arms and slapping them down on my voluminous skirts. "I have no idea what to do with all this stuff," I complain. "And if I don't get out of this corset soon, I'm going to pass out."

"I can help you with that." The corner of his mouth lifts in an irresistible smile.

"Here? In a garden?"

He just looks at me, and the memory comes flooding back. Oh, yes. In a garden. More than once.

"Oh," I say, and I blush again.

"I was merely going to suggest that you let me adjust your laces, love. Give you some more breathing room."

I glance around, but we're behind a set of bushes not visible from the main path, and there's nobody out here now that dessert is being served.

"Okay," I say, turning so my back is to him. His fingers are deft and quick as he unfastens my gown. I can feel the breeze on my skin, and I let out an involuntary groan at how good it feels.

His fingertips brush my skin, raising gooseflesh on my arms as he pulls at the corset strings, loosening them another inch. I feel him tie them off, then suddenly his hands are inside my gown, sliding over my shoulder blades as I feel his lips meet the back of my neck.

"You feel like my Jessa," he murmurs.

I look over my shoulder and his lips touch mine softly, and then he turns me so he can deepen the kiss. I lift my arms to circle his neck and it's like we ignite. My hands thread into his hair, clinging, and his hands move and shift across my back to my waist, pulling me in, and it's all I can do to breathe, despite my loosened corset.

His lips slide down to my neck again and I'm gripping his shoulders hard when suddenly, he pulls away and flips me back around so he can fasten up my gown.

I hear the sound of heels crunching on the gravel walkway that runs along the other side of the bushes a moment later.

"Jessamyn? Are you out here?" My mother's voice carries clearly in the night air.

I turn panicked eyes to Finn, who puts a finger to my lips, signaling me to keep quiet. He leaves the finger there, stroking it slowly back and forth as he smiles down at me. Finally, her footsteps fade into the distance, and I can breathe again.

I push his hand away and get hastily to my feet.

"Where d'you think you're going?" he asks, reaching out for my hand.

"I—I really should get back." I didn't come here to make out with Finn. *Did I?*

I take a deep breath in an effort to calm my racing heart, and I'm grateful that I actually can. "Thanks for the adjustment," I say. "That's so much better. Now, if you'll excuse me . . ." I scoop up my reticule and gloves, holding them both in front of me.

"I'll walk you inside," he offers, falling into step beside me. "No one will notice me in this crush." He puts his hands down deep into his pockets, just like my Finn does. I can't help but smile.

"What?" he asks.

"You do that just like my Finn. Your hands in your pockets."

"Is he very like me, then?"

"In some ways. You're a lot more . . . outspoken."

"So are you," he answers. "And that's all right with me, love."

His words do something funny to my insides. "Come on. I've got a party to escape from."

We step through the French doors, and I can't help but squirm a little. Finn steps closer, lowering his voice so we can converse.

"What are you doing?"

"My back," I say. "It's itching . . . ugh." I look up at him. "You didn't tuck in the ends of my corset laces. They're bunched up between my shoulders and tickling me."

He lifts his eyebrows apologetically. "Well, I can't very well adjust them again here, love. You'll have to retire to the ladies' salon. I'm sure one of the attendant maids there can assist you."

"You'd better get out of here before my father recognizes you," I say. "And I need to get home."

He reaches for my hand, pressing a kiss to the backs of my

207

fingers. I can't help but feel—and remember—how soft and warm his lips are.

"As before, Jessa . . . it's been a pleasure."

"Good-bye, Finn." I know I'm staring, but I'm somehow help-less to stop. The corner of his mouth quirks up.

"Right through there, love," he says, pointing the way.

"Yeah . . . I'm, uh . . . I'll just be going," I stammer. I turn to go, but I have to take one more look back. He's still standing there with that lopsided grin, and the butterflies are swarming in my stomach.

I look off toward the crush of women coming and going from the salon and heave a sigh before I head off into the fray. I make my way inside and push through the throng to put my hand to a mirror. Just as I start to transfer, a shout goes up. I could swear I smell the faintest hint of smoke, and then I'm through.

And I'm staring at myself in a small, circular mirror next to Ben's worried face as his arms tighten around me.

"It's definitely bruising," the lady from the historical society says as she shoves the compact mirror closer toward me. "Right there, on your cheek." She's kneeling next to me as well, and gently prodding at my face with her free hand.

My hand is resting on the mirror still, and I push it out of my way.

"I—I'm all right," I say. I think I am, anyway.

Ben is shaking his head. "Holy . . . !" He trails off, aware that there are a couple of kids on the tour. His arms are still tight around me, and I'm shaking.

"Are you okay?" he asks.

I look up at the small crowd of people gathered around me and my mind begins to slowly piece it all together.

I had been snapping pictures with Ben's phone, fascinated by the device and half listening to the woman from the historical society as she told us all about the Clock Tower Ghost from here atop the roof of Founder's Hall when one of the other women peeled away from the group and approached me. She wanted a picture of herself with the clock tower in the background.

I decided I needed to back up, since the spire of the clock tower was too high to fit in the picture along with them. Other me didn't think to zoom in or out. I started walking backward, and I heard the woman's shout just as I realized it was too late. I backed into a handbag someone left near the low wall lining the roof. My feet tangled in the strap and I went over, dropping the phone on the roof as I twisted, screaming. My right hand grabbed and clung to the edge of the wall.

Ben shouted, I scrambled to grab with my other hand, and Ben's hands closed over my wrists as he pulled hard. I came back over the wall, landing in a heap on the rooftop.

I can't speak just yet, and I can hear Ben panting from the adrenaline and exertion. I manage to sit up.

"I'm okay," I gasp. "I'm okay."

"I'm so sorry," the photo lady stammers.

"Did—did I break your phone?" I ask her.

"No, it's fine. Are you sure you're okay?"

I get up to my feet, but keep my hands on my knees, breathing deeply. I nod. "I'm a little scraped up, but I'm okay."

Ben is on his feet again as well, and he pulls me full into his arms again, hugging me tight.

"You scared me to death!" he exclaims. "I think you just took ten years off my life!"

He pushes me back at arm's length, looking me up and down.

"Are you okay? I thought we were gonna have to scrape you off the sidewalk with a spatula or something."

"Me too." I nod. "I think I wrecked my shoulder again." I give it a rub as I rotate it gingerly.

"It's not out of its socket," Ben says, pushing my hand away so he can push and probe. I smack his hand in retaliation.

"That hurts."

He reaches into his pocket, digging out his truck keys. "Let's go get you checked out, just to be sure."

"No." I shake my head. "It's just sore. I still have medicine I can take for it, if it gets worse. Let's just go home."

"You're sure you don't want me to call an ambulance?" Photo Lady asks.

"No, really—I'm okay. Just a little shaken."

I look back toward the wall, and the handbag is gone. Whoever wants me dead, it definitely isn't Ben. And they were right here, somewhere in the crowd. I scan the group, but I'm not seeing anyone suspicious. Several people have left, since this was the last stop on the tour anyway, and I'd brought the presentation to a stop.

As Ben leads me toward the stairs, the lady from the historical society reaches out, grasping my hand.

"Oh, honey," she says, shaking her head. "You have the worst luck."

I stare at the edge of the roof, three stories off the ground. I can't go on like this. I'm not going to let someone kill me in front of Ben, or Finn, or my parents . . . or Danny. I'm not going to let someone kill me, period. Something has got to be done.

And something tells me it's going to have to be me doing it.

31

Side by Side

"JESSA! IT'S TIME FOR YOU TO GO TO BED!" DANNY SAYS.

I am lying on my dad's couch, and it's nearly midnight. Ben brought me here over two hours ago, and my mind is still whirring between my memories of the ball and my other memories of nearly dying on a rooftop.

"What are you doing up?" I ask Danny. "You have work tomorrow. You should be in bed."

"I heard a noise and saw Finn," he tells me. "I was going to let him inside. It's cold."

"Finn is outside?" I sit up. "Where?"

"By the shed," Danny says. "I think he likes it there."

I move across to the sliding glass door that leads out to the patio and open it slowly, shivering a little in the cold night air. The shed is off the patio, but there's a four-foot gap between the back of it and the house.

"Finn!" I call in a loud whisper.

I see the shadows shift, and Finn emerges from behind the

shed. He glances around to make sure he's not being seen and walks quietly up to the door.

"What are you doing up?" he whispers. "You should be in bed."

"Danny saw you."

"Oh. Sorry." He shoves his hands in his pockets, and I smile.

"Why are you behind my dad's shed?" I ask.

He rocks back and forth on his heels, but he doesn't say anything. It finally dawns on me.

"You don't have anywhere to stay," I realize. "Because you don't have a counterpart here."

"No."

"But when Rudy brought you here—didn't he give you money or anything?"

"He did. He had money and clothing and a room at the YMCA waiting for me, but I wanted to stay close tonight. To keep an eye on you." His eyes slink away, and I wonder if he's still worried about Ben.

"Hi, Finn!" Danny says from right behind me.

"Danny, go to bed," I say, without looking at him. "It's late."

"Okay. Bye, Finn." He waves.

"Good night, Danny," Finn replies. "See you tomorrow."

"See you tomorrow!" Danny echoes, as he walks down the hall to his room.

I turn back to Finn. "Come on," I say, keeping my voice low so my father doesn't wake up. "You can hang in my room for the night."

He raises an eyebrow. "Are you sure?"

"Finn, it's freezing out here."

"It's not so bad," he says, but I can see his breath when he says it.

"Yes, it is," I say. He stares at me a minute, deciding.

"Yes, it is," he agrees, stepping inside. "It's really cold. And you've got a giant spiderweb behind that shed, did you know that? It's like a miniature spider city. It's really spectacular."

I lead him carefully down the hall and into my room, shutting the door as quietly as possible and locking it to be safe. I stand and listen for a moment, but all I hear is Danny's TV because he sleeps with it on all night. It should provide sound cover, since he's right next door to my father's room and I'm down the hall from both of them.

"I've locked the door, but my dad won't come in anyway. He has to be up early to drive Danny to the retirement home. He works there three days a week, with my mom," I explain.

"He's a busy guy," Finn says. "He told me he made Volunteer of the Year at the library."

"He volunteers there on Monday and Friday afternoons. Mom tries to keep him busy. And he loves meeting people, even if he doesn't always know what to say."

I turn back to Finn, who's still standing there with his hands in his pockets, looking mildly uncomfortable. It's quite a change, considering the Finn I spent part of my evening with earlier.

"You're staring," he points out.

"Sorry. I'm still trying to sort out reality here."

He gives me a look as it dawns on him. "You traveled?"

"Uh-huh. And when I came back, the other me had almost died."

"*What?*"

"I was with Ben—I mean, another Jessa was—at the ghost tour. I traveled back just as the drama was done. Apparently, my counterpart went a little crazy when she saw Ben take pictures with his phone. She borrowed it and was snapping pictures all over the place. Somebody asked her to take a picture of them, and somehow she tripped over a purse. Then she almost fell off the roof."

"The roof?"

"We were on the roof of city hall, hearing about the Ghost of the Clock Tower."

"So somebody planted the purse there," he says grimly. "Do you have any idea who?"

"No, she—I—was pretty overwrought." I remember her fear—my fear—and it's still so very real.

"I don't like when you travel without me."

"I wasn't without you. Technically."

He rocks back and forth on his heels some more, and I stare at a spot on the wall. The silence is awkward.

"Well . . . ," he finally says, "at least this time it wasn't my fault."

"That's a relief."

"Not really. It means our Traveler has stepped up his game. He's getting desperate."

"So now what? I can't have you sleeping in my backyard every night."

"If you've got an extra blanket," Finn suggests, "I can sleep on the floor. I'll leave before anyone wakes up."

"Yeah . . . sure, I think there's one up here." I walk over to the closet, reaching up to the top shelf. I'm too short and the blanket is pushed too far back—I can't get to it. I'm just about to ask him for help when I feel his chest press into my back, and his arm reaches around me to pull the blanket down.

"I've got it." He doesn't move away, and we're still pressed against each other. I close my eyes, remembering the feeling of his lips on my neck.

"Do you have a pillow?" he asks. He still hasn't moved. I turn, gesturing toward the bed. "You can have the other one," I say. Then my mouth opens and my voice speaks and from a far-off distance, I hear myself tell him that he can have the other side of the bed.

"You mean that?" he asks.

Do I? I think I do.

"I've got a full-sized bed—you can fit." I realize just how this must sound, so I add, "You just stay on top of the covers with the blanket, okay?"

"I'm okay with it if you are," he says carefully.

I slide into bed, straightening the blankets, and he takes his jacket and shoes off and climbs on top, spreading the other blanket over himself.

"Mmm." He makes an appreciative sound. "Much better than a spider-infested dirt mattress."

"I would imagine so."

He stacks his hands behind his head. "Hope I didn't bring any with me."

"Finn!"

"I'm teasing. I think."

We lie in silence for several long minutes, and I wonder if he might be asleep until he proves me wrong.

"So, where did you go? Anywhere I know?"

I consider that. It's not an outright lie if I say no. He's never been there, after all. He's too clever, though. He picks up on my hesitation.

"Anywhere I've *heard* of?" he clarifies.

I sigh. "Yes."

"You went back to see the pirate!" he says accusingly.

"Shhhh! Don't wake my dad up!" I whisper.

"Did you?"

"I saw him for all of ten minutes, Finn. Mostly I was at a party with my fiancé."

"You have a fiancé!"

"Shhhh!"

"Sorry. Just wasn't expecting that."

"It's not a love match or anything," I reassure him. "More of an arranged marriage. I'm an heiress over there. Anyway, the ball was hot, my shoes hurt my feet, my corset was worse than a medieval torture device, and I'm glad to be home."

"So this is better than hanging out with a pirate?"

"I wasn't with him very long," I say. "And mostly we just talked." *Mostly.*

He mulls that over. "Interesting."

I turn over on my side to look at him. "What do you care what I do in another reality, anyway?" I have no idea where I got the nerve to say that, but I did.

He turns to face me, too.

"I care about you, Jessa. No matter where you are."

My hand slides down to play with the covers, my fingers tracing the design on the comforter.

"Were we good friends—back in your world?"

"Yes. Best friends," he adds. "We went everywhere together."

"And my family?"

He sucks in a slow breath. "You didn't have one anymore by

the time we met. You never talked about them, and I never asked. I didn't have one either by then. I think that's why we latched on to each other. You used to call us 'two lost souls.'"

He smiles a little at the memory, while I let the pure awfulness of what he's told me sink in. Both of our families? Both of us alone? And then something happened to me over there and he was even more alone. My chest feels tight and I feel tears prick my eyes. The words tumble from my lips.

"Was it an accident? The way I died?"

I can feel his body stiffen from across the bed.

"No."

"Sorry. I know it's probably hard to talk about."

"It's okay. You're curious. I would be, too." He's keeping his voice neutral, but something tells me it's really not okay.

"I'm sorry, Finn."

I can hear him breathing in the darkness. "It's not your fault," he says.

"I know. But I'm still sorry it happened to you. I wish it hadn't." I feel a lump growing in my throat at the thought of what he's had to live through. "I'm sorry I left you there alone."

I feel his hand slide across the covers, and he threads his fingers through mine.

"You're here now," he says softly. "Get some sleep, Jessa. We need to rest."

I wonder if I'll be able to, after a conversation like this, but the warmth of his hand in mine is soothing, and my eyes grow heavy as I hear the sound of his breathing lulling my senses.

32

The Prophecy

EVENTUALLY, SLEEP CLAIMS ME. FINN WASN'T FAR BEHIND, because as I slide into my desk in the white classroom, Finn takes the desk next to me.

Mario is already there waiting for us, along with Rudy, who is tapping his fingers impatiently, glaring at the both of us.

"Another near miss," he snaps. He turns to look pointedly at Finn. "Where were you?"

"Jessa was with Ben, and since he'd kept her from harm a few days ago, I assumed he'd be watching out for her," Finn explains. "He was."

I turn to stare at Finn, because that's the closest thing to an endorsement he's ever given Ben.

"And you have no idea who set you up?" Mario asks.

"No. The other me was too busy falling," I say. "It was cold out—people were wearing hats and scarves. By the time I thought to look around, half the crowd had already left."

"Two attempts in one week." Mario shakes his head. "This is unlike anything we've ever seen before. Perhaps it's time to pull in some reinforcements."

"Out of the question," Rudy says. "We're diverting entirely too many resources to this. We need this resolved."

His attitude is really rubbing me the wrong way. I'm the one who's getting run over and thrown off buildings, for Pete's sake. I guess that's a real imposition to him. I've had it—with him, and with this whole situation.

"We need to go on the offensive."

Mario's head starts shaking even before I finish the sentence, and I push out of my desk to stand up.

"Look—I'm the one getting slammed around here. I'm the one with a target on my back."

"We're doing all we can, Jessa," Finn says.

"I know. And it's not enough. This . . . Traveler, whoever he or she is, is still getting through to me. And they'll keep on doing it until they get the job done." I clench my hand into a fist out of sheer frustration. "Whatever I did to piss this Traveler off, it must have been big."

"Jessa, sit down," Mario says.

"No! I'm done sitting around! We need to do something!"

"You need all the facts first," Mario says. "We all do. So sit down, and let me tell you what I've learned."

Rudy's eyes narrow. "You've discovered something? Why wasn't I informed?"

"I'm informing you now," Mario replies smoothly. "I know why Jessa has been targeted."

Finn reaches out for my hand and pulls me gently into my seat again. "Let's listen," he says. "If Mario knows the motivation, it'll give us somewhere to look."

"All right," I say, taking my seat again. "What did one of me do to piss this person off?"

Mario steps back, and the whiteboard behind him lights up.

"We're going to have a bit of a history lesson first," he says. "We're going back a few thousand years, before we began using Travelers."

"You haven't always had Travelers?"

"We didn't need them early on," Rudy says. "We used the dreamscape to communicate directly, through oracles, priests, and shamans. People were much simpler then, much more inclined to primitive beliefs. We directed the oracles, and they directed the people."

"And then mankind began innovating," Mario continues, as the whiteboard behind him lights up with civilizations and history progressing. "Science and industry ushered in higher levels of conscious thought and an endless curiosity about the world they lived in. People began moving away from their more primitive beliefs, and we needed to find a way to keep the reality streams in check."

"So you created Travelers?" I ask.

Mario's mouth tilts up at one corner. "No. You created yourself. We just realized your potential."

"Travelers just suddenly began appearing?" Finn asks. "What started that?"

"There was only one, to begin with," Mario says. "Think of her as a mutation of sorts. But she was born with the ability, and we learned a lot from her."

"Eventually, other Travelers began spontaneously emerging, and we realized the full potential we could draw from them," Rudy says.

"But the first Traveler was especially important. Her name was Viatrix," Mario says, and a woman's face appears behind him. She looks like she may be Greek or Roman from the hairstyle. "This is where you come in, Jessa, because you are her direct descendant, and the only living Traveler who can make that claim."

"So . . . another Traveler wants me dead because of my heritage?" I'm confused. Is this some kind of weird Traveler racism?

"Viatrix was the only one of her kind for many years—decades, actually," Mario continues.

"And in the course of our study of her phenomenon and its far-reaching repercussions, a prophecy was made," Rudy adds.

"What sort of prophecy?" Finn asks—and he's looking as uneasy about that word as I am.

"First, you have to understand that 'prophecy' is an archaic word," Mario says, giving Rudy a stern look. "Think of it as more of a . . . forecast. We cannot absolutely predict the future, not while mankind has free will. There are too many variables."

"And there's a forecast involving a descendant of this . . . Viatrix?" Finn asks.

"A time was foretold when the multitude of realities would become too great and too complicated to control as we've been doing," Rudy says. "When that occurs, a convergence can take place."

"And a convergence would be catastrophic," Mario says, "erasing all the reality streams, with the exception of the original stream."

"Which, unfortunately, we've been unable to locate," Rudy says. "The streams are too vast and variable. The time to trace it all back would be incalculable and take far more resources than we as Dreamers have to commit to it."

I feel sick to my stomach. Thousands of realities—millions of them, all wiped out. It's almost beyond comprehension.

"So where do I come into play?" I ask warily.

"You're the only one who can stop it." Mario walks back over to his desk and leans against it.

"Potentially," Rudy amends. "The prophecy was made that a Traveler descendant of Viatrix prime would have the ability to defeat the convergence."

"Viatrix prime?" Finn asks. "As in . . . she was in the original reality stream?"

"Exactly," Mario said. "And once the forecast was made, I began researching back, to find the origin stream. It's taken millennia, but I've put the final effort into it recently, in light of certain events. I now know that this Jessa is not only the descendant of Viatrix, but she's the descendant of Viatrix prime."

Rudy looks as startled as we are by the news.

"You're certain of this?" he asks. "Jessa's reality is the origin?"

"Absolutely."

"What do you mean, 'in light of certain events'?" I ask.

"The reality streams are beginning to splinter," Rudy says. "You haven't noticed the effect yet, and may not for some time if you are indeed within the origin. But in some of the later streams, the more recently created, we've seen fragmenting. Realities crossing or becoming skewed."

"None of it is catastrophic," Mario says. "We are able to contain it with some judiciously placed corrections. But it's there all the same and it's a constant battle to stay ahead of it."

Finn looks up at Rudy. "What happens if that continues?"

Rudy makes a face. "If it goes unchecked, chaos. Widespread and potentially uncontained chaos."

"Here's my theory," Mario says. "A Traveler—a very well-seasoned Traveler—has seen some of this splintering and reported it to their Dreamer, who would, of course, know the prophecy. Someone may be taking it upon themselves to make their job a little easier."

Finn's jaw drops. "You think there's a Dreamer behind this? They're trying to simplify by cutting out all the other reality streams?"

"But who?" Rudy asks. "I've been very thorough in my research regarding this rogue Traveler. My investigations haven't turned up anything."

"*Yet*," Mario qualifies. "If there's a Traveler, there has to be a Dreamer, which means someone is pulling the strings."

"Or it means someone has cut the strings and is working without a tether," Rudy says pointedly. "Either scenario is a disaster in the making."

"So what happens if there's a convergence?" I interrupt.

Mario gestures to the whiteboard, where thousands of intersecting lines begin to splinter, then morph together, condensing into one solid line. "If the convergence is allowed to occur, we reset. New reality streams would begin from the origin as before, but in a smaller and much more easily controlled fashion."

"But millions of people—"

"Billions," Mario interrupts me. "Billions upon billions. All gone. Vanished in an instant, as though they never existed at all."

I turn to look at Finn, and his eyes carry the same sick knowledge as mine. He will not survive this. He will be one of the billions, because he doesn't belong in my reality.

"They're all at risk," Mario says, as if reading my thoughts. "And you are the one who can save them all."

33

Together

I SHAKE MY HEAD FRANTICALLY. "YOU'VE GOT TO BE wrong. I'm not a savior. I can barely travel. I don't know the first thing about stopping a convergence!"

"We're in luck," Mario says. "Because whoever is behind this, I don't believe they yet know the first thing about starting the convergence."

"So it has to be triggered?" Finn asks.

"Oh, yes," Rudy says. "It won't occur spontaneously. There are certain tools that must be used, but without knowing the origin reality, they couldn't be easily found."

"I'll keep that from general knowledge," Mario says. "And don't discuss that anywhere that you can be overheard," he cautions the both of us. "Until we know who this Traveler is, we can't risk that information getting to them."

"Aren't they risking destroying themselves?" I ask. "If they're not from my reality? Why would they do that without knowing for sure?"

"Martyrs have existed since time began," Rudy reminds me. "Someone willing to perish for a cause they believe to be right can be virtually unstoppable."

"Rudy's right," Mario agrees. "Until the Traveler or their Dreamer slips up, we'll be one step behind, and they'll be closing in. You need to get off the radar."

"You mean travel," Finn clarifies.

"Yes," Mario says. "We need to throw them off your trail."

"What do you suggest?" I ask.

"Let me think on it," Mario says. "We'll do the transfer on Sunday, and I'll debrief you tomorrow, after I've had a chance to do some more research."

"I should look into options as well," Rudy offers. "Perhaps if we send the two of them to a reality that Jessa has never existed in, the Traveler won't think to look there."

Mario nods. "That's a good idea—not much chance of discovery when the Traveler won't know where to begin looking."

"I guess we'll just sit tight," I say, not really liking the sound of that.

"We won't leave Jessa's house," Finn agrees.

"If we're finished here . . ." Rudy gets to his feet. "I have work to do. We'll meet again this evening." With a nod to Mario, he steps through the red door and shuts it behind him.

Mario follows him, opening the door for us. "Go on," he says.

We start to step through, but Mario holds us back. "Wait," he says. "Before you go . . . I've just had a thought. I know exactly where to send the two of you."

"Someplace where Jessa doesn't exist?" Finn asks.

"No—she most definitely exists there. You don't, however."

I'm confused. "I thought we were deciding for the other way around?"

"We were, but . . . I'm working on a hunch. Trust me." He holds my eyes a moment. "You need to look for a girl wearing a black Ramones T-shirt."

"You're not going to walk me through a preview?" I ask.

"Not this time. You'll find her." He holds the door open. "I want you both to leave at nine this morning. I'll fill Rudy in. You two just stay until I give you instructions for a new location, if we need it."

"Wherever it is," I say, "at least there's good music."

Mario looks at me strangely.

"What?" I ask.

He shrugs and then gives me an odd smile.

"Nine, Jessa. Be prompt."

"I will," I promise. And then we step through the door.

Sometime before seven a.m. I help Finn sneak back out, and by the time I get my shower, my dad has taken Danny to the library for his volunteer shift. Then he's planning on driving over to Manortown to some electronics store there, and he won't be back till the afternoon. The timing will work out perfectly.

I'm scrambling eggs when a knock sounds at the door.

"Long time, no see," I say, smiling at Finn as I open the door.

"I waited till they were gone," he says, stepping inside.

"Are you hungry? I'm making breakfast."

"Yeah." His eyes light up. "I'd love some breakfast."

"It's only eggs and toast."

"Sounds delicious."

I wonder when Finn last had a home-cooked meal. The thought of the life he's probably lived squeezes at my heart.

"You ready to be a fugitive?" he asks, as I scoop out a large portion of eggs onto his plate.

"Truthfully? No." I grab the toast and put it on a plate in front of him before I sit down to join him at the table.

"It'll be fine, Jessa. You'll still be here, you know. Your parents and Danny won't suspect a thing."

"I'm not so sure about Danny," I say. "And what happens if this Traveler finds the other me? I'll never see my family again."

"It's not like he can go after you every hour or something," Finn explains. "He has to arrange events that end badly for you but have the least number of ripples as a consequence. The Traveler can't just assume getting rid of you takes care of everything. He's got to get rid of you the right way."

"Is that why he's been using you?" I ask.

"Probably. My guess is he's trying to frame me to throw suspicion off him. Only that didn't work so well when it was obvious I kept trying to protect you."

"Really?" I wonder why Mario didn't tell me that. If the killer is after Finn, too, or doing his best to put the burden of my death on Finn, then Mario knows I'm going to do my best to prevent that. That is, if I can see it coming.

"What are you thinking?" he asks, reaching out to take my hand.

"I'm thinking that Mario didn't tell me that because he knows I'll try to protect you."

I take his now-empty plate and walk it over to the dishwasher, and he gets up to follow me.

"That's not your job, Jessa," he says. "I can take care of myself."

"Me too."

"I know," he says. "But I'm going to watch out for you anyway."

"Me too—for you," I answer stubbornly.

"There's no point in trying to talk you out of it, is there?" he asks.

"Nope."

"Come on," he sighs. "It's nearly nine."

I give him a nod. "Let's do this."

He grasps my hand and leads me up to my bedroom to stand in front of the mirror.

"Remember," he says. "We're in this together."

"Together," I repeat, and the word causes a spreading warmth within me. Whatever is waiting for me on the other side of the mirror, I can face it. We can face it.

Together.

34

Silent

WE TRANSFER THROUGH INTO HER BATHROOM. I MEAN *my* bathroom. The first thing I notice is that it's cold. The second thing hits me a moment later, and I stand frozen in the middle of the bathroom, my feet rooted to the floor in shock.

Finn grabs me by the arms, instantly sensing something is very wrong.

I have the memories now. I struggle to find my voice, but it's not something this Jessa's brain does easily.

"Finn." My mouth struggles to make the words. "I'm deaf."

He's startled. I can see it on his face even though I can't hear a word he's saying as he replies to me. I make out my name as he says it, but that's all. I nod my head and say it again.

"I'm deaf."

It really is hard to speak, even though I know how to do it. This Jessa's brain has no use for speech, so it's like trying to use a door that's rusted shut at the hinges. I shake my head at Finn, letting him know I don't know what he's saying.

And then he surprises me. Finn knows sign language. And apparently, so do I, because I understand perfectly what he's trying to say to me.

You understand me? he signs.

Yes.

Smart Mario. The Traveler would never think to look here.

I would never think to come here.

Where are we?

I look around. *In a bathroom.*

I know. He rolls his eyes. *Is that snow?*

I look past him, out the window. *Yes.*

We make our way out into the bedroom and cautiously down the stairs. It's odd, trying to be stealthy when you have nothing to judge by. No footsteps to tell you if you're being too loud, no sounds from another room to tip you off—it's kind of freaking me out.

Finn holds up a hand and signs, *I hear Danny.*

We turn off the staircase into a living room that's a lot nicer than mine. The furniture is new and there is all sorts of fancy artwork on the walls. The room is lovely, but it looks like it's being used as a toddler playground at the moment. There are toys scattered everywhere, and Danny sits in front of the TV, rocking.

I walk around between him and the TV and try to sign. We taught our Danny some sign language when he was younger and not as verbal. Maybe we did the same here.

He pushes me away angrily and goes back to rocking. And rocking. And rocking.

I say his name and he jumps back. I've scared him. He immediately starts crying, and according to Finn, he's doing it loudly.

My mother comes tearing down the stairs, giving Finn a startled glance before wrapping her arms around Danny and rocking
him back and forth to calm him. She signs over his shoulder at me.

What are you doing? Who is this?

I can tell from the way she's gesturing that she's angry.

This is Finn. I know him from a project through school.

You need to clear out! You know how Danny is around strangers.

I nod, pulling Finn along as we make our way through the
house and out into the front yard.

He's nonverbal, I explain. *It must be so hard for him. He's a lot
more disabled here.*

What project at school? Finn signs. *In case she asks?*

*I attend an online school. Sometimes, we do group projects and
have meetups. If she asks, say it's science.*

An online school? Over the computer? Not a classroom?

I nod. *Is that where you learned sign language? School?*

My mother was deaf. She taught me.

He pauses a moment, and his eyes show a flash of pain.

*They killed her, along with my little brother. She didn't hear them
coming. I was gone, looking for food.*

I'm sorry, I sign. I don't know what else to say.

It was a long time ago, he signs back. As if that makes it better,
somehow. Not as horrifying, somehow.

I slide my arms around him and hug him tight.

He slides his arms around me in return, and I can feel the solid
strength of his heartbeat against my hand on his chest. It's

snowing and the falling flakes land on his hair and stick to his eyelashes, and he's looking down at me and his eyes are shining.

And then I suddenly remember that I've got a boyfriend in this reality.

I've got a boyfriend named Ben.

35

The Getaway

I FEEL MY PHONE VIBRATE, AND THE SMILE HITS MY LIPS before I can stop it. My hand reaches for the phone out of habit, and I feel warmth spread through me as I read the text message.

> Hey babe
> How are you feeling?
> Miss you much

We've been here six days. Six days of trying to adjust to a world of strange feelings and an entirely different lifestyle.

Finn glances over at my phone as I stare at it.

You need to answer him, he signs.

I know, I sign back. *Just give me a minute.* I set the phone down on the couch next to me, and then I sigh and pick it up again.

This is so hard. Ben is texting me a few times a day, and I'm yearning to see him. The minute I feel my phone vibrate, I light up like a Christmas tree—until I remember that this isn't me. Not really. I can't play this part, even if I feel like I know the lines. So I've told him I have mononucleosis and he can't see me in person for a few weeks because I'm contagious. It's the best I can do to preserve their relationship and keep it from playing havoc with me and my feelings.

I look down at the phone again, and I'm simultaneously wishing he'd leave me alone and really happy to know he misses me. My mind and my heart feel like they're being tumble-dried.

> **Hi handsome**

(My nickname for him.)

> **Miss you too, a lot**

(And I do. Oh God, I do.)

How much longer?
Maybe I could come by
and just not breathe or something?
I can hold my breath and kiss you ☺

I laugh at his suggestion, my face wreathed in smiles until I glance up and catch the look on Finn's face. It hits me right in the chest like a ten-pound weight.

Sorry, I sign. *It's rough. Having her memories.*

His face softens. *I know,* he signs.

I turn my attention back to my phone, reining in the nearly unrelenting urge to take Ben up on his offer.

> I won't take a chance
> at getting you sick
> we'll be together soon

I won't—

Not soon enough
I have that card that you
sprayed the perfume in
I open and close it all day long

> I have your hoodie
> wrapped around my pillow
> it still smells like you

I can't decide
are we pathetic, or not?

> Probably ☺

Wish we could be
pathetic together

> Me too

I look up from my phone again, feeling a weird mix of guilt and happiness. This time, Finn is making an effort to concentrate on the TV, I guess to give me some privacy. I still feel like he can read every emotion running through me, though. I'd better end this conversation.

> I'm getting really tired

Get some sleep babe
Love you

Love you, too

This week has been such an emotional roller coaster. In addition to adjusting to a world without sound, I'm having a really hard time living in my house.

My mother is rarely around. She's got a good corporate job in this reality—one that pays for this lavish house and a team of therapists and aides who cycle in and out of Danny's day, but her job keeps her working late almost every night, and by the time she gets home, she just wants to have a glass of wine and go to bed.

My dad in this reality is a complete nonentity. He walked out on us when I was three, and we haven't seen him since. This is unlike any version of my father that I could ever imagine.

Danny is surrounded by caretakers most of the time. I haven't been able to really interact with him much, and I get the feeling that like my Danny, he knows I'm an imposter. He just can't verbalize it, and he's keeping his distance because of it.

All in all, I feel like I'm not interacting much with my own family. The final cherry on top of this is that I'm warring with my own feelings on a daily basis. Finn and I are growing closer, and I know he feels it just as much as I do. He understands exactly what I'm going through in a way that Ben could never comprehend.

But this Jessa has been dating Ben for nearly a year. They met at her Mugsy's, and she taught him sign language. They're nearly inseparable, and they are in love.

They're really, honestly in love. She loves him—I love him—and the memory of it is so strong, it's wreaking havoc with my insides because I also want to spend more time with Finn, but I have to be discreet because I don't want to blow anything for my counterpart.

All this has made me edgy and emotionally raw. I feel like I can't share too much of it with Finn because it involves Ben so much, but I can't exactly tell Ben about all of this, either. Every time he texts me to check on me, I feel like I bleed a little.

Mario has been absent on the overnights, so I guess he's busy. Finn's hasn't had any contact with Rudy, so he's not getting any answers, either. I am ready to burst.

On Saturday, Finn meets me for a walk in the park and I just completely lose it on him.

He doesn't try to tell me it'll get better. He just tells me he's sorry, because he knows that sometimes, that's all you can say.

We are standing in the park by a pond, snow is falling all around, and I am cursing myself for not remembering to bring Kleenex, because I'm crying all over the front of his shirt. I feel him lift my chin, and he wipes my face with his fingertips.

Thanks, I sign.

I'm not blowing your nose for you, he signs back.

I laugh, and I'm sure it sounds as awkward as it feels. He doesn't seem to notice, though. He pulls me into him and I rest my face against his chest. He's warm and real and the only anchor I have in this swirling sea of feelings and frustration.

He pulls back and I feel him laugh.

What? I sign.

You'd better stop crying before you freeze to my shirt, he signs.

Right, I sign, stepping back.

He looks around, which is kind of silly, considering we aren't going to be overheard. Not unless somebody knows sign language.

Hey, he signs. *How would you like to get away from here for a little while?*

You mean away from the park, or "away" away?

He grins conspiratorially. *"Away" away.*

Won't Mario get mad? I don't want us to get in trouble and end up getting night terrors or something.

We'll only be gone half an hour. Besides, I have permission. Rudy and I talked last night and he suggested that I take you away for a little while. He thinks you're under too much stress. He'll handle Mario for you.

Do you have someplace in mind? I ask.

I thought a little glitter mousse might cheer you up.

I smile, my eyes darting around. It's like I expect Mario to leap out of the bushes like an avenging angel, ready to smite us or something.

Okay, I sign. *I'd love to. Let's get back home while Danny is busy with his therapist.*

Why? he responds. *We've got a pond right in front of us.*

Are you serious? It's freezing. We'll get soaked.

You'll transfer as soon as you touch it. If you do it right, the only thing getting wet will be your fingertips.

If I do it right, I qualify.

You have to learn sometime. He shrugs. *Come on. You've got this.*

He leads me over to the pond's edge. *We'll do this the easy way,* he signs. *But it'll get our shoes muddy.*

What's the hard way? I ask.

He points at the footbridge that arches over the water. *We jump.*

From the bridge? That's only about six feet above the water!

We'd have to shift fast, he agrees. *But I don't think you're ready for that yet. And I doubt our counterparts would appreciate slamming into an icy pond.*

No, definitely not, I sign. *Let's stick with easy.*

We crouch down at the water's edge, and he breaks through the thin ice. The water is crystal clear, and I'm easily able to see myself in the surface. I reach out, putting tentative fingers to the water as I stare at the other me, my mind filling with images of chandeliers and chrome and sparkling everything.

I push on the surface, and the water is so cold, it makes my fingers numb. I concentrate as hard as I can with my fingers freezing off, and my hand pushes down . . . right into the water, soaking my sleeve.

I draw back, making a startled sound as I shake the water off my frozen hand.

Don't get distracted, Finn signs. *You have to tune out the conditions around you and focus on where you want to go.*

Can't we just go back home and find a decent mirror?

Finn shakes his head. *You need to learn this. Someday, you may need to travel quickly, or under harsh conditions. Keep your focus, and you'll be fine.*

I rub my hands together, trying to get them warm, and I try again, gazing at my reflection in the water and looking closely as my fingertips barely graze the surface. It still takes two more tries and an achingly cold hand before things begin to morph before my eyes.

This time, instead of the easy give of water, it feels thicker, tighter. One strong push and I am through.

Whoa. So this is where I live over here. My room is a technicolor, glittering nightmare. Everything is in neon shades of yellow and pink, and I have what looks like four shimmering disco balls instead of light fixtures, and all four of them are spinning at different speeds. It makes me want to throw up. If Danny were here, he'd be crouched in a corner with his eyes shut.

I am suddenly filled with a wave of homesickness so strong it brings tears to my eyes and they spill over, sliding down my cheeks. I miss my Danny, singing along with Disney movies. I miss his goofy sense of humor and even the way he announces it like the town crier every time he farts. I miss climbing into my mom's bed at night, after Danny goes to sleep. I know she's tired, but she never tells me to leave. It's the only time we have really that's just for us, and we lie there and I talk about my day and we laugh and she lets me fall asleep there, if I want to. And when she turns out the light, she smooths my hair back and kisses my forehead, even though I'm seventeen. I pretend I'm asleep when she does it, but I'm really not.

"You okay?" Finn says, coming up behind me.

I nod, wiping my cheeks with the backs of my hands. "Just homesick." I give a watery laugh. "It feels so weird to hear. And talk."

"A big mouthful of glitter mousse might help the situation," he says.

"Lead the way." I slide my hand into his, and we walk down the hammered chrome staircase with the eye-burning fuchsia carpet and out through the multicolored front room with the rotating chrome fireplace.

I'm relieved to see that the street looks nearly normal. The exteriors of the houses are a lot more flamboyant, and the cars look like something out of a 1950s sci-fi movie about the future, but we're able to find our way to Mugsy's without too much trouble.

We get our mousse and slide into the booth. I don't even bother waiting till I've sat down—I pull a huge dollop off with my finger and cram it in my mouth.

I roll my eyes in ecstasy, not bothering to say how good this is. Finn knows. And he's right; I do feel a little better. I wish I could bring some of this back for my mom and my brother. I'm not sure if Danny would try it because it looks strange, but he'd love it if he did.

"You want a refill?" Finn asks, pointing to my nearly empty bowl.

"I do, but I'm also debating the merits of a cupcake." I hope other me can forgive me for sabotaging her diet this once. I need it.

"Why don't I go get both, and we can share them?" Finn suggests.

"It's obvious to me why I like you." I grin.

"Be right back."

Finn makes his way to the counter, and I spend a moment looking at the outrageous posters on the wall. Apparently, clowns are a major thing in this reality, and they all look demented in the posters. I cannot suppress a shudder.

My fingers are sticky from the glitter mousse, so I walk back to the bathroom to wash them before I add a layer of frosting. I've just finished drying my hands and I'm opening the door when it's suddenly shoved in from the other side. My mind barely has time to register the intruder before I'm pushed back and spun around, falling into the polished chrome wall.

I let out a sound of protest because I'm surprised, but my eyes are on the sparkling, gloved hand with all its bracelets and jewelry that comes down to hold my palm flat against the wall. My startled eyes lock on my reflection next to it. Before I can get my bearings, I feel a mighty push from behind, and then the grip on my arm breaks.

I am through. And I am all alone.

36

Walking on the Moon

THE LANDSCAPE AROUND ME IS AN ENDLESS SEA OF gray. It's unrelenting. Everywhere you look, there is almost nothing to break up the monotony. If my lungs weren't frantically sucking in air, I'd think I landed on the surface of the moon.

I guess I just met the other Traveler. And I think it's a woman. A very strong woman, apparently.

Where is Finn? Does she have him? I glance around frantically, but neither of them are anywhere in sight. No one's in sight. I am completely and utterly alone.

I get to my feet, rubbing my arms for comfort, and also because it's really, really cold here. The sky is overcast, and it looks like it might rain any minute.

I am standing next to a trickle of a creek, but it's clogged with garbage and chunks of charred wood, forming a stagnant pool. The water has a greasy coating. I can barely see myself, but I might be able to see well enough to use it. It's hard to tell with the hazy cloud cover darkening the sky.

I have no idea where I am, but the Traveler doesn't appear to have followed me. I crouch down next to the pool, holding my breath so I don't have to smell it. I reach out, clear my mind, and touch the murky, swirled reflection showing in the water.

My hand slides into a slick of goo and I pull it back, shaking the nastiness off it and wiping it against my jeans. Gross.

I take a deep breath, really concentrating this time, and I nearly fall in, trying to push through the water. I try one more time, willing myself to the other side, to Finn, and still I am here. Wherever "here" is.

I stand up, looking around, but I don't see a house or a business or anything that could possibly have a better mirror. And since I'm not smart enough to have thought to keep one on me—I make a mental note to do that from now on—I'm going to have to walk until I find something. I decide to follow the creek, hoping to find clear water somewhere, but it dries up not far from where I was.

I feel like I'm making pretty good time. A glance down at myself shows that I'm wearing what I wore at Mugsy's, instead of whatever I'd be wearing here, which means—I guess—that there *is* no me here. So the Traveler pushed me through to a reality I don't exist in. I'm also standing out like a sore thumb in head-to-toe gold and fuchsia.

I pick up my pace, wondering how long it's going to be before the Traveler finds me. Off to one side I see the only thing that could pass for cover. It looks almost like a landfill of some kind, made up of large piles of garbage and felled trees. It almost looks like a tornado was through and leveled a town and they pushed all the rubble into a long, long pile that stretches as far as I can see. I need to get on the other side of it, because the Traveler could be following, and soon.

Maybe I can find a broken mirror in the pile if I look. I just need to find a clear reflector to get me out of here. Murky, possibly diseased water is probably not the best way to go about this.

I walk for what feels like hours, but without a working phone—I can't get a signal at all—or a watch, who knows? It's likely been less than that, but it feels like a lot longer. I haven't found anything along the way that I can use as a mirror, either.

The sun is beginning to sink in the sky, and it's getting even colder. I'm starting to think that I'm not going to find shelter before evening when I find the road. It's half-buried under dirt and fine grayish powder, and chunks of it have crumbled off at the edges.

I follow the road in the same direction that I was walking toward, keeping to the edge of the rubble pile, and just as the sun drops to the horizon, I see the houses. It's a small town, and strangely, even though it's twilight, there are no lights, not in the street and not in any of the homes. I get a creepy sense of foreboding about this, and I slow my steps a bit, trying to pay closer attention, because I just kicked something hard as I was walking and it rolled off in front of me.

That's when I realize I'm walking through a graveyard.

I kicked a human skull, and there are bone fragments all around me. Not one of them is intact—all are broken, shattered. I crouch down to look more closely in the remaining dim light and I see the marks upon them—like they've been gnawed. The bones are of all sizes. Large adults. Smaller adults. Children.

I stagger to my feet as the horror hits me like an icy fist in the chest.

I am in Finn's world.

The Traveler doesn't need to follow me. She knows I won't live long. Not here.

The town in front of me now becomes a place to be feared instead of a safe harbor. I need to get out of sight. Who knows what's hiding there, waiting for someone clueless like me to stumble in?

But I have no choice. I have to go. I need to find a mirror. A puddle of clear water. A piece of polished metal. Something. And the houses in town are my best chance for finding any of those things. More than anything, I need to get out of sight, and I'm not about to curl up for the night on a pile of skeletons.

I make my way more carefully now, grateful that I have my hearing again, but starting at every sound in the deepening night. It's eerily quiet for the most part, but that just makes the tiny sounds stand out more when they occur. A shift in the rubble. Wind picking up. A thump that I can't define.

I crouch down, running as quickly as I can until I reach the side of a house, flattening myself into its shadow. I'm panting with exertion. I stand there a few minutes, waiting and listening.

And then I hear it. Far off and barely discernable. Could it be human voices? I can't tell for sure. I am tempted to hide in this building, but if they're looking for people coming in off the road, this would be the first place they'd look.

I stay flat against the wall, inching along until I get to a corner and can look around it very, very slowly. I don't see anyone in either direction down the street, but that doesn't mean they're not inside a building or something. I stop and listen again, but whatever I'm hearing is faint and far away. I think. I hope.

I decide to risk a run to the next house, and again, no one is there. I still feel like I'm too close to the road, though. I count down two more houses and wonder if I should risk crossing the street. Probably not.

I move around to the back of this house, still listening closely for voices, or any sound of people. I am torn between the need to get away and the need to stay clear of what is an obvious entry point to the town. I try the back door, but it's not budging.

I look up and down the street carefully as I move around to the front of the house. I can see in the dim moonlight that the door has been broken in and I stand in the doorway, listening, holding my breath to keep it from sounding in my ears. I take a step cautiously into the house. My foot crunches down on something and I freeze in my tracks, holding my breath again. After what feels like an eternity, I move once more, and everything sounds impossibly loud as my footsteps echo on a wooden floor scattered with debris.

The house is very dark, and I make my way blindly from one room to the next, finding nothing on the ground floor that could act as a mirror—at least not that I can see in the dark.

I make my way up the staircase as silently as I can, but the stairs creak badly and I am sure I heard something rustle. I bite down on my lip to keep from making a startled sound, and I wait. Breathe. Wait some more.

I make it up two more stairs and wait again before finally moving to the top of the staircase and working my way carefully down the hallway, my eyes straining to see in near pitch-black.

The first room I encounter is a bathroom, and I nearly shout with excitement. Where there's a bathroom, there's a mirror. I fumble around automatically for the light switch and realize how useless that was when nothing happens. The power must be out. I feel for the sink and find it, then reach my hand out and touch the glass above it. Yes! It's a mirror.

But I can't see it. If I can't see it, I can't shift. My hand reaches up to trace its outline. It's definitely large and attached firmly to the wall. Maybe there's something I can smash it with? I only need a good-sized shard. I feel around, but there's nothing in the room—just a sink and a toilet.

I lean against the sink, momentarily defeated. This bathroom has no windows, and it's as dark as a tomb in here. I'm going to have to find another mirror in a room with some windows, or a flashlight.

I step back out into the hallway, trying to move silently but failing miserably. There's just entirely too much debris to step on, and the floor—at least to my ears—is incredibly creaky. I step into one bedroom that's been made over into an office, feeling carefully along the wall. There's nothing that feels like a mirror. I move on to what must be the master bedroom, and I'm disappointed to discover that there's no bathroom suite attached. I ought to see a little better due to the windows in here, but there are heavy draperies blocking out even the slightest glimmer of light, and I open them carefully, just in case someone can see shadows moving in here from the outside. The windows still don't shed enough light with a pale moon in an overcast sky. It's useless. I close the drapes again.

I put my hands to the wall, inching along and feeling for a

bureau or any type of vanity table, when I hit the jackpot. A heavy, very ornate, and dust-covered mirror hangs on the wall over a chest of drawers. I clean its smooth surface with my fingers, crinkling my eyes as I strain them hard trying to see myself. I stare hard, touching the glass, willing myself to see more. Still useless.

I start opening drawers as quietly as I can, feeling around in the hope of finding a flashlight, and I go into full-body shudder as I put my hand in an enormous spiderweb. I shut the drawer quickly and have to force myself to open the next one, and then the next.

Still no luck.

Another slow walk around the house, along with drawer-opening in the office and another bedroom with a crib (but no mirror) and rifling through the kitchen drawers, gets me nowhere. Until the sun comes up again, I'm not going to find anything in the dark. I might as well just wait it out till morning, then open the curtains and shift back once the sun is up.

I feel across the top of the bare mattress on the bed and it seems to be clear, but a quick check of the closets doesn't find me any bedding and only a few articles of clothing that I can try to use for warmth.

I slide my arms into what feels like a ladies' blouse and then carefully reach out to guide myself onto the bed, hoping I won't be getting another handful of spiderweb. After another inspection, I curl up across the foot of the mattress.

I am exhausted, but every slight noise, every bump, every whistle of wind skitters across my frazzled nerves like nails on a chalkboard. Every creak and pop of the house is a gang of evil men who have been instructed to target me specifically.

I've got a mirror in front of me, and all I need is a little of the muted glow that passes for daylight in this place, and I am home free.

I lie in the dark with my eyes open wide, pulling my knees up into my body, and I try to keep warm.

37

Found

I REALIZE THAT I MUST HAVE DOZED OFF, BECAUSE I'M standing in the white-walled classroom. Mario comes through the red door and rushes over to me, grasping me by the shoulders.

"Jessa! You're safe!"

"No I'm not," I say, shaking my head. "The Traveler threw me into Finn's world, I think. I haven't seen anyone yet, but—"

I'm pulled backward through the red door with such force, my arms flail, reaching out for Mario. When I open my eyes, I am still lying on the dusty bed in the dark, and from the adrenaline pumping in my veins, it's clear that something has startled me awake.

I lie very, very still, listening.

There it is again. The voices.

They're getting louder, a lot louder. I can even make out the words.

"See . . . ? Footprints. We weren't over here today, and there was that dust storm yesterday morning. These are fresh."

"Keep it down. Let's start checking the houses."

"They're small feet."

"A kid?"

"Or maybe a girl."

"Yeah."

There was a wealth of inflection in that last word that makes my breath freeze in my chest. I have to get out of here. I can't just hide—they'll be expecting that. Plus, in the dark, I can't find a place that I know they won't discover in daylight. I have to get out of here, and I have to do it now.

It sounds like there are only two, or possibly three of them, and they were right outside this house somewhere. I curse myself for not thinking about the footprints. In the fine layer of ash that's settled over everything, the footprints would be clearly visible in the dim moonlight. I probably even tracked footprints onto the hardwood floors.

I get up and carefully pull back the drapes, checking the mirror across the room, but it's so dim, I don't know it'll make enough of a difference—I can barely make it out from here even with the curtains wide open. I run over to it anyway, pressing my hand against it, willing myself to emerge more clearly from the dark shadow barely outlined in the glass. I don't have much time, and every sound is reminding me that they're getting closer.

Nothing.

I can't afford to keep trying, and the mirror is far too large to take with me. Shattering it is out of the question—they'll hear that from a mile away—so I move on, down the stairs, not even entirely sure of where I'm going to go. If I could get around them somehow, maybe I could hide in the first house, since they will have already searched there if they came in off the road.

I have to make this fast. I get my bearings. The back door has rusty hinges and is likely to squeak. It's also on the other side of the house from where I want to go. I make my way to a room that will have a window on the side of the house closest to the one next door. I'm just going to have to hope they're searching each house together, and not individually all at the same time.

I manage to open the window in what would have been the dining room, wincing every time it goes up another inch because it makes noise. I get it open as wide as I can risk, praying that there won't be a breeze to rustle the drapery and put them on my trail again. If they have anyone stationed outside, they'll see me easily. It occurs to me that even if there's no one standing watch, they'll see my footprints again in the fine ash that seems to be all over the ground.

I look around quickly for something I can use to sweep my tracks, and I find a long-handled feather duster in a cupboard in the laundry room. It'll take extra time, but I don't have a choice. I grab it in my hand like a club and make my way back to the window, moving as quietly as I can. I can hear them more easily now with the window open, and they sound like they're checking a house across the street. I risk a quick glance out the window, and I can see them clearly now. There are three of them, and they are moving toward the house directly across from this one.

They all have knives of some kind clutched in their hands. *Probably to make it easier to skin you and eat you.* The thought digs into my brain with icy fingers, freezing me into immobility. Then

I realize I'm wasting a golden opportunity. Their backs are turned, and they're not yet in the house, where they could easily look out a window and see me.

I throw my legs over the windowsill and drop to the ground. I have the duster out and I walk quickly backward, sweeping it side to side, running as best I can while trying not to kick or trip on debris as I go. I make it to the side of the other house, then push on toward the back, just making it around the corner as one of them turns around.

I flatten myself against the wall, and I work on keeping my breathing even so I can hear them better. Was I seen? He was turning as I rounded the corner—it's entirely possible. I am shaking, and sweat drips down my back even though it is cold out here. *Please . . . please . . . please . . .* I am murmuring soundlessly as I strain to listen. After a few moments, it's clear no one is shouting an alarm. I move as quickly as I can, stepping around and over anything that might crunch or jangle or trip me, wincing when I stumble a bit and something clangs softly.

One more house. If I can make the run across, I can get to the first house and then maybe, while they're searching the other houses, I can run for the road and the rubble pile again, go back the way I came. Maybe I can follow the stream farther down and find someplace where the water is clearer. Why didn't I do that in the first place? *Because I'm stupid, that's why,* I mentally berate myself.

I edge up to the corner on the second house, moving my head by the barest fractions until I can see out. No one is there. I can hear them in the houses now, calling for me, promising me food, shelter, a helping hand. If I didn't know what Finn taught me, I would believe them. They sound sincere.

I take a deep breath and race across to the first house, half turning so I can obliterate my tracks again, and finally, I am safe up against the back wall. I need to try the door or find a way to get through a window, if I can. Once I'm inside, I might even be able to find a mirror and hopefully some more light. I try the back door, but it's not only closed but slightly warped and immovable. I start checking the windows and find that the one nearest the road has been broken out. I manage to get my leg over the sill by stepping up on a cinder block lying under the window. I reach inside to brace my hands against the inside of the window frame and pull myself over.

And a pair of hands closes down over mine, pulling me through.

I land on the floor in a heap and scramble up to my knees.

"I've got her!" a man cries out loudly. He's filthy and he smells indescribably bad and in the dim moonlight, I can see the contrast of his gleaming teeth against the darkness. He's grinning at me like I'm a five-course dinner.

38

Caught

"DON'T WORRY, HONEY," THE MAN TELLS ME. "I'LL MAKE you a deal before the rest of them get here—if you're nice enough to me. My name's Vince."

I get slowly to my feet and start backing toward the window. He steps in closer. "Won't do you no good to run," he says. "They'll be on you before you get far."

He folds his arms, straining to see me in the dim light.

"You're a real treat." I see his teeth again. "And I'm getting really tired of Josh. He's pushy. If you're nice enough to me and Bobby, we'll probably get tired of Josh before we get tired of you." He smiles again. "You think about that while we wait."

I am shaking all over, fighting not to pass out because I'm hyperventilating so badly. I'm going to have to dive through the window and hope I can outrun them. I'm still in my glitter-Jessa body, though. I may not be as malnourished, but I don't know how fast I can run. It's the only hope I have, and I have to go now, before the others get any closer. I don't know if I can make it, but I know I'm not going down without one hell of a fight.

I start to turn, but Vince second-guesses me, yanking me hard by the hair. I let out a scream as my head is twisted, hard, and he pulls me up against him. He grins in my face—like he's glad I'm fighting him. His breath is foul, and I feel like I'm going to vomit. How long do I have before the rest of them are here? Minutes? Seconds?

I do the only thing I can think of to do. I twist in his arms, then I cup my fist in my hand and I use the added force of it to push my elbow back into him as hard as I possibly can, just like Finn taught me.

He doubles over and the air comes out of him in a whoosh. His grip on my hair is momentarily loosened as my knee connects solidly with his head and I yank myself free, ripping some of my hair out as I go.

I try to run for the window again as I hear the door bang open behind me, but it's too late. Vince grabs my arm, swinging me down, and I hit the floor, hard. I roll to my knees, expecting him to come at me again, but my mind registers that I'm watching him struggle with someone else in the shadows, possibly the hated Josh. Maybe he overheard the plan and is eliminating his enemy first. Now is my chance. I have to get out of here.

They crash into the closet door and I am diving for the window, hitting the ledge painfully with my chest and scrambling to pull myself through. Two strong hands grab my hips, pulling me back in, but I'm fighting with all my might, kicking hard.

"Jessa!" comes a whisper, urgent and then repeated until I realize who it is.

Finn pulls me back against him, hugging me fiercely. "Come on! We only have a minute before they're all here." He leads me to step over Vince's body—I don't know if he's knocked out or dead, and I don't really want to know.

"We could run for it," I pant.

"We'll never make it," he says. "They're expecting that." He pulls me along, up the stairs and into a bedroom. Here, the windows face a mirror over the dresser, and there are no curtains to obscure the thin light of the moon. But is it enough? The mirror has a large crack down the center, and I can still barely see myself.

"I tried this in the other house," I tell him, gasping for air. "It didn't work. I couldn't—"

Downstairs a door flies open, and I can hear them pounding up the steps.

"Get your hand on the mirror and don't let go of me." He holds one hand in a steel grip and I concentrate as hard as I can, pushing on the mirror with my other hand next to his.

His face is shadowy in the reflection, and he's squeezing my other hand so hard it should hurt. Instead, I cling to it.

The other two men burst into the room a moment later, and I catch a glimpse of their startled faces in the mirror. They've brought light with them—a makeshift torch—and it's all we need.

Finn calls my name to get me to look at my reflection instead of theirs, and a heartbeat later, we are through.

We're back in the glitter world, in my bedroom.

I sink into the sparkling fuchsia carpet, putting my face into it, and I begin to cry, in great heaving sobs. I cannot stop shaking. I feel Finn turn me over gently, rolling me into his arms as he lies on the carpet next to me. He lets me get it all out, rocking me slightly as his arms tighten around me.

"Did they . . . hurt you? Are you all right?"

"All *right?*" I say incredulously. "I could have died! And so could you!"

"You're safe, Jessa," he reassures me. "Safe now."

"How did you get to me?" I ask, then I shudder, hard.

"Mario. I was meeting with Rudy, trying to get his help, when Mario interrupted us."

I set my head against his chest, and I cannot move. I am indescribably tired. The relief flooding through me is like anesthesia, and I feel like I could close my eyes and be unconscious without any effort at all.

He smooths my hair, pulling my head back a little so he can look me in the eyes. I bring my hand up to self-consciously cover my nose and mouth. I have rivers of snot running down my face.

"I have to blow my nose," I say.

"I've got it." He pulls away and gets to his feet, walking over to my nightstand and pulling two fluorescent tissues out of the gilded box next to my lamp. He kneels down, handing them to me, and I sit up, doing my best to clean myself off.

I stuff my head tiredly into my hands. "Oh God, Finn." I look up at him. "This is how you *lived?*"

His eyes shift down to look at the carpet. "Yes."

"Is that"—I can barely bring myself to ask it, but I have to know—"is that how I died? Someone like them?"

Finn's eyes lock with mine, and they are so haunted, I feel like

I can't breathe. "There were six of them, and they had you surrounded. They would have killed us both, but you would have taken a lot longer." His jaw is tight, and it takes a second for him to finish. "I managed to get my knife in your chest and ended it quick."

I look into his green, green eyes. "Am I the reason you stayed—over there? Even when you had it in your power to shift and get out of there?"

"Yes. I had no idea you were a Traveler, too, not then. You weren't aware yet."

"So you stayed around to protect me."

"Yes," he says, twisting a lock of my hair around his finger. "For all the good it did you. I ended up killing you anyway."

"You *saved* me from being tortured to death." My voice is surprisingly strong. I can't stress enough to him that there's a difference here.

"I know. But it was still my hand that threw that knife."

"If we hadn't been able to get away this time, would you have done it again?"

He swallows hard. "Probably. I don't know."

How weird is it to know how much someone cares about you by the way they're willing to kill you first? And I suppose it's equally weird that I would have done the same for him.

His hand comes up to cup my face, and I feel his thumb gently stroking my jaw.

"All I know," he says, and his eyes are burning bright, warming me and chasing all the cold away, "is that no matter how many times I lose you, I can't seem to let you go."

Then his mouth comes down to meet mine, and the warmth

bursts into flame inside me, stealing my breath and curling my fingers into the front of his shirt. He pulls away slowly, kissing the tip of my nose, then my forehead.

"I'll keep you safe, Jessa," he promises. "Anywhere you go."

"I want to go home, Finn," I finally say. "All the way home."

39

Torn

AFTER TRANSFERRING BACK TO MY DEAF SELF—WHICH didn't take long, since glitter me really wanted to get home—I put in a call to my deaf counterpart, and she answered almost instantly. It occurs to me that as hard as it is, she likely misses her life as much as I miss mine. Finn and I arrive in the bedroom of my reality and it's Sunday morning.

I turn away from the mirror with a huge sigh of relief.

"I know this body had a good night's sleep last night, but I still feel exhausted."

Finn pulls me in close, wrapping his arms around me. "You've been through a traumatic experience," he says. "It's a perfectly normal reaction."

"I need to get a grip on myself."

His hand comes up to slide around the back of my neck. "I've got you," he says, and once again, his lips are on mine.

My hands slide up over his shoulders and time slows to a crawl.

There's only him and me and the absolute *rightness* of the feel of him against me.

He pulls back and gives me a smug little grin. "Tell me the truth," he says. "Am I a better kisser than the pirate?"

I give him a wide-eyed, innocent smile in return, choosing my words carefully.

"Nobody kisses like you, Finn," I reply.

He rolls his eyes and pulls me in, kissing me again, and I'm losing myself in it—that is, until my bedroom door opens.

There stands Ben, right behind Danny. I give a squeak and hastily step out of Finn's arms.

"Danny! You could have just told me Ben was here!"

"Hi, Jessa!" Danny says. "When did you come back? You should lock your door!"

"Yeah, St. Clair," Ben says flatly. "You should lock your door."

The look on his face hits me hard and then the memories rush in, swamping me.

I sink down on the bed as he storms out, with Danny right behind him.

Oh, the memories. So many memories . . .

I'd arrived here, thrilled that I could hear—this was my deaf self's third time traveling, and I hadn't yet been to a reality that held Ben—or Finn for that matter. Not that Finn would matter to the other me—I had no experience with him at all. But Ben . . .

I gasp aloud and tears pool in my eyes as the memories flood over me, drowning me in emotion. I'd spent most of that first weekend with Danny, delighted that he could speak, and since I was at my dad's house, I was getting to know my father—a father *that*

Jessa never knew. I went back to Mom's on Sunday afternoon and when the doorbell rang, I opened the door and Ben was standing there. He said "Hey, St. Clair," and oh . . .

I heard his voice for the first time. The very first time. It was warm and wonderful and I couldn't help but throw my arms around him. I put my head to his chest and listened as he laughed, trying to figure out what had gotten into me. When he spoke again, my fingers touched his lips in wonder.

And then my lips touched his. Of course they did. This was Ben, and I love him.

From that moment on, we were inseparable. I told him that nearly falling off the roof made me realize what he meant to me—which I thought was a great cover story at the time. Ben didn't question a bit of it. He told me he'd been crazy about me for months, and he asked if Finn was out of the picture. I assured him that he was the one I wanted, and that was that. Ben and I were dating. I hadn't told this Ben yet that I loved him, but oh, I'd made sure he felt it.

My mind plays over cuddling on the couch, dinners with my family, stolen kisses in the hall at school.

"Uuuuhhhhgggghh." I bury my face in my hands.

What a way to totally mess up a friendship. Oh my God, what am I going to say to him? The last thing I want to do is hurt Ben's feelings. I need to find out just how invested in this new definition of us he really is.

"Maybe you can tell him you were doing research for a story," Finn says, trying to make a joke. It's clear he finds this just about as amusing as I do. Which is not at all.

I automatically hate the other me. Who do I think I am,

playing with Ben's feelings like that? I should be ashamed of myself. *Stupid other me.* I am really, really mad at me for this. I wish I could give me a piece of my mind. I catch a glimpse of my reflection in the mirror.

"Do you realize what a mess you left me?" I ask myself.

She's not there, of course. She's probably with Ben.

"I have to talk to him," I say to Finn numbly. "Let him down easy."

Finn sits down next to me. "There's no such thing, you know. He likes you. A lot."

"Oh God." I bury my face in my hands again.

"Now you've granted his heart's desire, and you're going to have to find some way to tell him it was all a big mistake."

I get up and walk over to my window to look out, and Ben's truck is still in front of my house. Which means he's waiting downstairs to talk to me.

40

Ben

I CAN HEAR BEN MAKING SMALL TALK WITH DANNY, and I wonder what I could possibly say to Ben to let him know that the last week of my life with him was a total anomaly. He's either going to think I'm completely nuts or toying with him.

I have no idea how to handle this. Worse, I'm feeling guilty, because truthfully, other me has enjoyed all of this. Too much.

I feel a very weird mix of confusing feelings, as I have other me's memories fresh in my mind, of Ben with his mouth on mine and those perfectly muscled arms around me. These are mixing with my near-death rescue by Finn and the tenderness he's shown me in the aftermath. The way I feel when he holds me is just different. There's a rightness about it—just as there was a rightness for my other self when I was with Ben.

I reach the bottom of the stairs, and he's stopped talking to Danny. Instead, he's looking at me with a wealth of pain in his eyes.

"Hey," I say.

"Hey," he says. And my traitorous mind goes back to yesterday, when the other me walked down these stairs, and he called me beautiful, the way his eyes brightened, and that easy grin he broke into when he saw me. My heart gives a lurch and I take another deep breath, trying to push all that out of my mind.

Danny breaks the ice.

"Jessa! I'm winning!" he yells gleefully as he points at the TV screen. "Am I good at this, Ben?"

"You're a killer, Danny. I should know better than to play with you," Ben says.

Danny turns his baffled face to Ben. "I don't kill you. You died." He looks up at me. "Me and Ben were playing but he died, so he said he was going to go wake you up. I didn't kill him."

"He didn't mean it like that, Danny," I explain. "When someone says you're a killer that way, it means you're good at something."

"It's mean to say I killed somebody," Danny says.

"Ben wasn't being mean. He said it because he likes you. He meant you're good at the game."

"I'm good at this," he says matter-of-factly. "I'm winning. Are you going to stay here now, Jessa?"

"Yeah, Danny," I say, eyeing him warily. "I live here, remember?"

"Is Finn still here? Can he play the game with me?"

I feel Ben's eyes on me, and his whole body is frozen.

"Danny, Ben and I are going to go out for a little while, okay?" I tell him. "Just keep on playing."

"Okay. I'm a killer. Ben says so."

I fold my arms across my chest and we walk to the door. I keep my eyes on Ben's rigid back and I hate myself. Oh God, do I hate myself. I want to find a mirror, reach through, and punch me right in the wandering mouth.

We walk outside to his truck, and he turns to face me, leaning his back against the door.

"Ben . . . ," I start. I look at him, and the urge is overwhelming to wrap my arms around him. This is Ben. *Ben.* And she—we— love him.

He shakes his head, and I see his jaw tighten, like he's keeping himself from saying something.

"I'm sorry," I say, and the tears start to slip out. "I'm so sorry." I put my hands over my face and start to cry, big, heaving sobs, and I don't know how it's even possible that I have any tears left after all the crying I've done this morning. I hear him sigh and feel his hand settle tentatively on my shoulder.

"Talk to me, St. Clair. What's going on?"

"It's . . . complicated."

"What's complicated?"

"Everything. I don't know what to tell you."

"About me? Or about him?"

"Both, I guess." I look at him and realize that's a cop-out. I have to be honest with him. I owe him that. I force myself to meet his eyes.

"You, mostly," I say, and the tears start up again.

"So this whole week was . . . what? An accident? An experiment? What?" His arm drops. He's getting mad now. He can barely get the words out, and I am drowning in misery for it.

"No! It's not like that!"

"Then what are you doing? With him?"

Oh God, I am so bad at this. "It's not like I don't . . . care about you. I do. I just . . . I've done some thinking."

"And you think you'd rather have Finn," he says flatly. "Or would you rather just string us both along until you figure it out?"

"That's not fair!"

"Not fair? *I'm* not being fair?"

He storms around to the driver's side of the truck and gets in, turning the keys in the ignition.

I follow him, and I reach out and stop the door as he tries to shut it.

"Wait, Ben—where are you going?"

"I'm fixing to go home. Wouldn't want to risk having your *boyfriend* see us together," he snarls. "He just might feel like he's been played or something."

He pulls the door closed with a bang and revs the engine, and I step back as he pulls out and drives away. I stand in the street until he turns the corner and I can't see him anymore. I want to just sink down to the ground, but the neighbors are probably all looking at me.

I wipe my eyes and cheeks with my fingers and take a couple of deep breaths before I walk back inside. Danny turns to look at me as soon as I open the door.

"Did you kill Ben because he's your friend?" he asks.

41

Revealed

I GO RIGHT UP TO MY ROOM AND THROW MYSELF DOWN on the bed to get the rest of my cry out. After the couple of days I've had and the situation with Ben, I am heartsore and still exhausted. My bed is soft and warm and I feel like I'm sinking into it, growing roots that burrow down.

"Jessa?" Finn's voice carries from the doorway.

He carefully sets down two giant cups of Mugsy's coffee on my nightstand and closes the door behind him.

"So your day can only go up from here," he quips.

"Don't even joke like that," I say, staring up at the ceiling.

"Sorry."

I turn my head to look at him as he sits down on the bed. "I didn't hear you leave."

"I snuck out the back."

"I really don't want coffee," I say.

"I brought cookies, too."

"I want to throw up."

"Then I guess some glitter mousse is a bad . . . idea." He trails off, and his mouth parts slightly. He starts slowly shaking his head.

"What?" I ask.

He turns to me, and with one word, he pulls me out of my misery.

"Rudy."

"*What?*"

"The Traveler isn't the one trying to kill you. Rudy is."

I am instantly awake enough to sit up.

"Rudy!"

Finn makes a grim face. "Rudy was the one who sent me to you in the first place. He sent every Finn he could to every Jessa, and they started dying, didn't they?"

"But—"

"It's been so obvious we were blind to it. Rudy left before Mario sent us to your deaf reality, didn't he? And we were safe there."

It's beginning to dawn on me. "And when we showed up at glittery Mugsy's . . ."

"A place we've been known to frequent," Finn reminds me. "We were easy prey. Rudy even suggested to me that I should take you away for a while. Once we got there, he knew exactly where to send you."

"But he can't come into reality, can he?"

"He's not working alone," Finn said. "He's got a follower who's a Traveler. Maybe more than one. He's directing them, and now he knows for sure he's got the right Jessa, doesn't he?"

My chest freezes in fear. "You can't go to sleep," I whisper. "If he knows that you've figured it out, he'll find a way to kill you, too."

"You have to talk to Mario. Now. And I have to stay awake until he tells us what our next step is." He reaches for one of the cups of coffee and takes a long drink.

As tired as I am, I'm not sure I can sleep. My heart is pounding too hard. We've got a practically omnipotent being with control over God knows how many other Travelers trying to wipe out most of the universe, with us in it. Who could sleep in the face of that?

"I don't know if I can," I say shakily.

"You've got to. Can you take something?"

"I . . . uh . . ." My mind is racing. "I think there's some NyQuil in the bathroom."

"Will it put you to sleep?"

"Knocks me right out," I answer. "I'll get it."

I run for the bathroom, stopping along the way to let Danny know I'm feeling sick and I'm going to lie down—that ought to keep him from disturbing me. Finn can play video games with Danny and keep him distracted—and himself awake. I grab the NyQuil and step back into the room, twisting off the cap and pouring out a dose.

"Down the hatch," I say, chugging it back.

I set the bottle down next to Finn's coffee and lie down on the bed. My hand reaches for his.

"Be careful, okay? If you have to leave me and run, do it."

"I won't leave you," he says.

"I told Danny you'd play a game with him."

"That's as far as I'll go," he swears.

"And you'll need more coffee. My mom drinks decaf." I can

feel the medicine making me foggy, but I have to make sure he'll be safe.

"I'll get more coffee if I need it. And then I'll come back. I promise."

I nod, and my head is starting to feel heavy. "Stay till I'm sleeping."

The bed dips and he eases down next to me. "No problem," he says, stretching out at my side. I turn and scooch into him, spoon-style, and his arm comes around my middle.

"Finn?"

"Yeah?"

"I'm afraid."

"You've been through a lot, Jessa."

"I'm afraid for *you*. What if something happens to you?"

I feel his hand come up, and it gently plays with my hair, his fingers combing through the strands as his voice calms and lulls me.

"I've been traveling for a while now," he reassures me. "And we know where the danger is coming from. Once Mario's involved, this will all be over. And then you and I get to figure out where we go from here."

"What if I don't want to go anywhere? What if I just want to stay plain old Jessa?"

I hear him chuckle. "You could never be plain old Jessa."

"What if I don't want to travel?"

"Then you don't." His fingers are still stroking my hair, and my eyelids are getting heavier as the minutes pass.

"I don't want you to go away," I tell him.

"I told you I'm not going anywhere."

I turn my head to look back at him, and it's not easy to do because I'm definitely feeling light-headed from the NyQuil.

"I mean after. After this is all over. I guess you'll want to go back to whatever you were doing before."

"What I was doing before was looking for you," he reminds me. "And now I've found you. I'm not going anywhere."

I feel his lips against my temple, and I close my eyes, savoring the sensation. He's warm against my back, and where his arm circles my waist. His fingers are in my hair again, and then through a fog, the bright white of the classroom hits my eyes. I immediately tense and turn my head, looking around.

"Rudy won't be joining us," Mario tells me as I take my seat. "You can relax."

"You know?"

"I had a hunch, after our last session. It's confirmed now—and he's on the run."

"What's going to happen to Finn? He can't stay awake forever."

"No, he can't. I've been given permission to take on a second Traveler—which is not generally allowed—but this is an extreme circumstance."

"Rudy has a second Traveler," I say.

Mario nods. "Yes, he does. He's been using Finn for information about you, and another Traveler to do the dirty work where you're concerned. Arranging for all your calamities to revolve around Finn ended up causing more suspicion, instead of diverting it."

"You'll take care of Finn?" I ask. "He'll be safe?"

"I can't guarantee that," Mario says quietly. "Not any more than I can for you. Forecasting can be uncertain when you're dealing with people of free will. We deal in suppositions and potential outcomes, not absolutes. But at least we know what we're up against."

"Easy for you to say. You didn't lose a best friend shortly after almost being tortured, killed, and eaten by cannibals. And now I still have to watch my back."

"The Traveler is still out there." Mario nods. "He's sure to try again."

"Or, *she* is," I add. "I think it was a woman who pushed me through into Finn's world. I couldn't see her face, only her gloves and jewelry. It all happened too fast."

"You should have known Rudy was going to watch there—he knew how fond you two were of the place." Mario's tone carries a world of consternation.

"Thank you for helping me."

"I had a feeling Rudy would look for a reality that could do his dirty work for him," Mario continues. "Add in the fact that Finn would be reluctant to go back to his own reality, and it was perfect for Rudy's purposes. The Traveler couldn't have ever had a counterpart there, so that might give us a starting place for narrowing down who it is. The trick was figuring out *where* in that reality the Traveler would send you, and when you fell asleep, I found you."

"I was only asleep for a minute or two," I say.

Mario shrugs. "I work fast."

"Well, let's keep that reality off the travel list as far as return visits, okay?" I shiver again, remembering. Rudy wasn't playing games. Rudy really did want me dead.

277

"So . . . what now?" I ask.

"Rudy can't kill you directly—normally, he can only use the Traveler to influence events around you in order to facilitate your death," Mario answers. "But he's gone rogue, and he's desperate. I need to figure out exactly what he's planning to do to be sure we're countering properly. Stay alert, stay with Finn, and I'll let you know what the next steps are as soon as I can."

"I'm not just going to sit around waiting for someone to kill me again," I tell him. "Or Finn. We've got some clues, and I'm going to start following them. I can start with the lady at the historical society—she can give me the list of people who bought tickets to the ghost tour. If we can find the Traveler, maybe we can ask some questions and figure out what Rudy's doing."

Mario gives me a grudging nod. "Whatever you do, make sure Finn is watching your back."

"And I'm watching his."

"You're more important." His eyes hold mine. "We can't allow the convergence, Jessa. Too much is at stake."

Finn, I think. *Finn is at stake. And all the other Moms and Dannys and Dads and Bens—and Jessas.*

The fate of them all, resting on me, and I have no idea what I'm doing.

42

Missing

I WAKE WITH THE ALARM CLOCK WHEN IT GOES OFF, and with no sign of Finn. I've slept through the night, and according to Danny, Finn said good-bye around seven o'clock last night. That doesn't mean he left, though. Without me awake enough to open the door and sneak him back in, he probably sat outside all night. At least the cold would have kept him awake.

I text him to let him know I'm heading out; then I dress and hurry out the door to school, expecting he's going to fall into step beside me. He doesn't, and by the time I reach the school, the first frisson of unease is unfurling in my stomach. I figured he would be waiting for me at school, but he's not there, either. I give his phone a call this time, but it rings and rings. And rings.

I'm starting to feel some panic, and to make it worse, Ben is leaning against his locker as I walk in, and he turns pointedly away the second he sees me.

I know he doesn't want to talk to me, but I need his help.

"Wait! Ben!" I call out to him as he's walking away. He takes a few more steps, and then he finally stops. He doesn't bother turning around.

"What?" The irritation in his voice is clear.

"Please." I move around in front of him. "Ben, I need your help. I know this is the last subject you want to talk about, but have you seen Finn?"

"He take off on you?" Ben asks, and he looks like he doesn't particularly care if that's what happened.

"No," I snap. Then my eyes fill with tears. "I don't know. He's gone. And he's not answering his phone or his texts."

"He's probably just running late."

"No, that's not it. He's gone. He's just gone." My voice cracks on that last word. "Otherwise he'd be talking to me."

Ben bites his lip. "Did you tell him? About us?"

I look up at him guiltily. "Yeah. I did."

"Maybe he's reevaluating after hearing that."

I know I deserve that, but it stings anyway.

The bell rings for class, and Ben looks backward over his shoulder. "I gotta go."

There is no sign of Finn in calculus, and the panic is turning into an outright fear, trickling down my spine. I slide into my seat next to Ben in Mr. Draper's class, and I'm nervously drumming my fingers on the desk. Ben looks over at me, but when I catch him, he just turns away.

When the bell rings, I am out of my chair and walking before I even realize it. I am barely able to see through the fog of fear that is overtaking me and the sting of unshed tears in my eyes.

What if Finn fell asleep?

Oh God, why didn't I think to check outside the house? If he's asleep, he could be in danger.

I am just reaching for my phone to text him again when it suddenly vibrates and my message icon lights up again. I look down at the screen, and it's all I can do not to shout.

Finn. Hallelujah!

I slide into my seat in creative writing class, and all the air comes out of my lungs in a whoosh of relief.

Good morning

> Good morning???
> I've been worried sick about you!
> Where are you?

It's good to know you worry

> Of course I do ☺
> When am I going to see you?

I think that depends on you

> ??

How badly would you like to see Finn again, Jessa?

I stare at the phone, feeling like someone has their icy-cold fist wrapped around my stomach. And not just any someone.

> You work for Rudy?

Yes

> Is Finn hurt?

Not yet

> What do you want?

Meet me after school
The bridge in Founder's Park
You know which one

> I want to talk to Finn.
> How do I know you
> haven't hurt him?

Almost a full minute passes, and then the Traveler returns a video. It's only four seconds long, and it's clearly Finn. He's got a cut on his left cheek and he's squinting from the flash. Everything around Finn is dark. There's nothing in the background that can tell me anything. I can see in his eyes that he's desperate to tell me something, but all he manages to get out before he's cut off is "Jessa—"

I switch to text, punching the keypad angrily.

> I can turn this entire conversation
> over to the police, you know

You won't.

Whoever this Traveler is, she's awfully sure of herself, and a few seconds later, I can see exactly why. She's attached a picture. At first it just appears to be some random crowd scene, but then I zoom in and see clearly that it's my mom and my brother. They're in the parking lot at the retirement home, and they're talking to a co-worker, completely unaware that a murderer is right behind them.

I am going to be sick. I fight the nausea back, and try not to hyperventilate. Ms. Eversor finally strolls into the classroom with her coffee mug clutched in her hand, calling out a cheerful good morning in a voice that makes me want to scream at her.

She moves to the whiteboard and turns her back as she maps out the next issue of *The Articulator*, so I carefully pull out my phone, watching the video again and again. I even turn my phone into the light and up the brightness on my screen in an effort to see his surroundings. I don't know why I bother. He's probably in a closet. Or a car trunk. Or his own grave, for all I know.

Oh God. Why did I think that?

I've got to get out of here. I have to find Finn, but how? If Finn were here, he'd probably come up with something, but I can't seem to focus. My mind has been taken over by a blank wall of panic.

What if he's hurt? My stomach roils at the thought.

"So, Matthew and Evan," Ms. Eversor says cheerily. "You will cover the sports for this issue, but touch on more of the human interest, you understand? It's not enough to know we won. We must know what makes an athlete *want* to win, yes?" She looks over her shoulder at me.

"Jessa! You will be on assignment to give us more on the town history. Tell us something filled with intrigue. Everyone loves a scandal!"

I put my hand up.

"Ms. Eversor? Can I be excused to the restroom, please? I'm feeling sick."

It's not a lie. My stomach is a huge knot of worry and stress, to the point where I feel like I'm going to throw up from it. I have to find Finn. *Now.*

She looks concerned. "Let me write you a pass," she says, heading over to her desk.

I get up and follow her on shaky legs, doing my best to blink back the tears that might betray me.

She finishes signing with a flourish, holding the pass out for me to take, when suddenly, I freeze with my hand extended.

Another memory rears up, the memory of a sequined, gloved hand complete with jangling bangle bracelets, pushing against a polished chrome wall. Bracelets like the ones right in front of me.

That was right before she'd tried her best to kill me.

43

The Other Traveler

I LOOK WITH DAWNING HORROR AT THE HALL PASS IN my hand. That script. That curling, beautiful script. I saw it on a Post-it note that was placed on an article in a yellowed newspaper—an article that directed me to chase a ghost story that happened on a bridge.

Eversor opens her file drawer to put the notepad with the passes away, and I see her purse sitting inside. Her large brown purse. A large brown purse that's exactly the same shape and size as the one I tripped over on the roof. And how easy would it have been for her to suggest to Chloe that someone else could fix the lights on the stage if she was afraid of heights?

I am starting to shake, but I manage to fold my hand around the pass and remember to keep on breathing.

"Jessa?" she asks, still smiling that overly concerned smile. "Are you all right?"

"I—I really have to go," I stammer, keeping my eyes on her the whole time, just waiting for her to spring. She remains as she is, with her smile firmly in place.

"I hope you feel better," she says. "If you need to go to the nurse, stop back and I'll escort you there."

"Thank you. I will." I edge toward the door, still not entirely sure I'm going to make it.

She smiles placidly, and I say nothing else to tip her off. She's holding all the cards, or at least the only card I care about: Finn. I suddenly want to hit her right in the face. No wonder she was late to class. She spent her advisory period kidnapping Finn and torturing me.

I give her a nod, hoping she can't read the wild panic in my eyes. Then I walk calmly out to the hallway. I swear, I can feel her eyes on me, but I'm not going to turn around and betray what I know.

I pass my locker, and I keep on going, with my eyes locked on the door at the end of the hall. I'm not even going to the restroom. I'll deal with the repercussions later. I have to get out of here.

"St. Clair!"

I turn panicked eyes to Ben, and then my head swivels to look back. Eversor is watching me, with a smile that doesn't quite reach her eyes. Is she going to kill me? She can't do that—not here. Not in front of everyone. Can she?

I don't want Ben in her line of fire, so I deliberately ignore him and keep going.

I get a few more steps before he trots up next to me.

"What's going on?" He's looking at me like he's actually concerned, so I guess my poker face isn't as good as I thought it was.

"Why are you out in the hall?" I say, forcing a smile and hoping I look something close to normal. I don't want to glance toward Eversor again.

"I'm going to the library to do some research," he says.

"I have to go," I tell him. He reaches out, putting his hand on my arm.

"You're shaking," he says, surprised. "What's the matter?"

"Just walk with me," I say under my breath. "I've got to get out of here."

I look back over my shoulder again, trying to make it look casual. "She's not watching anymore. Good."

"Who?"

"Ms. Eversor."

"Why would she be?"

"It's a long story. Keep walking."

He looks back now, too. *What is going on?*

He's seriously confused and I don't blame him, but I don't have time to talk.

"I have to get out of here. Finn is in danger."

"Wait—what? Danger?" He stops again and I make an exasperated sound.

"Look, just trust me, all right? Walk." I give him a push from behind. "Walk fast. Let's get outside and I'll explain."

Of course, I have no idea how I'll explain this. We're out the doors, and I pull him to the side, up against the building.

"Do you have your truck here?"

He looks at me blankly. "Yeah. Why? What's going on, St. Clair? What do you mean, 'Finn is in danger'?"

"Not just Finn," I say, gesturing wildly. "But Danny. And Mom.

Please, Ben—I know you're still mad at me but . . . can you help me?" I'm pleading, but I don't care. I need his help.

He puts his hands up. "Slow down. Just start at the beginning and—"

"I don't have time for that!" I explode. "We have to get out of here! Ben, please!"

He's looking at me like I'm nuts, and I know that's exactly how I sound, but he finally pulls his keys out of his pocket and points toward his truck.

I run across the parking lot with him close behind, and I clamber into the truck, where I sit on the passenger side panting and looking around wildly.

"Drive, Ben. Just drive."

The urgency in my voice affects him, and he puts the truck in gear, pulling out of the parking lot. He stays away from the center of town, taking us instead to the outskirts, where the local shopping center stands. He pulls into a spot on the far end of a grocery store parking lot, puts the truck in park, and shuts it off.

Then he turns, taking both my hands in his.

"What's going on, St. Clair? Talk to me."

I shake my head, not knowing where to begin. "Finn is in trouble. And so am I. And now, so are you." I press my hands to my cheeks, sucking in a deep breath.

"What kind of trouble?" he asks. "What did he drag you into?"

"I can't give you all the details, okay? But you have to trust me. Eversor's got Finn, and she's using him to get to me. And now, since she's seen us together, she'll probably go after you, too."

"Wait—are we talking about Ms. Eversor? The *teacher*?"

"She's not just a teacher. She's sort of a criminal. And Finn and I found out about it and now she wants us dead."

"Eversor." He says it perfectly deadpan, and I realize there's no way in hell I can make him believe me.

"I know it sounds crazy, Ben. I know it does. But you have to believe me. She's got Finn, and she wants me. I have to save him."

He leans back in the seat, rubbing his neck. "Okay. Let's go see the police." He starts to turn the keys in the ignition, but I reach out, stopping his hand.

"No. No police. She'll hurt my mom and Danny if I call them—she made that clear. And she can get away from the police too easy." I sound completely crazy, I know. "I have to figure something out."

Ben looks at me strangely. "You really think she kidnapped a student?"

"She wants me to meet her at the bridge in Founder's Park after school, but I don't know if she's holding him there."

"Jessa—"

I turn to look at him full-on. "Where could she take him—and me—that no one would hear us? Someplace where she could easily arrange an 'accident' if she needs to?"

"I don't—Jessa, this is really . . . crazy." He's struggling for words. "This is crazy," he repeats.

"I'm not making this up," I tell him. My mind is whirring, trying to figure out where she could possibly be keeping Finn.

"Wait a minute—she took a picture of my mom and Danny, and it was definitely today because Danny was wearing that same sweatshirt this morning," I say. "Eversor's free period is right before my class. I know because sometimes she's up at the teachers' lounge and we start class late because she's not back yet."

"She took a picture of your mom and Danny?" Ben is sounding alarmed now—I think he's finally realizing this is serious. He glances down at my phone as I bring the picture up.

"That means she spent her free period over where they work, at Haven House," I say. "The retirement home is on the west side of town. What's out that way? Where could she stash him—and take me—that's close to there?"

"She's stalking your family?" Ben asks, shaking his head in disbelief. "What the hell is Finn involved in?" He sucks in a breath. "Did she plant that purse? On the roof?"

"Wait—you saw her there?"

"I thought I did. She was wrapped up in a scarf. I was just about to ask you if that was her when you went over the edge. I didn't think anything of it."

I show him my phone again. "Eversor sent me video of Finn as proof he was still alive." *Then.* The thought creeps into my head and I tamp it down, hard. I push the play button, and Ben watches with me.

"It's hard to see anything," Ben says, tilting the screen left and right. "He's all lit up and it's dark behind him."

I study Finn's face again, wishing I could talk back to those expressive eyes. Tell him it's going to be okay. Then I notice what he just did. I punch pause, and then pull the video back a second. Yes, there it was. His eyes were locked on the camera, looking right at me, and then all of a sudden they darted down.

She's only filmed him from the chest up, and I can't really see what he's trying to get me to look at, if anything. His hand comes up to his chest, making a pleading gesture as his eyes try to tell me . . . what?

I let it play to the end again and then I watch it play once more. This time, I keep my eye on that hand. Maybe he's pointing at something. Maybe he's—

"He's giving me a word!" I shout. "He's signing! She doesn't know that he can sign!" And now, thanks to my forced assumption of an alternate life, so can I.

I play the video again, and it's crystal clear. His hand, open, brought up and placed palm-down against his chest. I took it as a sign of entreaty, which she must have done as well. But it's not.

It's the sign for a word. *Mine.*

"Mine," I say. "Is the mine near there?"

"The old Greaver mine," Ben says. "The entrance is sealed off, but it would be less than ten minutes from where your mom and Danny work. Right up in the foothills."

His words bring both panic and elation. Of course. The mine would be perfect. It's on the outskirts of town, it's deserted, and no one would think to look for us there.

"But it's been boarded up for eighty years," Ben says. "I don't know how we'll get in."

"If she found a way to get in," I say, "so can I."

"So can we," he corrects me, but I stop that train of thought immediately.

"No. No, Ben." I shake my head emphatically. "She doesn't know you know anything about this. Go back to school and stay there. I'll find Finn and then talk to Mario—"

"Mario?" His eyebrows come up.

"He's sort of like a policeman. He's after Eversor."

Ben digests that for a moment. "What have you gotten yourself mixed up in, St. Clair?"

"You wouldn't believe me if I could tell you—and I can't. The less you know, the better." I wrap my arms around myself.

"Wait. She's at school . . . ," Ben says.

"Yeah?"

"So, if she's keeping him in the mine, he's unguarded right now."

"Unless she's keeping him somewhere else and moving him later," I point out. "But you're right—as far as creepy hideouts go, that's a good one. Nobody ever goes there, since the collapse shut the mine down. It's not safe."

"Then we should go now," he suggests, "while she's still playing teacher at school. Don't wait to go meet her."

"Ben . . ."

"I'm not letting you go alone," he says firmly. "You're wasting time."

He looks at me mutinously and I finally relent.

"Maybe we can find him and get him out of there," I agree. "And if he's not there, at least we've eliminated one place. We'll keep looking."

I wish I had time to take a nap and talk to Mario, but I don't know how I'd possibly explain that to Ben. He's right, anyway. There's no time to waste. I have to search for Finn now, while she's otherwise occupied.

If she hasn't killed him by now.

The thought wraps around my mind and strangles me, making

it hard to breathe. It can't be true. It can't. I'd know. I blink hard, but the tears fall anyway.

"We'll find him." Ben reaches across and takes my hand again after he starts up the truck and backs out. I stare blindly ahead, barely feeling his hand holding mine, and grateful it's there.

Hang on, Finn, I think. *Just hang on.*

44

Like a Knife
in My Chest

WE MAKE IT TO THE MINE IN LESS THAN FIFTEEN minutes—one of the perks of living in a small town, I guess. We find a place to park behind some trees that's far enough away not to arouse suspicion, but close enough that we can run for the truck and make it quickly if we have to.

It occurs to me that we have no weapons on us. I don't know what we'd use, really. Neither of us owns a gun, and it's not like we can carry a knife into school. I suppose we could have dropped by one of our houses and grabbed a butcher's knife or something, but that would have wasted valuable time. Every second is going to count if we're going to get in and out before Eversor arrives.

"You stay here," Ben says. "I'll go inside and look for him. You stay out of sight."

"Are you crazy?" I look at him incredulously. "You're not going without me. Besides, I'm the one she wants. If she finds me out here, she'll just kill me and then sit here and wait for the two of you."

Ben doesn't look happy, but he doesn't argue with me, either. He opens up the glove compartment, rummaging around. "Hold on," he says. "We're going to need some light."

He pulls out a small flashlight, and of all things, a pack of glow sticks.

"My mom keeps them in there for when she babysits my nephews," he says. "The drive from my sister's house is a long one, and if they're getting crazy, she just tosses the pack back to them."

"Well, we can use them. Let's hope we can find a way in."

The way in ends up being no obstacle at all. There's a large section of board that's simply lying propped against the opening and is easily moved out of the way. Ben shoves it to the side, and we give each other a look.

"That was way too easy," Ben says.

"Yeah." I look over my shoulder again, as I've been doing constantly since we got here. "Let's just get in there and get out."

He steps in first, reaching back to take my hand and pull me through.

"Watch your step," he warns. "There's stuff all over the ground here."

He trains the flashlight on me, and I snap a couple of glow sticks, giving them a shake to make them light up. The mine is pitch-black, and I can hear water dripping somewhere in the distance. It's chilly already, without the sunlight on our backs.

"Let's go," I say, taking the lead. I stop every couple of minutes to listen, and occasionally I hear a scrape or the sound of a pebble scattering along with the water, but it's all very faint. It's most likely from whatever animals have made this place their home. I try to remember if bears are native to this area. I sincerely hope not.

I'm trying to walk as fast as I can, but there's a tremendous amount of debris in some places. The Greaver mine was closed down sometime after the Great Depression when a collapse took the lives of over two dozen men and rendered the mine unusable. The owners lost everything between the collapse and the charges of negligence that faced their business afterward. The Greavers were all but run out of town at the time, ruined financially and socially. The mine has been boarded up ever since, with nothing done beyond the recovery of the bodies—the ones they were able to recover, anyway. I shudder at the thought of the ones that are still in here. *Oh please, don't let me see any bodies. And don't let any of them be Finn. . . .*

I'm so lost in that thought that I round a bend in the tunnel and a second later, I'm pulled backward as Ben grabs a fistful of my sweatshirt and yanks me toward him.

I start to let out a shout and immediately cover my mouth, hoping I didn't alert Eversor, if she's somewhere behind us. Ben steps forward carefully, peering over the edge of what looks like an elevator or maybe a ventilation shaft. I peer down with him, but it's completely black. I take one of the glow sticks and drop it down. It takes a few seconds before I hear a muted splash and a very faint glow lights up the shaft. Well, at least we can see it now.

"You need to be more careful," Ben urges. "We're getting into the working areas now. There are going to be shafts and maybe even old explosives lying around. Watch your step."

I nod, moving away from the edge. I won't be any good to Finn if I'm dead at the bottom of a mine shaft.

We're traveling more slowly now, and it's maddening. Every second we take is another second that she can be closer to us. Or another second that Finn could be bleeding his life away. Ben stumbles over a pile of twisted metal that blended right into the rock and goes staggering, falling heavily into one of the posts. I grab him, steadying him before he falls any farther, and a rain of fine dust and tiny bits of rock falls all around us. I can see the outline of another shaft ahead. They must have them at certain intervals throughout the mine. I break open another glow stick, tossing it down the shaft so we can see it on the way back.

No wonder she chose this place. It'll be easy to dispose of the bodies.

I suppress a shudder and we keep moving, and we're doing fine for a while until I catch my arm on something sharp that's sticking out from a wall. I let out a startled sound that seems to echo through the place in an astonishingly loud way.

It only takes a second, and I hear him.

It's the faintest, strangled kind-of sound. One someone would make with a gag in their mouth.

"Finn!" His name bursts out from my lips, along with a sense of relief that it's not too late. We find him a few hundred feet ahead, around another bend and just past another shaft. Ben grabs my glow stick to mark it as I rush over to yank the gag off Finn's mouth. She's tied his hands and feet, and he's sitting against a wooden column that's warped far more than I'm comfortable with.

"I need some light!" I crouch down next to him as Ben shines the flashlight on Finn's wrists.

"Jessa," Finn says quickly. "It's Eversor! She's—"

"She's working for Rudy, I know."

"Careful," he says urgently. "Don't yank too hard—this is a load-bearing column."

"How did she get you?" I ask as I pull at the ropes, leaning down to get my teeth in them so I can untangle them. After a few moments, one of the knots starts to slip free and I'm able to tug it loose. Once his hands are free, Ben focuses the light on Finn's ankles and Finn starts to work at the knots, but his fingers are too numb and much larger than mine. I push his hands aside and take over, conscious that every second we waste is one less second to get far away from here.

"She was watching your house. When she saw me, she knew we were both back."

"Back?" Ben looks confused.

"How?" I ask.

"Because I wouldn't have disappeared if you were here," Finn says. "When I left to get coffee, she followed me to Mugsy's. She came inside, told me she had a flat tire, and asked for my help to change it."

Ben gave him a look. "That's what you get for being a good guy," he says.

"So I see you got my message?" Finn asks me, smiling. The action pulls at a cut on his cheek, and I see him grimace.

"Yes, and hopefully she doesn't know that," I answer him. I help him to his feet a bit clumsily, and then I slip my arms around him.

"Are you all right?" I hold him, reveling in the feel of him, safe in my arms.

"I am now." He squeezes me tight. "You shouldn't be here." He looks across at Ben. "And you shouldn't have brought her."

"You ever try to talk her out of something?" Ben asks.

Finn raises his brows. "Good point." He gives Ben a nod. "Thank you. I would imagine you have a lot of questions."

Ben lets out a sound between his teeth. "That's an understatement. But they can wait until we're someplace safe." He looks over at me, and then back to Finn. "Then we need to talk."

"Fair enough," Finn says. "Let's get out of here."

He takes my hand and indicates that Ben should lead the way, since he's got the flashlight. I give Finn one of my glow sticks and start to move forward, but I slam into Ben, who has suddenly stopped moving. Finn's hand jerks mine back, trying to pull me behind him.

"Jessa! Get back—"

He doesn't need to finish. I can see her. Eversor is clearly visible in the light of Ben's flashlight, and so is the gun she has trained at Finn's head. I pull my hand away from his and step forward.

She maneuvers herself between us and any sort of escape, and then she sets a heavy glass lantern down on the rock floor, where it lights the room with a muted glow.

"Oh, but you've made it easy for me," she coos. "All three in one place. I knew you wouldn't disappoint me."

"You've got to listen to me," I say to her, smacking at Ben's hand and pushing Finn with my shoulder as they both try to pull me back.

"You have such talent, Jessa," she says almost sadly. "One of my favorite pupils, truly. But this is necessary. A necessary evil."

"You can't do this," Finn tells her. "Think of all the repercussions."

"We deal in trade-offs every day," she snaps. "Stop this one from crossing the street, and they may go on to marry that one two years later. Remind that one's child to return his overdue library book, and he's kidnapped and murdered on his way to the public library by a serial killer. The tougher laws that come from public outcry save countless lives. We let people die every single day, and all for the greater good."

"Rudy is lying to you," Finn says evenly. "He lied to me, he lied to Jessa, he lied to Mario. What makes you think you're getting accurate information?"

"There are rules!" Eversor exclaims. "Your Dreamer has a plan, and you follow the plan! Rudy wouldn't lie."

"Please . . . ," I plead. "We're talking about people. We're talking about families." *We're talking about my family*, I think but don't say. "You're going to help Rudy kill billions of people!"

"Not kill. Simply remove. Billions upon billions, if you also count their descendants." She shrugs. "It's the way we operate, Jessa. Surely you've learned this. We can't get involved. Just consider this another job." She smiles a little too wide to be anything but creepy. "But it is all for the greater good, you see? Rudy is doing this to simplify. We crave simplicity. It is in our very nature. He wants what is best for us all."

Ben holds up his hands defensively and walks forward, keeping his eyes on the crazy teacher with the gun. "Listen," he says cautiously, "I'm not part of this. And I left my truck out front. Any cop patrolling will see it. They'll have to come check things out."

She gestures with the gun, motioning for him to get back, and he does.

"And what a shame when they find what's left of your bodies in the mine, buried under a collapse." She steps forward to tap on the wooden column gently with the edge of the gun, drawing our eyes to the deep score marks she must have put there earlier. "Once I've taken care of you, this will only need one good push. Teenagers are always ignoring warning signs." She makes a tsk-tsk sound with her tongue. "And your poor mother, Jessa! Meeting two boys here at the same time? What will she think of you?"

I have a sudden picture in my mind of my mom and Danny, standing alone outside the mine, with their arms around each other. I can feel their grief like a living thing, eating my insides, and I am burning with anger. As furious as I am about what Rudy is trying to do to me, the effect on my family just seems so much worse, for some reason. And what about Ben's family?

Finn has no family, not anymore—but he has me. He has me, and I will stand for him. I will stand for him, and for all my families, across all the realities. None of them deserve this.

I back up a little, snaking my hand behind me and feeling around until it lands on a crumbling crevice in the rock wall. I push back and feel the edge of a good-sized stone. I start working it with my fingers behind me, back and forth, rocking it to free it. It's not much, but it's the only weapon I've got.

"You're a Traveler," Finn says. He's got one eye on me and he's clearly trying to stall her. "You of all people should know that actions have consequences—and not always good ones."

"We lose a little more every day as each world splinters and fragments and re-forms into other realities. The possibilities are becoming too infinite. We must return to a state of *control*. Rudy is the only one brave enough to make the tough choices. The ones that will restore order."

I dig my fingers farther under the rock, feel warm blood on my fingers as I tear up my knuckles, but it's starting to shift now. Back and forth, back and forth . . .

"Oh, but it is such a shame about you, Finn," she says apologetically. "You had such promise. Rudy always thought so."

"I don't give a damn what Rudy thinks," Finn snaps. "And you're a fool to believe anything he says."

"Year after year, century after century," she says with a flamboyant gesture of her hand. "We hesitate and we doubt ourselves, making only the smallest changes, the ones with the least risk. We need a leader who isn't afraid to take those risks, to move mankind forward with purpose and vision. To make the sacrifices that must be made. You, Jessa, are one of those sacrifices."

She sighs, and her face settles into determined lines. As she centers the gun and squeezes the trigger, I pull my arm back and throw the rock as hard as I can.

I hit her wrist, sending the shot wide and making her drop the gun. Ben is closest. He and Eversor both make a dive for it, but my eyes are on Finn as he staggers back, slamming into the wooden post and raining dirt and small rocks on us. He's clutching his shoulder, and blood is running down his arm.

"Finn!"

"It's only a graze," he says. Then his eyes widen as he looks past me. "Ben! Don't let her—"

I whirl just in time to see Ben holding the gun on Eversor, who has crawled over to the lantern. She puts her hand to the reflective glass, and in the blink of an eye, she vanishes.

The gun drops to the ground with a clatter as Ben stares, openmouthed. "What the hell!" he says in disbelief. He turns to look at us. "What just happened?"

But there's no time to answer him. A second later, a cracking sound turns into thunder as the post crumples and rock rains down all around us.

"Run!" Finn shouts, as everything shakes. A giant cloud engulfs us, throwing dirt and debris into our mouths and eyes. I feel a hand latch on to my arm, yanking hard, and we run, coughing and feeling our way along the wall. Ben's foresight with the glow sticks helps to dimly illuminate the way out, and we stumble forward until the air begins to settle. It's still so thick, I can't see much, and the dust chokes my throat as I hold on to that hand like a lifeline.

I swipe at my eyes as the flashlight switches on, shining first on me, then around. It's reflecting off the dust, but it's enough light for me to see that it's Ben's hand I'm holding. The flashlight is in his other hand.

And I can't see Finn.

I call his name once, then again, coughing to clear my lungs so I can call him louder.

Ben's hand tightens on mine.

"Jessa," he coughs.

I wave my other hand, trying to clear some more of the dust, and I look around wildly.

"Finn!" I call out again. "Finn!"

I pull my hand from Ben's so I can feel my way along the wall and back the way we came, but he moves to get in front of me.

"Don't go back there," he says grimly. "Stay here—I'll look."

"No! Finn!"

I push past him and I am running, stumbling, falling to a pile of rock and debris so monstrously wide and tall, it's impassable.

I skid to a stop, tearing up my knees as I scream Finn's name. I'm grabbing rocks and throwing them, determined to dig my way through.

"Stop!" Ben's voice is urgent behind me. "You might bring more of it down! Stop!"

But I've found him. I've found his arm and it's ominously still. Ben shines the flashlight down, and he reaches across me, putting his fingers to the wrist to feel for a pulse. He pulls his hand away, and something breaks inside me as he silently shakes his head.

"No! No! No, please! Finn!" I squeeze his hand, willing life back into it. "Finn. *Finn*."

I begin throwing rocks like a madwoman; my fingernails break off and blood pours from my knuckles. I can feel the pile shifting and sliding, sending rocks down that bounce and strike me.

"Jessa! We have to get out of here!"

I can hear Ben's voice, but I've got to get to Finn. It can't be too late. It can't be.

"Jessa," Ben says urgently, wrapping his arms around my waist and pulling me back. "Come on! We need to get out of here. It's still not safe!"

"I didn't get to say good-bye." I can hear my voice echo off the walls, high-pitched and shrieking. "We didn't even say good-bye!"

The rocks shift again, sliding fast and covering Finn's body completely as Ben drags me, kicking and fighting, through the tunnel. The mountain groans and shudders around us, but I can barely hear it over my own screams.

We emerge into the bright light of day, and I fall to my knees, so full of anguish I'm sure I'm going to die of it. I stuff my fist against my mouth to keep from screaming again. I know if I let myself start, I'll never be able to stop.

Ben drops to his knees next to me.

"Are you okay, St. Clair?" His hand comes up to gently smooth back my hair. "Jessa?"

I can't answer him. I hear him let out a huge breath as he pushes to his feet and digs out his phone.

"We have to call the police," he says, pacing. "But I . . . I mean . . . how do I explain about Eversor? I don't even . . ."

My head snaps up. "You can't do that."

"We have to tell them about Finn," he says quietly. "His family will be looking for him."

"He doesn't have a family," I say, and the pain washes over me again. "He didn't have a family. He was alone."

"What are you saying?" he splutters. "We can't just—"

"He didn't belong here!" I shout. "He shouldn't have been here! He only came here to save me and now he's gone!"

I cross my arms to my chest, and my forehead meets the ground again. "He's gone." I say it again, as I rock and rock, fighting with everything I have to keep it all in and failing as the tears pour from my eyes. I feel Ben's hand on my back, and I cry for a very, very long time. Finally, I can't cry anymore.

"You need to tell me what's going on," I hear Ben say softly. "All of it."

"You'll never believe me," I answer, not even bothering to look up. "None of it will make any sense to you."

"None of it makes any sense *now*," he retorts. "A crazy teacher threatened your family, tried to murder us all, and disappeared before my eyes! What the hell!"

"My family!" I reach out, gripping his hand. "Ben, my family! Please—take me to my mom—and Danny. Please! I'll tell you everything—just . . . later, okay? I need to know they're safe."

He pulls me to my feet, and we run for the truck. As we drive away, my eyes linger on the mine, and the coldness inside me spreads, leaving me hollow.

45

Aftermath

IT'S A FIVE-MINUTE DRIVE TO THE RETIREMENT HOME, and to my relief, my mom and Danny are fine. Mom is a little shaken when she gets a look at us—filthy, scratched, and bleeding. My numbed mind can't even come up with anything, so Ben does it for me.

He tells her I was researching another ghost story, and he'd agreed to drive me to a spot in the foothills on our lunch break. We'd taken a tumble down a slope, so he brought me straight to her.

She bought it, but she's pretty pissed at me for my carelessness, considering my arm still isn't entirely better. I can't stop shaking, and while she calls me out of school and goes to collect Danny, Ben makes me drink a cup of coffee from the vending machine. He watches over me like a mother hen as I drink every bit of it.

We follow Mom and Danny home, and we both sit quietly as she fusses over our scrapes and cleans and bandages all our scratches. Once we've both washed up, we stand staring at each other in the living room, and I have no idea what to say.

The last thing I want to do is talk. A curious numbness has set in. I can hear Danny starting up a game of Mario Kart in the other room, and I'm absurdly grateful for the background noise. I'm too empty to be surrounded by quiet.

Ben sits down on the couch next to me, wrapping an arm around me and pulling my head to his shoulder.

"It's okay," he says, and I wonder if he's saying it to me or for himself. "It's all going to be okay."

We stay that way for a long time, and somehow, eventually, I drift off.

I am sitting at my desk in the classroom when Mario steps in through the red door. Even in here, I feel the weight of Finn's death. It's all I can do to lift my head and look at him. He sits down at the desk in front of me, turning in the chair. He reaches out and takes my hands in his.

"Jessa . . . I'm so very, very sorry."

I nod. There's nothing to say.

"Rudy is on the run," Mario says.

"How does that work? It's not like he can come into our world."

"No. But the dreamscape is virtually endless," he says. "We're looking where we can, following every trail, but . . ."

"But I'm still in danger," I sigh. "I don't care."

"Eversor is still out there. We need to get you to safety."

"Where?" I snap. "Where is there that could possibly be safe for me? Or for anyone who knows me?" I shake my head. "I'm staying where I am. I want to be home. If I get killed here and end up trapped in some other body in another reality, that's worse than dead."

"Very well," Mario relents. "For now, you stay home. We'll find him, Jessa," he promises me. "He's going to need to regroup to work around us, and that's going to take time. We can use that time to get some work done."

"I'm not up to traveling," I say. "Not now. Maybe not ever." I know I'm dreaming, but my voice breaks as my throat tightens.

"Jessa." Mario's voice softens. "You haven't lost Finn, not really. You'll see him again."

All Finns are Finn. He told me so himself. He's Finn no matter where he is. I feel my eyes filling with tears, and I begin to shake all over now. I am torn. I feel the grief ripping through me, the sheer impossibility of all this. I can barely speak around the lump in my throat.

"You can't do that to me. I can't see him again."

"You will eventually, Jessa. I'm sorry if that's difficult, but it is what it is."

His eyes are apologetic, but I want to hit him. I want to claw at his face and scream until he's sorry enough. Because he's not sorry enough. I sink back down into my chair, and my hand is tight against my chest. I feel like I can't breathe.

"You're going to see him again and again," Mario offers sympathetically. "It can't be avoided. You have to learn to let it go."

"Let it go?" I turn disbelieving eyes to Mario. "I *lost* him." My voice cracks on the words.

"And you can find him again. You *will* find him again, the next time you travel. You need to make peace with that." He shoots me another apologetic look that doesn't do anything for my sore heart.

I tear my eyes away from him and look down at my hand. I watch a tear splash on the back of it.

"You're not giving me a choice?"

Mario gives me a look that says *No, not really.* He reaches out and tries to take my other hand, but I pull it away.

"I'll try to limit your exposure to him for a while," he promises.

A while isn't long enough, but I know better than to argue. I just nod mutely.

"Eventually, Jessa, you'll have to get through this. You do understand that?"

No, I don't. It's too raw. I can't do this. How do you walk and breathe and function in worlds full of ghosts?

"Here," he says, getting out of the desk in front of me and moving back behind his teacher's desk. He opens a drawer and reaches inside.

"I brought you something. Maybe it'll make you feel better."

He gestures to me and I walk over as he sets down a dish, filled with sparkling glitter mousse, right in the center of the desk. I look at it in disbelief.

A hundred memories fill my head, sharp and poignant and overwhelming, and I wonder if my Finn was replaceable to him—another death among the thousands he's seen or possibly even influenced across thousands of realities and thousands of years. Finn was a speck. A number in a sequence. A momentary bump on a long road that a bowl of glitter mousse will easily smooth over.

My hand sweeps out, flinging the mousse off the desk, and I watch it shatter against the wall.

"He was more," I say to him through gritted teeth. "His name was Finn, and he was *somebody*. We're all somebody."

In two steps, I wrench the red door open. It slams behind me and I wake with a start as my mom calls my name from the laundry room.

Ben looks down at me and I take a moment to get my bearings.

"You ready to talk?" he asks in a low voice.

"No," I sigh. "But I guess I have to do it anyway."

46

Explanations and Allies

"ARE YOU TWO HUNGRY?" MY MOM CALLS OUT AS BEN helps me off the couch.

I know I won't be able to eat, and Ben comes to my rescue.

"We'll eat later," he lies. "We've got a lot of history homework to finish up."

"Another project?"

"Something like that," I call back. "We'll be upstairs if you need us."

I drag myself up the stairs, with Ben behind me, and I hear him shut the door. A long silence stretches between us and I sink down onto the bed, not sure what I should tell him. I don't want him knowing too much, but he has to know why a person was murdered in front of him, by a teacher who wants to deconstruct the universe.

The grief washes over me again, and I bury my face in my hands. I feel Ben sit down next to me, and his hand rubs my back.

"C'mere," he says, pulling me into his arms. I put my head on his chest, and the tears pour out silently. I cannot allow myself to make a sound because if I do, I won't stop until I'm screaming. He rocks me gently, letting me get it out.

Eventually, I calm down, empty again and feeling like my limbs are filled with lead. He picks up the hem of his T-shirt and wipes my eyes.

"Tell me about all this when you're ready," he says. "It doesn't have to be right now."

I sigh heavily. "No, let's get it over with."

I step out to the bathroom, splash some water on my face, blow my nose, and pull myself together. Ben is still sitting on the bed, waiting patiently.

"First of all," I say, closing the door gently behind me, "this is going to sound completely crazy."

"I just watched a teacher try to murder us right before she vanished into thin air," Ben says, working hard to keep his voice down. "And I seem to be the only one who's questioning any of that."

"I know, I know." How do I explain this? He's right. I ease down next to him on the bed.

"What did you mean when you said Finn isn't from here? Was . . . was he an alien?" Ben asks cautiously.

I nearly laugh at the absurdity of it, but then I realize what I'm about to tell him is equally absurd.

"No. He was a Traveler. And so am I. We can move between realities." I stop to clear my throat. "I know that sounds crazy, Ben, but it's true."

"And Eversor . . . ?"

"She's a Traveler, too. If we can see our reflection—in a

mirror or a piece of glass—we can use it like a portal. It takes us to another reality."

"You just . . . disappear? Like she did? Poof?"

"Something like that. And we don't always disappear. Most of the time we trade with someone on the other side."

He digests that for a moment, but his face makes it clear that he's not any less confused. "Are *you* from here? This reality?"

"Yes. I only just found out I could travel." My eyes meet his. "But the Jessa you were dating last week wasn't me."

He opens his mouth, then closes it. Then he opens it again. "How?"

"We switched. I was in her reality, hiding from Eversor. She came here. We were trying to throw her off."

"And that Jessa just up and decided I was boyfriend material?"

I sit back down next to him. "No. In her reality, you two have been dating for almost a year. She's in love with you, Ben."

Something flares in his eyes, but he bites his lip hard and tamps it down. "And you came back without knowing what the hell was going on."

"I knew," I say. "I get all of her memories. She gets all of mine. We're the same person, just in two different places."

"So did you feel any of that? What she felt?"

I make myself look him in the eyes. I owe him that much. "I felt every bit of it."

He lets out a long stream of air through his lips and shakes his head, still trying to wrap his brain around it.

"I hated hurting you," I say. "I'm sorry." The tears start again, and he shushes me, bringing his fingers up to gently wipe my face.

"It's okay, St. Clair. At least I know what's going on now." He wraps an arm around me and pulls me in again. "You're one of the freaking X-Men and didn't tell me. Some friend."

I laugh explosively, my shoulders shaking, and then I sit back up and look at him.

"It's not over yet," I say. "Someone was giving Eversor orders, and they're both still after me. We're not going to be able to hang out for a while—until I get this sorted out. I don't want you put in danger."

"Tough luck," Ben says, grasping my hand. "I'm signing on as a junior X-Man, and you're not keeping me out of the club."

"Ben—"

"I mean it, St. Clair. I'm in."

"I can't make you a Traveler," I tell him. "It doesn't work that way. And you could get hurt. Or worse." I swallow again, not wanting to think about worse.

"You're stuck with me," he says. "I've saved your butt too many times. And I'm fixing to save it again, if I have to."

47

The Comforts of Home

"TAKE IT BACK!" DANNY CALLS OUT. "TAKE IT BACK!"

"All right, all right . . . gimme a second." I grab the DVD remote off the table and reverse the movie a half-dozen frames.

"Right there!" He points. "Watch!"

I hit play and lean in to see what he's talking about.

"You're right!" I turn to look at him. "When Iron Man headbutts Thor, it dents his helmet. Holy cow!"

"I don't know how either of you can see anything in that movie," my mom calls out from the laundry room. "It all goes so fast in those fight sequences."

"That's why it's called *action*-adventure," I say.

"They shouldn't fight," Danny says. "They are friends."

I walk over and lean in the doorway of the laundry room. After the events of yesterday, it's almost bizarre to have this slice of normalcy. I'd say it's comforting, but the knowledge that someone's trying to murder most of the universe—including me—is never far from my mind. Normalcy is a temporary balm, and always will be until I find a way to get this target off my back—and the backs of all the people I care for.

Mom looks up from the pile of laundry she's sorting.

"What's up?" she asks.

"Are you going to watch with us?"

"Huh? Oh, you guys go ahead." She gestures with a dirty hand towel. "I need to get a load put in and then I need to fold all that." She points at the basket full of clothes she just pulled out of the dryer.

I pick up the basket. "Why don't I bring it out to the couch and we can fold while we watch?"

"Okay." She smiles. "I can make us some popcorn, too."

"I'm already on it," I tell her. "Danny!"

"What?" he calls from the living room.

"Popcorn!"

"Okay!"

I can hear him stomping over to the kitchen and pulling open the pantry doors.

"I'll make two!" he calls out gleefully.

Mom closes the washer door and starts it up, and then follows me out. I set the laundry basket down by the couch, and Danny pauses the movie while Mom waits in the kitchen for the popcorn to finish in the microwave.

"I'm gonna go back," he says. "For Mom."

"So she can see the helmet?"

"Yeah. 'Cause she missed it."

"What did we do before microwave popcorn?" Mom muses as she pours the popcorn into a bowl. "You know, we used to make it on the stove top. Back in olden times, I mean."

"Yeah, you're *so* ancient," I say, rolling my eyes.

Danny turns to look at me as he cues up the DVD. "When you miss something, you should go back," he says matter-of-factly.

My mind turns his words over, then runs them through again.

When you miss something, you should go back.

I look over at my mother—my far-from-ancient mother—and a thought takes root.

We need to go back.

I have an ancestor who, by all accounts, was the one and only Traveler who began it all. And a group of Dreamers—at some point in time—decided I'm the one to stop the ending of it all.

How? It's not enough that they know it's me. Somewhere, someone must have predicted *how*. Maybe no one could agree on the forecast, but the answer had to have been considered. Maybe even discarded. Or maybe Mario knows and just didn't think I could handle it yet.

My sleep was dreamless last night. Whether that was out of respect for my pain, or anger at my outburst, I don't know. Today, I am still hollow, but the empty places are slowly being filled with questions.

Tonight, we're going back to the beginning, and I don't care if I fill up ten journals full of notes in dreamland. We're missing something, and we need to go back.

"Jess?" Mom interrupts my train of thought. "Popcorn?" She holds out the bowl.

"Are you staying here tonight, Jessa?" Danny asks.

Mom thinks he's asking if I'm going out, but I know he's

asking more. He's asking if I'm going to stay his Jessa, just like he's my Danny.

"I'm staying here, Danny—with you and Mom."

I'm their Jessa, but I'm more now.

I'm everybody's Jessa. And I'm going to find an answer.

Epilogue

HE WATCHED THEM LOWER HER INTO THE GRAVE.

Her mother stood, weeping softly, holding her son's hand as she tossed the first rose onto the lid of the coffin. It took some time for the well-wishers to file past, tossing their flowers, one at a time, yellow roses, signifying loss.

He looked across at her parents, moved by the grief in their faces. For all their occasional differences, it was clear they'd loved her.

They'd loved her as he'd loved her. Still loved her.

Slowly, the townspeople and friends took their leave, climbing into their vehicles to join her family at their home, eating delicate finger sandwiches and talking in hushed tones.

He made his way to the grave, holding his rose—a vivid red for the vibrant young woman, lying cold in a grave that she didn't deserve.

He would find the one who did this, and he would make them pay. He offered it as a vow, murmured over a corpse that had no business being sheltered in a coffin so soon.

He tossed his rose and bid his final good-bye.

And as he stepped aboard his ship, he saw his reflection in the portal glass, and he realized it didn't really have to be good-bye.

Not if he didn't want it to be.

Acknowledgments

I have an enormous list of people without whom this book would never be. First and foremost, to Holly West and Lauren Scobell, for noticing a book with a handful of great reviews but not a lot of buzz around it, and then for having the foresight and patience to help me shape it into so much more. Thank you for taking a chance on me, for holding my hand, for brainstorming and poking and prodding and cheering me on from the margins with a well-placed remark. You made me a better writer.

To my many blog and fan-fiction readers—you've been so incredibly loyal and supportive, giving me the confidence and the courage to push myself as I never had before, and oh, has it paid off in so many ways. Thank you for reading, thank you for retweeting, for reblogging, for Facebook sharing, for shouting me out in fan forums, and for beta reading in the early stages. You're the best, all of you!

To Gary, the creator of LiveJournal Idol, and all of my former competitors there: I was just a girl who liked to tell stories until all of you came along. That contest was grueling and challenging and exhilarating. It gave me my start, and with a few of my best entries in hand, it gave me my first paying writing job. You made me think it was possible, and I cannot thank you enough for it.

To my friends and neighbors, who listened to me gush when I thought up a plot twist or gripe when writer's block hit, who mowed my lawn or invited my kids over to your house so I could write, who preordered my book the second it went up on Amazon, who introduce me to their friends as "My friend the writer" (thank you for that): I owe you a mountain of debt for it all. These past years haven't always been easy, and you stuck by me through the downs and cheered from the sidelines when it started racing up. I am so very lucky to have all of you.

To my family all over the country that I talk to more on Facebook than in person: Please know how much your support means to me. You never once told me this was a waste of my time. You never once told me that the obstacles were too high, or too frequent for me to be anything less than utterly successful. You never doubted that I would be, and I put my faith in that so many days. You got me through.

To my children, who have seen my face over the screen of a laptop for several months, who heard "hold that thought" so many times while Mom finished writing her thoughts down, who put up with the perpetual stack of laundry at the foot of my bed and the occasionally cranky demeanor of a woman under a deadline: Please know how very much of this I owe entirely to you. You are my inspiration, my joy, my brightest and best gift to humanity. I love you.

And finally, a big thank-you to the good folks at Antonio's pizza, for letting me sit in that booth and just write. And write. And write. Nobody makes a cheesesteak like you do.

FEELING BOOKISH?

Turn the page for some

Swoonworthy EXTRAS

*Special thanks to Chef Dominic Orsini at Silver Oak Cellars for his collaboration on this recipe.

GLITTER MOUSSE
Makes 6 Servings

1 cup heavy whipping cream
8 ounces cream cheese, softened
⅔ cup powdered sugar
½ teaspoon vanilla extract
6 tablespoons lemon juice
2 tablespoons grapefruit juice
¼ teaspoon blue food coloring
3 tablespoons sugar
white decorative sugar
blue decorative sugar

1. In a large bowl, using an electric mixer, whip heavy cream until stiff peaks form. Set aside.
2. In a separate bowl with an electric mixer, whip cream cheese until soft and fluffy, about three minutes.
3. Mix in powdered sugar, vanilla, lemon and grapefruit juices, and blue food coloring.
4. Slowly fold in half the whipped cream mixture, until combined, then fold in the other half.
5. Cover bowl with plastic and refrigerate for two hours.
6. While the mousse is chilling, prepare the parfait glasses. Mix the sugar and one tablespoon of water in a small saucepan and place over medium heat. Stir and heat the mixture until all the sugar granules have dissolved.
7. Next, prepare six parfait glasses by brushing the insides with sugar syrup and sprinkling each glass with blue and white decorative sugar.
8. Finally, gently add chilled mousse to prepared glasses, top with more blue and white decorative sugar, and enjoy!

A Coffee Date

between author L. E. DeLano and her editor, Holly West

Getting to Know You

Holly West (HW): What was the first romance novel you ever read?
L. E. Delano (LD): That would be *Shield's Lady* by Jayne Ann Krentz (aka Amanda Quick), if memory serves. If not, probably something by Johanna Lindsey.

HW: I *loved* Johanna Lindsey. Great classic romance novels. Who is your OTP, your favorite fictional couple?
LD: For books, I'm going to be unorthodox here and choose Katniss and Gale. I loved Peeta, but he didn't have enough fire in him for Katniss, I think. I love a tempestuous pairing, and they definitely were.

HW: I totally agree! Team Gale, all the way! Do you have any hobbies?
LD: I love to bake, I love to travel, and I am such a Netflix binger. You have *no* idea.

HW: And my favorite question: If you were a superhero, what would your superpower be?
LD: I'd want to be able to freeze time, even if it's only for a few moments. Sometimes you just need to live a moment a little longer or delay the inevitable long enough to get your stuff together.

The Swoon Reads Experience

HW: What made you decide to post your manuscript on the Swoon Reads website?

LD: I figured I had nothing to lose. I'd polished it, workshopped it, had beta readers hash it through. I knew it was a good story—I just needed someone to notice it!

HW: What was your experience like on the site before you were chosen?

LD: I thought it was tremendously helpful. Anytime you can get someone from your target demographic to read your book and give you feedback, it's a very good thing.

HW: Once you were chosen, who was the first person you told and how did you celebrate?

LD: I hung up my phone and my kids heard me yelling. In fact, I think the whole neighborhood heard me yelling. Then my kids went away for the weekend, so I was actually all alone and seriously broke at the time—and so unbelievably happy. I danced in my living room and life was good.

The Writing Life

HW: When did you realize you wanted to be a writer?

LD: I've never *not* been writing, but I had planned on being an actress. I did that for a while, but never stopped writing while I was. I just didn't put an effort into really getting a book finished until 2014 or so.

HW: Do you have any writing rituals?

LD: Absolutely none. Really! I have a son with autism, so finding a quiet, undisturbed place to write is honestly just impossible. That's made me such a better writer—I can write anywhere and pretty much under any circumstances.

HW: Where did the idea for *Traveler* start?

LD: When I was six, we were living in England and I saw a BBC production of *Alice Through the Looking Glass*. After the show was over, I passed by an ornate mirror we had in our hallway, stopped to stare, and I swear to you, I saw my other self blink. I still get an uneasy feeling if I look at a mirror too long.

HW: Do you ever get writer's block? How do you get back on track?

LD: Oh, I get writer's block all the time. I mean *all* the time. There's only one cure for that: You write. Even if it's bad, even if it takes the plot in an odd direction, even if you have no idea where you're going with it. You can always fix it later, but you can't do that if there's nothing to fix.

HW: What's the best writing advice you've ever heard?

LD: From every writer ever: Just write. Just do it.

TRAVELER
Discussion Questions

1. Mario has a lot of influence and power as a Dreamer. Do you think he's looking out for Jessa, or does he have his own agenda? Would you trust him?

2. Why do you think Finn tries so hard to keep an emotional distance from Jessa in the beginning?

3. Do you think Jessa's life experiences make her a more resilient person? And if so, do you think she will be a better Traveler?

4. If you were to see your family in another reality, perhaps slightly or—as in the case of Danny—*very* altered, would it be frightening? Or intriguing?

5. Do you think Jessa should feel guilty for letting Pirate Finn kiss her a second time? Would you have kissed him?

6. Jessa doubts her own writing talent after finding out her dreams have been influenced. Do you think that finding out her dreams were real has any bearing on her talent as a writer?

7. With her newfound ability, Jessa can now live many lives. Do you think she'll still want to live in her "home" reality, or will she become more independent, like Finn?

8. How do you think Jessa and Ben's dynamic will change now that she has the other Jessa's memories of her time with Ben?

9. Would you find it difficult to let a different version of you live your life for a while? Would it be hard to trust yourself?

10. If you could alter one decision you made in your life, then climb through the mirror and live in that altered reality, how do you think your life would have changed?

Fighter. Faker. Student. Spy.

Reagan was born to be a spy,

but will she turn her back on the world's
top secret agency for love?

ONE

"Reagan, everyone is going on Saturday," Harper says, in between bites of overcooked meat loaf and runny lunchroom mashed potatoes. "You'll be, like, the only senior not there."

"I'd rather eat glass," I say, taking a long swig of Vitaminwater. I ran six miles before school and my body is in dire need of electrolytes. I can feel it. I hate getting up early to train, but it's a million times better than waiting until the afternoon. I'd much rather be hanging out or studying with Harper and Luke, but skipping is not an option. I made that stupid mistake only once and that was enough for me. My parents were the kind of pissed that bypasses the yelling and screaming phase and goes straight to the silent treatment and punishment. They gave me a training session the next day that made my legs shake for an hour. A twelve-mile run followed by five hundred push-ups, a thousand sit-ups, and two hours of Krav Maga. Pure hell. In most households, I'm pretty sure that'd be considered child abuse. But what was I supposed to do? Call Child Protective Services? Tell them my parents forced me to work out for six hours because they're operatives for a part of the CIA the world, even most of the US government, doesn't know about and I'm training to be an operative too? I don't think so. So every morning, I pull my butt out of bed at five on the dot to train before school.

"I don't understand why on earth you would want to miss one of Mark's parties," Harper counters, tucking a loose strand of her long, wavy blond hair behind her ear.

"You know my two party rules," I reply, counting them down on my fingers. "Number one: Drinking Mad Dog 20/20 will make you sicker than eating at a strip club buffet. Number two: No good ever comes from attending a Mark Ricardi party."

Mark's gatherings at his parents' estate outside the New Albany Country Club community were sort of famous. I've only been to one of his parties and left before things got totally out of control, but the stories that come out of that house . . . my God. People always end up going skinny-dipping in the pond or losing articles of clothing (or just their dignity) during tequila-induced twerk-offs. Someone always gets into a huge fight or breaks something or cheats on their girlfriend. People always leave Mark Ricardi parties with the taste of expensive liquor and regret in their mouths.

"We'll take a vote when Mal gets here," Harper says, and takes a swig of her pop.

"I'll take a vote right now. All those in favor of not holding your best friend's hair back while she throws up in the master bathtub, please raise your hand," I say, throwing my hand straight up into the air. Harper narrows her hazel eyes at me, then smiles, exposing the tiny gap in her two front teeth that I love and Harper hates. She says she wishes she would have gotten braces back in middle school when everyone else's teeth were jacked up. She's thought about getting one of those clear plastic retainer things to fix it, but I continue to talk her out of it. I think the gap makes her look like a supermodel.

"Hey, that was the easiest party-fail cleanup ever," Harper says, reaching across the gray laminate table to slap down my hand.

"It was disgusting," I reply, my arm still high in the air. "I almost threw up next to you and I was stone-cold sober."

"You're so the good little mom of the group," Harper says, batting at my hand again. "I totally H your Gs right now."

"You totally what my what?" I ask.

"H your Gs," Harper replies and rolls her eyes. "Hate your guts."

"No way, you totally L my Gs," I say and laugh. Love how we both do that: Abbreviate things to the point people don't know what in the world we're talking about. We have some regulars, like RTG, which means "ready to go." PITA means "pain in the ass." SMITH means "shoot me in the head." Those are probably the favorites, but we both come up with ridiculous new ones every day that make our friends roll their eyes. But whatever, it's our thing and we like it so WGAS? Translation: Who gives a shit?

"Hey, MacMillan," a voice calls at me from the lunch line. I turn around to see Malika carrying a blue lunch tray. "Share my nachos?"

"Always," I answer, and spin back around.

MacMillan. Out of all my Black Angel cover-up last names, MacMillan may be my favorite. I've always been Reagan. But I've been lots of Reagans. Reagan Moore. Reagan Bailey. Reagan Klein. Reagan Schultz. No one has ever known my real name. Reagan Elizabeth Hillis. It's been so long since I've said my real name out loud that sometimes I have to think about it. It sounds crazy that I'd actually have to use any brainpower to know my name, but while it's only for a fleeting moment, sometimes I do. I've heard my mother say the older she gets, the more she really has to think about how old she is. When you're seven or seventeen, you never have to think about your age. She says as you get older, there's that split second where she has to ask herself, *Wait, am I forty-eight or forty-nine?* That's how I feel about my real name. And the more new last names I get, the longer that beat is in remembering who I really am.

It always happens the same way. As soon as I'm comfortable with a last name, I'm forced to forget it. My parents' cover will be in jeopardy or we're being watched and we'll have to get out of town. And every time we load up the car in the middle of the night and drive down our street for the last time, I feel like a piece of me is stripped away. I've never told my parents that. I don't want to make them feel bad. But it's like a version of myself—Reagan Moore or Bailey or Schultz or whoever I was there—dies and becomes a splintered shadow for anyone who ever knew that Reagan. When I get my new name and new cover story, it's like that Reagan—that fractured piece of myself—never really existed. I don't talk about it. I don't tell anyone the truth about where we were or what my life was like. I have to make up a whole new set of lies and repeat them over and over again until they become truth. I make the girl I was just a few months ago disappear.

"Hey, girls," Malika says, setting her tray down next to me. She lifts up her left leg to climb over the bench, forgetting about her very short red skirt.

"Holy inappropriateness," Harper says, covering her eyes with both hands.

"What'd I do?" Malika asks, settling into her seat.

"You kind of just gave the entire school a look at the goods," I say and pat her bare knee.

"Well, it's not like I'm not wearing underwear," Malika says, and throws her slick black hair over her shoulder.

"Yes. I like the pink flamingos, Mal," Harper answers, and gives her a wink.

With a Japanese mother and Pakistani father, Malika is hard not to notice in WASP-y New Albany, Ohio. Plus, she's what I like to call stupid pretty. So beautiful, she strikes you dumb and stumbling.

"Malika, what do you think this is, a strip club?" a voice says from behind me. I know who it is before I even turn around. Everyone knows the low, raspy voice of Madison Scarborough. "But then again, it's nothing half the guys in this room haven't seen before."

"Hey, I'm only a make-out slut," Malika says, pointing a finger to her chest. "I don't take off my clothes."

"Whatever. A slut is a slut," Madison says, rolling her startling blue eyes. I open my mouth to zing her but she's already turned on her heel to head to the field hockey girls' table.

"Don't worry," I say, linking my arm with Malika's. "I'll get her back later."

I learned how to hack into computers during one of my summer training camps in China. In about ninety seconds, I can hack into the school's computer system and change grades, attendance records, anything. It's child's play compared to the other systems I've mastered. By tonight, Madison will have a D in physics and the field hockey captain will be promptly benched for Saturday's rivalry game against Upper Arlington. I'll change it back Monday. Madison totally deserves the D for all the mean-girl crap she pulls on a daily basis. But I only use my spy skills for short spurts of vengeance evil.

The rumor-spreading, shit-stirring Madison Scarborough is what bonded us last year. I noticed Harper and Malika on my first day of school. Malika because she's gorgeous and Harper because she has the type of effortless coolness money can't buy. But they didn't hang with the field hockey and lacrosse crowd, the self-anointed "popular" girls. They were what Madison and her friends liked to call "fringers." Invited to the big parties but never the exclusive sleepovers or birthday dinners. They were known around school but never the center of attention. They quickly became my target group of friends. I needed to get into a small, uncomplicated group and blend as quickly as possible, so when I caught wind of terrible rumors Madison was spreading about them, I knew it was my chance.

Madison has had the same boyfriend for over a year: A preppy lacrosse senior who wears salmon shorts and mirrored sunglasses at parties and uses the word *summer* as a verb. Even with a d-bag boyfriend, girls think twice about getting involved with anyone Madison's ever dated. When Madison's ex-boyfriend asked Harper to homecoming, she spread a rumor that she was a lesbian and that none of the field hockey girls felt comfortable sharing a locker room with her. Then when

Madison heard that Malika kissed a guy who dumped her two years ago, she started a rumor that sweet Malika made a sex tape even though Mal had never even had sex. Still hasn't.

During study hall, I hacked into Madison's Twitter account (@PrincessMaddie. Cue the eye roll) and had Mal and Harper help me compose a stream of hilarious apology tweets to every person she'd ever terrorized. They were deleted twenty minutes later but that act cemented my place in our little group.

I almost hate to admit that my motive to befriend the fringers was part of my training because I sort of love everything about them. I love that Harper eats all the orange and purple Skittles because she knows how much I hate them and how her shoelaces are always coming untied because she refuses to double-knot. I love how Malika is deathly afraid of spiders but has seen every slasher film ever made and how she's still a virgin but has a hilarious goal of making out with a guy from every continent. They've become real friends now and not just part of my never-stand-out strategy.

"Got to love a guy in uniform," Harper calls over my shoulder, and whistles a loud catcall. I turn around in time to see Luke Weixel's creamy cheeks turn a dusty rose. He shakes his head at Harper, his lips crinkling into a crooked smile, before turning his pale blue eyes to me.

It's uniform day for the Junior ROTC and Luke looks extra sharp in his dark pants and tan button-down shirt, decorated with colorful medals, arc pins, and accolades. Six foot three with hair the color of summer hay and defined cheekbones, Luke always has girls swiveling in their seats or craning their necks to stare, but he looks especially stunning in uniform. It's not just the way the uniform makes him look but how it makes him feel.

He stands a little taller, walks a beat faster, and smiles a little wider in that uniform.

I raise my right hand to my forehead and give Luke a tiny salute. His crooked smile cracks wide, unmasking a pair of dimples so charming, even if you were mad at him, one smile would make you forget why. We hold each other's stare for a moment before he steps out of the lunch line and heads for our table.

"Hi, girls," Luke says, sliding into the seat next to me. He purposefully bumps his shoulder into mine, the right corner of his lip rising into a sideways smile. "Hey, Mac."

Luke is the only one I let call me Mac.

"Hey, soldier," I reply, my voice shyer than I expected it to be. Luke rests his strong arms on the table next to mine. Our skin is separated by my thin cardigan, but even the slightest touch from him manages to make my body buzz. Harper eyes the two of us and from the slow rising smile on her face, I know my olive skin is turning crimson.

"Luke, help us," Harper says, pulling her wavy hair into a messy bun. "Reagan is refusing to go to Mark Ricardi's party."

"What?!" Malika practically screams, then pouts. She loves a good and rowdy Mark Ricardi party.

"Oh, come on, Mac," Luke says, his smile still lopsided but wider, exposing his white, perfectly straight teeth. Orthodontists make a good living in this town. "Mark's parties are always epic."

"Yes. Epic disasters," I rebuff, but can't help but match his grin. It's annoyingly contagious.

"How about this?" Luke negotiates. "We go, sit in the corner, and watch the disasters unfold together."

Luke and I have done that before. Sat shoulder to shoulder

at parties, laughing as we make up the dialogue between fighting couples and drunk lacrosse girls. My stomach, even my face hurts from three-hour giggle sessions with him.

"Pleaaassseeeee," Malika begs, her eyes closed and hands collapsed together in painful prayer.

"Okay, okay," I say, throwing my hands into the air in defeat. The three of them cheer in unison and exchange a round of high fives.

"I better eat if I want to make it to lab on time," Luke says, standing up from his seat and resting his hand on my shoulder. "See you in a bit."

Luke's fingertips graze against my shoulder blades as he turns on the heel of his freshly polished JROTC boot and walks toward the lunch line.

The rush that takes over my body every time I'm near Luke drains from my blood, and as he disappears from my sight, my sharp senses return. Every muscle in my body tightens as I turn to my left and lock eyes with a man whose stare is so penetrating, I can feel it from hundreds of feet away. He's tall and strong, his eyes intense and dark, dressed in a janitor's navy-blue uniform. But I've never seen him before. He holds my stare for a moment, then looks away. He fumbles with the garbage bag in his hands, struggling to open it up. I watch as he tears at the black plastic, gets frustrated, and throws it to the ground. As he looks back up at me, a hundred pins prick my spine. My eyes follow him as he spins around and plows his way toward the dining hall door, knocking into a student with so much force, she winces in pain. I wait for him to stop or look back or apologize. But he doesn't. He puts his head down and keeps going.